GLOVER'S MISTAKE

Also by Nick Laird

NICK LAIRD

GLOVER'S MISTAKE

FOURTH ESTATE • *London*

First published in Great Britain in 2009 by
Fourth Estate
An imprint of HarperCollins*Publishers*
77–85 Fulham Palace Road
London W6 8JB

www.4thestate.co.uk
Visit our authors' blog: www.fifthestate.co.uk

1

A catalogue record for this book
is available from the British Library

HB ISBN 978-0-00-719750-7
TPB ISBN 978-0-00-731991-6

Typeset in Minion by Newgen Imaging System (P) Ltd,
Chennai, India

Printed in Great Britain by Clays Ltd, St Ives plc

Mixed Sources
Product group from well-managed
forests and other controlled sources
www.fsc.org Cert no. SW-COC-1806
© 1996 Forest Stewardship Council

FSC is a non-profit international organisation established to promote the
responsible management of the world's forests. Products carrying the FSC
label are independently certified to assure consumers that they come
from forests that are managed to meet the social, economic and
ecological needs of present and future generations.

Find out more about HarperCollins and the environment at
www.harpercollins.co.uk/green

To EJ

three in the morning

the club

At the kitchen table he'd turned a page of *Time Out* and there was her face. He'd been so shocked that he'd started to laugh. She was still beautiful – though squinting slightly as if she'd just removed a pair of glasses. Did she need glasses now too? He snipped out the inch-long update with nail scissors, folded it and filed it in his wallet. The exhibition, 'Us and the US', featured several British and American female artists, and it opened in three days.

When he reached the drinks table and lifted a plastic tumbler of wine, he noticed, with unexpected anger, how the suits had real champagne glasses. Money grants its owners a kind of armour, and this crowd shone with it. They were delighted and loud, and somewhere among them was Ruth. He headed towards her work and hovered.

There.

She did look good; older, of course, and the hair now unnaturally blonde. Her nose was still a little pointed, oddly fleshless, and its bridge as straight and thin as the ridge of a sand dune; one lit slope, the other shaded. A tall man in a chalk-stripe suit held forth as she twisted the stem of her empty glass between forefinger and thumb. Her unhappy glance slid round the group. As one of the men whispered into her ear she turned away, and her eyes had the same cast as in the lecture hall, when she would gaze longingly over the heads of the students towards the exit.

'Hello, oh excuse me, I'm sorry, Ruth, hi.'

David used one elbow to open a gap between the speaker and Ruth, and then slotted himself neatly into it.

'Hello.' The voice was lower than David would have guessed but instantly familiar. She still dressed in black but the materials had been upgraded. A pilous cashmere wrap, a fitted silk blouse.

'You taught me at Goldsmiths, a long time ago now.' He was staring too intently and looked down at her glass.

'Oh, sorry. Of course, yes. What's your name again?'

She presented her hand and David shook it firmly. He said there was no reason she'd remember him, but she repeated the name, making an American performance of the syllables: Dav-id Pin-ner. The three men had regrouped, and Chalk-stripe was still mid-anecdote. Ruth touched David's hand for the second time.

'Shall we find a drink?'

The queue was five-deep around the table. David knew he should stand in line for both of them, letting Ruth wait at some distance from the ungentle shoving, but to do so would be to lose her immediately to some suit or fan or journalist. Then Ruth stopped a waitress walking past, a black girl with a lip ring carrying a tray of prawns on Communion wafers.

'Can I be really brazen and ask you for some wine? Would that be okay?'

She appraised them: David left her unconvinced, but Ruth, five foot five of effortless poise, carried them both easily. The wealthy expect and expect, and are not disappointed. When the waitress smiled in confirmation, her lip ring tightened disagreeably against her lower lip and David had to look away.

'If you just let me get rid of these ...'

He was nervous, and kept pushing prawn hors d'oeuvres into his mouth before the present incumbents were swallowed. Ruth picked a white thread from her shawl and said, 'But what do you do now? Oh, I've lost your name again. I'm just terrible with names. I forget my daughter's sometimes.'

David, chewing furiously, pointed at his mouth.

'Of course ... God, Goldsmiths.'

She said it dramatically, naming a battle they'd fought in together. After swallowing, David repeated his name and said he was a writer. This was not particularly true, at least not outside his private feeling.

'Huh. So I managed to put you off art. Or maybe you write about it? Is this research?'

David thought she was very gently making fun of him. 'No, I teach mainly, though I have reviewed—'

She shifted register and dipped her head towards him. 'Look, I'm sorry for sweeping you off back there. The baby brother of my ex-husband had decided to explain to me how exactly I'd fucked up his life.'

'God, I'm sure you could do without that.'

The immediacy, the easy intimacy, was surprising, and it had startled him to hear himself repeating *God* in the same dramatic way she'd said it. Did she mean she'd fucked up the ex-husband's life or the ex-husband's brother's? He could imagine how she might unmoor a man's existence.

'You don't have a cigarette, do you?'

'Oh, I don't think you're allowed to smoke in here.'

'They won't mind. They're all very ... Ah, here we are. Darling, you're an angel. A punk-rock angel.'

The 'punk-rock', David thought, showed Ruth's age.

'It was kind of you to come and see the exhibition, you know. I managed to lose touch with everyone I knew at Goldsmiths.' Her dark eyes cast about the room. David waited for them to settle on him and they did. 'It was a very difficult time for me ... coming out of one thing, moving into another ... Maybe you heard about it.'

David pursed his lips and nodded. He had no idea what she was talking about. Her tongue was very pink and pointed.

'For so many years London was somewhere I just *couldn't* come to, and now I've taken this residency here for a whole ... Oh, stand there for a second. I don't want to have to deal with Walter yet.'

Ruth edged David a few inches to the left.

'Who am I hiding you from?'

'Oh no, I'm not really hiding. He's a friend. Walter. The Collector.'

'Sounds sinister.'

'Oh, it *is*.' She swept her wine glass in a small circle for emphasis. 'When Walter buys you, you know you're in demand. And he keeps *on* buying you until your price is high enough and then he dumps your stock and floods the market. Or' – the glass stopped in its circuit – 'until you die, and then he plays the investors, drip-feeding your pieces to the auctioneer.'

'A bit like a banker.'

'He used to be. I think he still owns a couple.'

David glanced around the room. He wanted to see him now. He needed to get a good look at the sort of man who owned a bank or two. Instead he noticed the grey-haired man in the chalk-stripe approaching them. Hurriedly he asked, 'So are you based in New York?'

'Ah, there you are. Richard Anderson's looking for you.'

'Richard Anderson?'

'He's doing a special on young new artists.'

'I'm neither young nor new, Larry ... this is David, an old student of mine.'

'It's very nice to meet you.' David was anticipating nothing, so the warmth, when it came, felt considerable. The man looked like a perfect lawyer, clean edges, something moral in his smile.

'Larry, where exactly is the club you were talking about?'

'Oh, it's just off St Martin's Lane. The Blue Door. Do you know it?'

He looked expectantly at David, who rubbed a finger on the tip of one eyebrow and pretended to think. 'The Blue Door? I'm not sure.'

Ruth placed two fingers on David's arm – he felt it in his gut – and said, 'We're going on there later if you wanted to come. There'll be a few of us. David's a writer.'

Chalk-stripe's interest had already passed. He glanced at his expensive watch and was all business.

'Hmmmm, what time is it now? Half-eight. We're probably heading over in, what, half an hour? Forty minutes?'

That night her exhibit was a sheet of black papyrus, four or five metres wide, that hung from floor to ceiling in the last room. Up close, its homogeneous black grew to shades of charcoal and slate and ink and soot, and its smooth appearance resolved into the flecked composition of chipboard. Its surface was wounded in a thousand different ways: minute shapes were pricked and sliced and nicked in it. There were Ordnance Survey symbols – a church, crossed axes – but also a crown, a dagger, a mountain, a star, miniature semaphore flags. And tiny objects – all silver – dangled or poked through it: safety pins, bracelet charms, an earring, a pin, what must be a silver filling. The man beside David pointed to the largest object, low down in the astral canopy, and said he was sure that the St Christopher medal, just there, must represent the Pole Star.

The gallery lights at that end of the room had been dimmed, and the work, *Night Sky* (*Ambiguous Heavens*), hung a foot away from the wall. Fluorescent strip lights had been placed behind it and shone through the fissures in the paper. As it wafted gently in the convection currents, breathing, it made a far-off tinkling sound. The conversation with Ruth had left him charged. He wanted to be affected, to give himself up to something, and standing a certain distance from the black, and being a little drunk, he felt engulfed. This was Ptolemaic night, endless celestial depths of which he was the core and the centre. Everyone around him disappeared, and he imagined himself about to step into the dream stupor of outer space.

David watched, he drank, he waited. He spent some time in front of a massive LCD sign that took up an entire wall of the gallery. As he watched, a single number rose astonishingly quickly, in millisecond increments. His heart sped. Death may be hidden in clocks, but this was a kind of murder. After a minute or so he felt hunted and light-headed. Every instant added to the total on the sign came directly from his reckoning. And a certain sequence of those digits was the moment of his death.

He slipped out for a cigarette, but at nine o'clock he was Ruth's guardian angel, floating a few feet behind her as she said her goodbyes. When they climbed the steps to Waterloo Road, Larry strode energetically to the central island to hail a passing cab. You could tell he was born to hold doors and fill glasses, Larry, to organize, facilitate, *enable*.

The view from the bridge was spectacular. The restive black river, slicing through the city, granted new perspectives. The buildings on the other side were Lego-sized, those far squiggles trees on the Embankment walk. Even though Larry and the taxi driver were waiting, Ruth stopped for a second to inspect the night, and stood gripping the rail. The normal sense of being in a London street, of trailing along a canyon floor, was replaced by the thrill of horizons. The sky was granted a depth of field by satellites, a few sparse stars, aircraft sinking into Heathrow.

Larry and Ruth talked for the length of the journey as David roosted awkwardly on a flip-down seat. Ruth's piece had been bought before the opening – by Walter – though Larry had retained rights to show it. When the gallery owner opened his notebook to check a date, David noticed that *$950k* was scrawled by the words *Night Sky*. He listened to everything very intently. Away from the public crowded gallery, a new, personalized part of the evening was actually beginning. Somehow there were only three of them, and he felt nervous. When the cab pulled up he tried to pay for part of the fare, but Larry dismissed him with a rather mean laugh that took the good, David thought, out of his gesture. The club was situated down a narrow alley and behind a blue door that appeared abruptly in the wall. David hurried through as if it might vanish.

Larry flirted with the girl on reception, signed them in. They followed him through a warren of low-ceilinged, wood-panelled rooms. Each had a tangle of flames a-sway in a grate and much too much furniture. And each was full of people in various modes of perch and collapse, laughing and squealing and whispering, demanding ashtrays, olives, cranberry juice with no ice. As he trailed after, David adopted a weary expression: if anyone should look at him they would never know how foreign he felt, how exposed and awkward.

Larry spotted a spare corner table and charitably chose the three-legged stool, leaving David the rustic carver. Ruth settled into the huge winged armchair, arranging her black shawl around her. David realized he'd been unconsciously pushing his nails into his palms, leaving little red falciform marks, and he stopped, forcing his hands flat on his thighs. He normally spent the evenings on the internet, chatting on a forum, but that night he was an urban cultural participant, engaged with the world, abroad in the dark.

'So what did you guys think of the exhibition?' Ruth asked.

This was his chance and David began talking immediately. He had given it much thought and started listing pieces and their attendant strengths and problems, then discoursing generally on the difficulty of such an undertaking, the element of overlap and competition with other artists, what the curator should have considered doing differently. Ruth was smiling, but the more he talked, the more solid her mask became. When she nodded in anticipation of saying something, David concluded, snatching his cigarettes with a flourish from the tabletop, 'But I would say – and I know this sounds a little crawly – but I thought your piece was the most involving. I felt drawn into examining the *nature* of darkness, how it's actually composed.'

He found he was sitting forward, almost doubled over, and he straightened up. Ruth smiled and said, 'Crawly?' but he could tell he'd talked too much. Larry had a bored, paternal grin on his face, and he waved his hand, dispelling some disagreeable odour. The waitress slouched across.

When Ruth made some slightly barbed reference to *pure commercialism*, David sensed a chink between them and tried to widen it. He waited ten minutes and then asked about money, about how art could ever really survive it. Larry grimaced, and explained that art and money were conjoined twins, the kind that share too many vital organs ever to be separated. Ruth balanced her chin on her small fist and flicked her gaze from her old friend to the new. David said that sometimes the most private, secretive art is the strongest. It had to relinquish the market to be truly free. Surely Larry wasn't saying that Cubism started with the rate of interest on Picasso's mortgage.

Larry frowned, forced to detonate David's dreams. 'Well, the fact is, not everyone's Picasso.'

'I think Larry's trying to tell you that minor artists, like me, need to make saleable *products*. Is that it, darling?'

'You're certainly not minor.'

'I'm certainly not *a* minor.'

Larry gave a loud guffaw and patted the back of her hand. Ruth ignored him and lifted David's cigarettes; he passed her the lighter and she drew one out of the packet, pinching it in half to break it in a neat, proficient movement. She noticed David noticing.

'Can't stop, can only downsize.'

Watching her, David found himself reminded of the finitude of earthly resources. She expected, and the taking was so heedless she had obviously acclimatized to prosperity at an early age. When the time had come for her to order a drink she'd spoken quickly, astonishingly, in a volley of Italian. The reluctant waitress had beamed, revealing one deep dimple, and replied in the same ribboning cadences. Later, when David leant across and told Ruth how much he liked her charcoal-coloured wrap, she said, 'Well, that's really something. It's a bit Raggedy-Ann now, but you know who used to own it? Audrey Hepburn. She was a great friend of my mother's.'

Men who own banks and Audrey Hepburn. A sheet of black paper for one million dollars. David lifted the edge of the shawl then, and pressed his thumb in the cashmere. It was soft as baby hair, as kitten fur. He thought of the symbolism of the act, touching the hem of her garment. He had a terrible tendency to think in symbols. He knew it made him unrealistic.

nutter

Blame is complicated but some of it must be David's. It was a Thursday night weeks later, and as the tube slid alongside the platform Ruth held tight to the bar, bracing herself for the lurch. She noticed a young man suddenly uncoil, a few seats down, and bounce to his feet. He was right behind her at the barrier, when she couldn't find her ticket, and she stepped aside to let him pass. Outside on the pavement, the man was peering into the window of an estate agent's, his head almost touching the glass. She walked down the High Street, took the second road on the left and, after a few moments, heard footsteps and looked back. He'd turned the corner too.

Something in her registered his presence as aggressive. But still, it was possible, she told herself, that he hadn't even noticed her. Or that he hadn't noticed he was scaring her. This was England. There was a thing called cultural difference. She quickened the percussive step of her boots and clawed round in her bag, locating her keys and jiggling them into her fist, so the sharp parts faced outwards. There was also a thing called sexual assault. Maybe she should stop and let him pass. But then they'd be only a couple of metres apart. Maybe she should knock on the door of a house, somewhere lit up. Further along, brown leather in street light, a man unlocking his car. Just as she tensed herself to shout, he climbed in and the door of the car banged shut. The words died in her throat.

The car's tail-lights receded, exited right. She glanced back and the man stopped, and she thought of playing Grandmother's Footsteps with Bridget in the yard on Sherman Street. The grass had almost been hidden by pink cherry blossom. An image of Bridget's tiny hands, a doll's hands, pouncing on her, Bridget screaming and giggling. She started walking quickly again and a white cat slinked out from behind some bins. That did it: she broke into a run, her canvas bag slapping awkwardly against her side. Flight heightened her panic. In the noise her motion made, she was convinced she could hear him behind her, running, and if she turned now he would be there, six foot of shadow coming towards her, coming right for her, and would say nothing, do something ...

Number 87. She vaulted up the steps and jammed the button for C, the top-floor apartment. David's. The man was strolling now, thirty, forty metres away. It was fine. Was it fine? As he approached, she managed to pout disdainfully and stare past him, but kept her finger pressed on the buzzer. He was almost at the bottom of the steps, and then he was there, and he stopped. It was real. He was here to harm her. She stared and he stared back, his face a private smirk, the whole world some obscene joke. He was forcing himself into her consciousness, into her life, and she could do nothing about it. She made a shooing gesture at him, and then suddenly she was out of bravery: her knees went. She grabbed at the doorway for support. The man pulled his hands out of his black anorak and held them out, palms up, as if to say *Cool it, let's take it easy.* But before he could speak, she cut in, her voice unnaturally high.

'No – fuck *you.* I think you should walk on by, sir, and leave me alone.' The 'sir' took even her by surprise. He took a step back and shrugged, still bemused.

'Well look, I'm sorry but—'

'If you try anything, I *will* kick you. I will kick the *shit* out of you. I'm not interested ...' She trailed off. Her American accent, minimal normally, sounded loud and false and ridiculous to her own ear, but she held his eye and nodded, to assure him she was serious. He sank his hands back into his anorak and leant against a lamppost as if he could quite happily wait there for eternity.

Upstairs David picked up the intercom handset: 'Hello?'

'Open the door. A man followed me and he's right *here.*'

'*What?* The buzzer's broken. I'm coming down.'

Three floors up, in a steamy kitchen, David grabbed the first heavy thing to hand and descended the stairs three at a time. When he yanked open the front door, Ruth pawed at his arm, pulled him out onto the porch.

'This man has been—'

David patted the fist that gripped his shirtsleeve. 'Ruth, meet James,' he said, there and then corrupting the future. She made a series of fathoming blinks and offered a panicky smile. David repeated: 'This is James, my lodger.'

Ruth stood stiff with embarrassment, both hands clutching her shoulder bag.

'Flatmate,' Glover corrected, signing *Don't shoot,* as he came up the steps. Ruth shook his outstretched hand, and noticed his engaging smile, his steady blue eyes.

'I'm so sorry about freaking you out. I'd no idea ...'

David backed against the hallway wall to let her pass, knocking unclaimed post from the radiator. Behind her, Glover widened his eyes at him as if to ask *Who the hell's this nutter?* Ruth tugged the weapon David had picked up, a blue oven dish, from his hands.

'And what's with this? Were you gonna make him a casserole?'

the intricate machinery

They climbed the stairs to dinner in procession – Ruth, then David, then Glover. It had been some time since the communal hall had seen any love. Handlebars, furniture, umbrellas and shopping bags had scored and scuffed the once-white walls until now they resembled the notepads in stationers used to test pens. The bare bulb hung limply. The radiator had leaked last winter and rust in the pipes had left a dark blotch, Africa-shaped, on the carpet. The man who came to read the meter had asked David if it was a bloodstain.

'I'm sorry – James – I'm sorry for getting so hysterical down there.'

'No, not at all. As much my fault as yours.'

'You really should have said something and reassured her.'

'I tried but she told me to shut up. In fact *she* threatened *me*.'

'I did, it's true.' Ruth laughed. 'You know what it is? I think it's that everything's so terrible everywhere, I'm just waiting for something to happen to *me*.'

She looked around the kitchen, taking in the slatted calendar for the Fu Hu Chinese takeaway, the cupboard with the missing door, the tannic stains of damp on a corner of the ceiling. David would have felt embarrassed, but he had a hunch that Ruth liked to slum it occasionally. She was privileged enough to feel at home anywhere, and to equate squalor with authenticity.

She leant against the steel sink, peering out of the window, and David stood beside her and followed her gaze down to the lit squares of distant kitchens, the empty trays of pale grey garden.

'If I lived here I'd spend all my time looking at this view.'

He helped her off with her yellow wool coat, and she was tiny inside it and dressed, as expected, in black. He felt he'd removed the protective cover of something and was inspecting the intricate machinery. There was something raw and breakable about her. Things had not, David knew, been going at all well. In New York someone called Paolo had broken her heart.

'It's great you could come round.'

'Oh, I have vast amounts of free time. New city, no social life. And didn't we have fun in Larry's club?'

'Do you remember that basement bar afterwards? With all the bikers?'

'They sang "Happy Birthday" to the barmaid.'

Glover left to change out of his work clothes, and David felt a pang in case his flatmate missed something, some further evidence of how close they were. Yet when he looked back to Ruth he could think of nothing to say. He eased out the cork with a pristine *cluck*. It would take some time to remember how they fitted together. She was reading a poem on the door of the fridge, standing with her hands on her hips as if she might start stretching. Her hairstyle was shorter, blonder, straighter-edged, the clothes more fitted; it was as if the focus had been sharpened.

'So what have they actually got you doing, then, as artist-in-residence?'

David had served up the pasta bake, cut the baguette, forked out the spinach and rocket salad, and now stood holding the back of a kitchen chair, rocking gently on the balls of his feet. He felt curiously passive and wanted to exert some dominion over the room.

'Walter's organized this great flat in the Barbican, and a studio ten minutes away. As a space it's wonderful, this washed-out English light coming through the skylights – it's an old factory of some type, though I'm not sure what it made.' She frowned at the mystery of industry.

'But what are *you* going to make?' Glover said, pouring more wine. The confidence with which he addressed her struck David as slightly presumptuous. He wasn't even supposed to be in tonight. He was meant to be at work.

'Which reminds me,' David said, 'we should talk about our project at some point.'

'I can't think about that at the moment.' She gave a little shiver of her shoulders, and David tried hard to keep smiling. 'I've got a million things to do right now. Did I tell you they're doing a retrospective here in London, at the Institute of Contemporary Arts? And yesterday I spent three hours talking to students, though that was actually kind of fun. I forgot about that.' She threw David a wide-eyed glance, and he looked away. Each time his eyes met hers he felt a charge of something, a little rolling emotion that would gather, if he let it, to an avalanche.

'I was very young, of course, when I taught David – not much older than him, really.'

You were twelve years older, a small, uncharitable part of him wanted to say, *exactly the same as you are now.*

'David's teacher. So it's you we should blame.' In his laughter, Glover's eyes became two slits in his face, two scars.

'Not *all* the blame, I hope.'

David felt an uncomfortable passivity again. The oven had made the kitchen hot and he hoisted up the steamy sash window behind the sink; immediately September began to cool the room.

'You only taught me for a few months, and to be honest,' he laughed – at what he wasn't sure, 'I think the damage was already done.'

They were christened that evening. After dinner they adjourned to the living room and Ruth's phone rang. At the sound Ruth looked sulkily around her, then lifted her canvas bag from the foot of the sofa and began to go through it, extracting an over-stuffed black leather wallet, two purple silk-bound notepads, a hardback of Chekhov minus its dust jacket, a small Maglite torch, a silver glasses case, and then a phone the size and shape of a silver glasses case.

'Her mobile's not very mobile.'

'It must be twenty years old.'

Ruth ignored them, wincing at the screen before answering it.

'Hi, Karen, hi ... No, that was from earlier. I straightened it out. I just didn't know which form they meant ... Right ... No, I'm with a friend ... No, I'm at the boys' flat ... Yes, tomorrow's fine ... Okay, great.' She plunged the phone back in her bag. David realized she'd hung up without saying goodbye.

'The boys?' he asked.

After broaching a bottle of Amaretto that Glover located under the sink, Ruth announced that she was going to the National Gallery the next afternoon.

'Is there something in particular you have to do?'

'Oh, I don't know, not really. I want to drop in and take a look at a few pictures, and then go somewhere else and think about them.'

Glover slapped his hand loudly against his chest in the gesture of allegiance. 'Well, I've got to work, but David's free, aren't you?' There was a hint of laughter behind his voice; he didn't even understand that David would want to go.

'I could check online and see what exhibition's showing.'

'Or we could let it surprise us,' Ruth said. David thrilled a little at that *us*.

'You should drop into the Bell afterwards, sit and have a proper think about those pictures.'

David thought Ruth might take offence, but Glover had judged it finely. Through it all he possessed a firm sense of what people wanted from him.

The evening was out of the ordinary. David felt good. Here was difference and it was fine. Ruth on his sofa. An artist. An American. A woman. When Glover rang her a cab before heading, finally, to bed, there were just the two of them at last. David half-hoped and half-feared that a further intimacy would develop – as if now they'd lean in close and start declaring the stark facts of their lives – but it turned out Glover's absence bred a vague uneasiness. When he disappeared, the strain of carrying on a one-to-one took hold, and Ruth checked her watch, then leant her chin on her hand, spacing four fingers along her jaw. David imagined them on his fleshy back, indenting. They were waiting for the buzzer and when it eventually went, they both started slightly, relieved. A chaste kiss on her hot cheek and she vanished. In bed he noticed, for the very first time, how the galaxies of Artex on his ceiling all swirled clockwise.

with a capital A

Raining when he woke, and so dark he thought it must still be night. Footsteps scuffled on the stairs and the front door banged: Glover was leaving for work. It was already after ten. A sheet of A4 on the kitchen table:

D, Thanks for dinner. Did you like the way I set you up? I'm on till six if you want to pop in later. God Save The Queen, J

The sign-off was a rejoinder to *Who Dares Wins*, which David had used on a note about milk and toilet roll a few days ago. It had been proverbs until recently. Had he set him up? Did he mean he'd set up a date with Ruth for him? Or did he mean he'd tricked him into going? David didn't know. He crumpled up the note and dropped it in the pedal bin.

They'd agreed to meet outside the National Gallery at two, and he arrived ten minutes early. The rain had eased but not stopped, and the vista from the portico was still uniquely uninspiring: London done by Whistler, arranged in black and grey. Ragged, pewter clouds turned on Nelson's head, so that he alone was all that held the heavens up. Lutyens's limestone fountains were blown to spray and rain danced on the surface of their pools in time to the Cocteau Twins' 'Iceblink Luck'. Everything today had kept rhythm with the tunes on his iPod: the shunting of his tube carriage through its rock-wall galleries had accompanied The Clash, his footsteps on the underpass at Charing Cross had syncopated perfectly with the Blind Boys of Alabama. And now not even the Great British weather could puncture his mood. He was thinking about Ruth.

He had not been a success at Goldsmiths. Too shy and self-conscious in groups, he had fastened to students who showed him kindness and then been peeled, not kindly, off. Slowly he found a few friends with corners, who like him were awkward, and whose expectations had been comparably reduced. There was Adam, a tiny, witch-faced historian with a tinny, nasal voice; Michelle, a chubby goth who smoked all the time and looked skywards when someone addressed her; and a gentle nervous Chinese boy called Wu, who was almost certainly gay and had, David learnt from the alumnus magazine, hanged himself three years ago. He tried not to think of that time in his life. It was all too ambiguous, shameful and strange. He'd been vengeful then and quick to take umbrage, had found refuge in books and movies, and as a general policy scorned the world. It was only since he'd begun teaching himself and had made his own students laugh that he'd realized misanthropy could be taken for wit, and had found some semblance of pleasure in anger and cynicism.

But he still remembered anyone who'd once been nice to him, and that morning had pulled two cardboard boxes out from under his bed. It was a blue file, its spine entitled *From Easter Island to Henry Moore – Versions of the Human*. On the inside flap he'd written: *Ruth Marks, Visiting Artist – Introductory Module on Sculpture*. As he flipped through it, what came to mind was the moment he'd first seen her. He had slid, a few minutes late, into the back row. In various dark layers, with a black headscarf over her blonde hair, the new lecturer was gripping each side of the podium as if she might fall. She had huge dark eyes, deepened with a ring of kohl, and spoke with excessive solemnity, trying to convince them that she was a serious proposition. The sobriety, though, couldn't stay completely intact.

21

Her voice would crack with emphasis, she'd accidentally enthuse. She had an ardour that came with practising the art, a passion the professional tutors had lost.

David's own journey to art, or Art as he always thought of it, had been a wrong turning. He was never quite sure why he'd been accepted onto the foundation course in the first place. Even now he was embarrassed by the sight of a watercolour from his A-level year that still hung in his parents' downstairs toilet: an acid-green sky against which a singular figure in black trekked over the crest of a mountain. All his work had featured a lone individual in a vast backdrop, and only recently had he realized the link with the image of the sage on the mountainside, of Jesus or Muhammad in the desert, of Buddha by himself beneath the Bodhi Tree. He too, David Pinner, had been looking for enlightenment. And it had come, after a fashion: at Goldsmiths he met real artists, those whose panicked relationship with their materials betrayed not a fear of mediocrity, of exposure, as his did, but a recurring, unanswerable compulsion.

He pretended for a while; then stopped pretending. After one of Ruth's lectures, he decided to stay behind and tell her he was changing courses. The hall's draughty windows were mirror-backed by the darkness of the winter afternoon, and stirred with his reflection as he walked towards the front. His steps echoed. Her hair in two Teutonic plaits, Ruth rustled across the stage in a madeira hippy skirt with tassels and small round mirrors sewn into it. She was folding her notes, too tightly to use again, scrunching them into a paper bolt.

'Ms Marks?'

She looked up, mustered a smile. 'Ruth. Please.'

'Ruth. Hi. I wanted to say firstly that I'm finding your course really fascinating—'

She gave a rueful little laugh; the tassels swished as she moved towards her bag. 'Well, isn't that kind. I wish they all felt like you do.'

Some of the students had left, noisily, during the lecture. Ruth sometimes got lost in her text and repeated herself. Other times she simply stopped and stared over their heads.

'Oh, they just want to get home. It happens on Friday afternoons.'

'Really?'

David nodded bravely, saddened by his fellow undergraduates' priorities.

'Still, today's did *not* go well …' A bell rang in the corridor outside and stopped. 'If it's the handout, I don't have any more copies now but next week—'

'Oh no, I got one of those. It was more of a general thing.' Up close the long nose became a little sharp, though it contained all the intelligence and glamour of European Jewry and sat, to David's untutored Old World eyes, a touch uncomfortably with the Aryan hair. 'I just wanted to thank you for your lectures. They've made me think in ways about things …'

She smiled uncomfortably. He realized he was giving the 'It's not you, it's me' speech and stopped. She waited for a few seconds, then swung her velvet bag up onto her shoulder and helped him out. 'But you wanted to tell me you're leaving the course?'

He was dropping art altogether and changing to English literature. They ended up sitting on the stage steps and talking for almost fifteen minutes. She asked David about himself and his family, and he found himself telling her. About being the only child of a philistine butcher and a woman fuelled by tension. He had never had any support. He needed the support. Why could they not have given him their support? When he'd begun to cry – for all frustrated artists, for all hampered ambition, for all the sensitive souls in the world – she'd dredged up a tissue stained with make-up from her bag, and had praised the bravery of his difficult decision. He often thought about how kind she'd been to him, and how attractive he'd found her own weird mix of confidence and fear. He'd kept that tissue in his pocket all evening, and the next day had been reluctant to bin it, although he had. Years later, in a second-hand book shop in the Elephant and Castle, when he came upon a glancing reference to her in *A Guide to Contemporary American Art*, he ran his fingertip along her name and bought the book.

■ ■ ■

David felt abashed on entering the National Gallery. When they climbed the great staircase, the awe of scale meant he was whispering, and by the time they came to the art, entering a room where portraits hung on thick gold chains against the crimson walls, and a cornice was piped like icing around the ceiling's edge, both had fallen silent. Ruth stared at each picture and he followed, a masterpiece or two behind. David noticed he was walking in a formal, measured stride, much like the Duke of Edinburgh, and he'd even tucked his hands, rudder-like, behind his back.

When he joined her in front of a self-portrait by Murillo, brushing his duffel coat against her shoulder, she gave a raspy little sigh of satisfaction. It was a picture of a picture, with a frame within the frame, and the painter-subject, a lump-faced dignitary with a suspended moustache, reached out of his own portrait and rested his hand on the inner surround in a neat *trompe l'oeil*.

'The fingers are very fine, aren't they? It gives real space and depth, but it's also Murillo saying' – she raked the air in front of the picture – '*look*, I'm the only one who can decide the reality of the art, or the art of the reality.'

David nodded, not quite sure if her chiasmus made any sense. Nonetheless a statement was plainly called for: 'It looks *exactly* like a hand.'

She stopped in reverent silence before a Michelangelo. *The Entombment* showed a naked Jesus being lifted up by John the

Baptist and two others. To the front right of the picture was a blank in the shape of someone kneeling. The creases at the top of Christ's thighs made the upper half of an X, marking the spot where his penis should be, but in its place there was only another blank, a cob-shaped void. I know how that feels, David thought. He put his hand in the pocket of his duffel and pressed it against his unresponsive crotch.

'There's something astonishingly modern about it,' Ruth said at last, picking her words slowly, 'and his mastery of the line's incredible. It's only through these contours' – she gestured again, spell-casting – 'that we experience the figure having volume and weight. It gives me a visceral reaction.' She shivered, or pretended to shiver. David thought how pointless the phrase 'visceral reaction' was.

'Who's the missing person?'

'The Madonna. Isn't it almost as though Michelangelo couldn't bring himself to make her visible, couldn't make her witness her son's entombment?'

'Hmmm,' David encouraged.

'Though apparently he was waiting for ultramarine to paint her blue cloak. The lapis lazuli he needed could only be gotten from Afghanistan.' There was a pause and then she tried a little political satire: 'Nowadays they'd just invade it.'

As they headed past Leicester Square station and up Charing Cross Road towards the Bell and Crown, Ruth, like one of Prufrock's females, was still talking of Michelangelo. She explained to David just why he was the supreme artist, how he represented the culmination of *disegno*. Just then a bicycle rickshaw went past, ferrying a bridal couple. The man, his hair slicked back as if he'd surfaced in a pool, grinned idiotically and waved. Poking from a millefeuille wedding dress, a wreath of white flowers in her hair, the bride was tossing confetti at passers-by. A trail of it stuck flatly to the wet road. Their cyclist was pumping his thigh muscles under a flapping, neon-blue rain poncho, and ringing his bell over and over. David couldn't tell if they were genuine or some kind of publicity stunt, but was amazed when Ruth waved back, and even more amazed when he did too.

Glover acknowledged them with a solemn wink, and they waited and watched him serving. He had an undeniable elegance behind the bar. For a big man he possessed grace. Simultaneously he poured two pints, listened to a customer's order, laid a banknote in the bed of the till, plucked up change, laughed at something, cracked a comeback, and all the while nodded his head to the R'n'B that slinked from the speakers.

He wouldn't take money for the drinks, a first as far as David could remember. He just shook his head and mouthed *no*, though David noticed him glance to the side to check whether Eugene, his slight ginger colleague, was watching. After passing across two glasses of red, he propped himself on his elbows on the bar, flexing his tennis-ball biceps.

'So how were the pictures? You get plenty to think about?'

There was an edge of banter to everything. Glover and David became her wayward boys, cocky and mocking and sly. It seemed to fit their three personalities, the little hierarchy of ids and egos and superegos. It was flirtation, David supposed, and surprisingly he was good at it. The Bell's manager, Tom, came up from the cellar wearing a tight silver shirt – David whispered to Ruth that he should be put in an oven and basted regularly – and then Glover finished his shift and joined them on the other side of the bar.

They moved to a table, and when David produced his gift shop postcards Glover stared at each in turn and said, without a hint of humour now, how beautiful they were. Ruth began to repeat some of the things she'd said in the gallery, and her lack of irony drew something similar from him. She talked about painting the way Glover talked about cars, with a personal, urgent pride in what others had made. David told them his own theory of art – which was that the finest pictures by the old masters featured either a monkey or a midget, or even, as in the Veronese they'd seen that afternoon, both. The classic double, he called it.

■ ■ ■

'She comes in every day at noon and orders a half of cider. Sits just over there.'

'With the *Mirror*.'

'Right, and her Dunhill Lights.'

'With a mirror? Why does she bring a mirror?'

'The *Daily Mirror* newspaper. And it used to be her husband, Ray, who'd come in for a Guinness every afternoon, but Ray's dead of a heart attack. I'd never even seen her, Irene, before. Then on the first day she came in she sat and cried.'

'She's on pilgrimage really, honouring his memory. Didn't Raleigh's wife carry his head around with her for years?'

'In a velvet bag,' added David.

'She likes to do the crossword. And she told me once the flat was just too empty without him.'

David, who had heard the story before, had seen Irene for himself. She'd had her pack of Dunhills propped open beside her and was filling in a puzzle book, pencil poised, one eye screwed shut against the thread of smoke unspooling from the fag clamped between her lips. The mouth itself was caved in and gummy like a tortoise's. The smoke, and her thinness, had left the impression she might actually be evaporating. Helmeted with a lavender-grey perm, draped in a shapeless maroon cardigan, she had an untied lace on one of her child-sized Adidas trainers, and the loose, lank, trailing thing struck David as desperately sad. The thin gold wedding ring on her finger was not a symbol of devotion but a statement of loss: it said *what you love you will lose, and for ever.* When she'd shambled to the bar and bought some cheese and onion crisps, the whole effect was somewhat spoiled. According to Glover, Ray had been an absolute bastard: he said Tom had always called him Wifebeater No 1, which led David to presume there were others.

Ruth was meeting Larry at eight, so David walked her down to the cab office on Greek Street. As he kissed her goodbye he pressed his fingertips, ever so gently, against the small of her back. When he got home he googled *disegno* and wrote an entry about it on The Damp Review. It was the Italian word for drawing but meant, apparently, much more than that. As Michelangelo had perfected it, *disegno* was a sublime kind of problem-solving, and the work of art an ideal solution, reconciling the often conflicting demands of function, material, subject, verisimilitude, expressivity … David got bored with typing the list out, and cut and pasted the rest of it … formal beauty, unity and variety, freedom and restraint, invention and respect for tradition. He also posted a second entry prescribing a trip to the National Gallery for anyone bored with shopping, or Hollywood, or crappy weekend newspaper supplements.

collective nouns

On The Damp Review David posted critiques of films mostly but also his thoughts about books, TV shows, plays, restaurants, takeaways, whatever took his fancy. Or didn't. He found it easier to write on disappointments. Hatreds, easier still. And it was his: *they* might have the television, the newspapers, the books, but the internet was his. Democratic, public, anonymous – it was his country and he felt grateful to be born in the generation that inherited it. He didn't tell his family or friends about his site. Not even Glover knew what he got up to in his bedroom.

He'd begun another little project recently, gathering information on all the people he'd lost touch with over the years. He didn't contact anyone directly but followed the footprints they left on their strolls through the virtual world. His nemesis from primary school had become a scuba instructor in the Virgin Islands. He found some photos on Rory's brother's Flickr account that showed a burnished and shaggy dropout hoisting a tank of air, thick-skinned as a seal in his wetsuit. David and he had been love rivals for Elizabeth S——, who he also found, eventually, on Facebook. She had retained her tragic, android beauty, though she was now holding a kid of her own.

He'd joined Friends Reunited under the pretence of being another boy from his class, the only person he'd ever hit, now a leading banking litigator. David took his bio from the law firm's website, where a photo showed him still to be the vulnerable and round-eyed, slope-shouldered boy he'd known. Then he searched MySpace for students at PMP, the private college where he taught, at the same time as checking Arts & Letters Daily, where he found an interesting article on the life of Chaucer. He printed out eight copies for his A-level group and was trying to staple the sheets together when he heard Glover come in from church.

An old western was on the television in the living room. Glover had changed his clothes and now lay on the floor with one arm tucked up into his red T-shirt. The shape of his fist bounced gently off his chest, like a beating cartoon heart.

'I think this is bust.'

Glover looked up as David wagged the black stapler, pulled the arm out from under his T-shirt and motioned for David to throw it. He caught it neatly, sat up and turned it over in his hands, as if looking for its price. Then he snapped it open and nodded.

'It's jammed. I can see it. The magazine can't push up to the top.'

'The magazine of staples?'

'Yep.'

'That's very nice.'

'One of the best.'

Last year David had photocopied the list of collective nouns for animals from his old dictionary at school and stuck it to the fridge. Glover and he had got into the habit of repeating them, and occasionally testing each other. ('A sloth?' 'Bears ... A fluther?' 'Jellyfish.') David didn't know exactly why he'd grown so fond of them. They seemed to hint at all the differing ways to proceed. A labour of moles. A zeal of zebras. A shrewdness of apes. With Glover, from the very start, David felt they fitted; that they lived in the same collective noun. He wanted good things to happen to him. He wanted good things to happen to them both. Glover worked the offending staple out with the point of a biro.

'Ah, cheers.'

'Interesting yesterday, with Ruth.'

'Was the Bell not pretty empty for a Saturday?' David clacked the stapler lightly a couple of times.

'I know it sounds stupid, but I never considered a painting as *representing*, instead of just straight depicting.'

David thought it did sound stupid and it made him feel fond of his friend – it was these little reminders of Glover's very average mind that made his good looks so much easier to stand.

'If I'd had a teacher like that I might have done my homework.' Glover lay back down on the carpet, where two cushions angled his head to the screen. They watched four men on horseback ford a river, then arrive in an empty one-street town. A man dived through the window of the saloon and began shooting at them.

David said, to no response, 'Sugar glass.'

Glover had slipped his hand back up into his T-shirt and was gently tapping on his chest again. The cartoon heart. He was always in such a good mood after church. David didn't think it was righteousness particularly, or smugness; more that he'd done his duty and could now relax. Still, it was intensely irritating. David felt excluded from his happiness, his secret. Over another burst of gunfire he said, 'How was God today?'

'Fine. Thanks.'

'What did you learn? What was the sermon?'

Glover sighed and blinked hard at the screen.

'Do you really want to know?'

'Of course.'

'Ermm, something like, without a shepherd sheep are not a flock.'

'Correct. They're not. They're autonomous.'

'They're sheep.'

'*Autonomous* sheep.'

An outlaw was hiding in a barrel with a shotgun, staring out through a knothole in the wood. David prodded again. 'You don't have to sneak off, you know.'

'I don't *sneak* off. You're not up when I leave.'

What's the opposite of coincidence? What's the word for nothing happening that might suggest a hidden plan? Glover found significance in the darkest corners of his life. Whatever found him could not have missed him, whatever missed him could not have found him. Once, when David had been turned down for the job of Deputy Head of the English Department, Glover had assured him that everything happened for a reason. David hadn't protested, but at that moment some deep tectonic movement had occurred. They might share the same flat but they lived in different universes. Folk-tale determinism! David was not surprised by much in the routine progress of his days, but that surprised him. If life turned on any principle it was haphazard interaction and erratic spin. He thought it much too obvious for argument: you make your own luck.

They were silent as the adverts came on. Glover and David considered themselves expert judges of the female form. There was an unspoken question when a woman was sighted which required a binary answer. It seemed as if they were simply being honest, and it made David feel masculine – not macho, not manly – to talk that way. Often, if they were in a bar or on a street, it would be a nudge or a directed glance to alert the other's attention – although Glover was picky. A beautiful Indian girl in full sari was selling teabags to them now and, without prompting, Glover said no, her shoulders were too wide.

the drogue

They had met in the Bell two years ago. David was trying to mark essays when the barman put some folk music, extravagantly loudly, on the stereo. Miming how to twist a dial, David said, 'Sorry, mate, could you turn it down a bit? Too much accordion for me.'

'My dad used to play the accordion.'

David smiled weakly, showing no teeth, trying for polite dissuasion.

'He met my mum at a church concert. Without the accordion I wouldn't be here.' The barman grinned – a kind of slackening that made his face charming.

'Does he still play?'

'On state occasions.'

Wearing a grey T-shirt and dark blue canvas trousers of the sort David associated with plumbers, the barman was athletic-looking with very square shoulders; and these he hunched forward as he rested against the glass-doored fridge, so his T-shirt hung concavely, as if blown on a washing line. The hair on his head was short, black, artfully mussed with wax. David's mother would have said he had the forehead of a thief, meaning it was very low, but his eyes would have won her over. They were widely spaced and a light, innocent blue. The way his heavy eyebrows sloped towards a neat, feminine nose seemed to grant his face sincerity. David liked him – James Moore Glover – at once. A friendship, too, is a kind of romance.

Glover did all the newspaper crosswords when it wasn't too busy, and since David always sat at the bar, marking at lunchtimes, or for an hour after work, he was often on hand to help. And talking in the sardonic, ruminative, unhurried way of two men who happen to be in the same place, they discovered that they made each other laugh.

A few months after Glover had started in the Bell, he looked up and scratched unthinkingly at his cheek, where light acne scars were still visible, and David noticed he wasn't working on a crossword. He was circling flat-shares in *Loot*. He'd been staying with his boss Tom and Tom's girlfriend, but the couple were splitting up and selling their flat; he had to move out.

After a pint and a half of German lager David said, 'Mate, you know, I've a spare room. You could stay there if you're stuck.'

Glover arrived with Tom, his worldly goods in the boot of the bar manager's BMW. It turned out the bar manager was also Glover's cousin. David and he disliked each other instantly. Tom remembered him from the pub, he said, as if that was somehow damning and odd, and he walked round the flat with a cursory, dismissive air; he'd seen it all before, or if not exactly this, then something close enough. He said, 'Going to make tea for us then or what?' and as David carried the tray through to the living room, he heard him whisper to Glover, 'You'd best make sure you've a lock on your door.' After he'd left, David had made it plain that this certainly wasn't that kind of set-up, and Glover appreciated, he thought, his candour. James had six wine boxes of books, several bin bags of clothes and a five-foot bay tree in an earthenware pot. The tree had a slim trunk and a perfect afro of thick, waxy leaves. The pot got cracked on the door jamb and they replanted it into the plastic red bucket David used for the mop. It was still there now, in David's living room, in its temporary home.

Glover's stopgap fix also settled into permanence. Initially circumspect, tidying up, knocking on doors, apologizing for polishing off the milk, they quickly developed the shorthand of flatmates. Glover came from Felixstowe on the Suffolk coast and his low-pitched voice had the slightest suggestion of an East Anglian accent: he lengthened vowels and weakened the second syllable in *thinking, drinking, something.* He didn't take sugar in his tea. His sudden violent sneezes seemed to come in threes.

He was muscular, and stayed fit by running every day along the river and the wind-picked streets of south-east London, his iPod strapped to his waist, his footfalls keeping time with his soundtrack of deep house. Glover claimed that he used to be *a lot bigger*, meaning fatter, and then at the end of his first year in college at Norwich he'd taken up jogging, and now greeted each day with the devotions of a hundred press-ups and sit-ups. David disliked and admired and envied that disciplined part of his flatmate. Glover's orderly mind was dominated by its left hemisphere. His toiletries stood grouped at one end of the window-sill, all their labels facing forwards; David's were scattered throughout the bathroom, or propped upside down in various corners, distilling the last of their contents into their caps. While Glover wired plugs, changed fuses, replumbed the leaky washing machine, David made cups of tea and hovered. He could ask Glover about cold fusion, about the white phosphorus the Americans were using, about a car's suspension, about enriching uranium, and Glover would explain it with a nerdish enthusiasm. The television occasioned some of his greatest triumphs. A programme about land speed record challengers led to an explanation of how those parachutes that shot out behind the vehicles worked. He fetched an A4 pad and a pen from his room, drew some diagrams to illustrate the dynamics of a drogue (his word). His measured speech, with its tiny lilt, sped up with excitement, and David felt he was one of those swollen, empty parachutes, dragging behind, slowing him down.

David liked the fact that Glover knew, that someone knew, how everything functioned. It was reassuring. These exchanges of information were interspersed with the usual male distractions: anecdotes, comparisons and lists, the one-upmanship of clambering humour; someone would say something funny, and the other would take the conceit one step further. And when Glover cracked up, the husky rev of his laugh never failed to ignite David's. Watching him put up the shelves that had been leaning in the hallway for three years, David asked if he ever thought he might go back and finish his degree: he'd dropped out of a mechanical engineering course. Glover had a screw in his mouth, and it fell on the laminate floor, hitting his foot and skittering across to the doormat.

'Yeah, thing is, I came back after the first summer looking a bit different. It was weird. I'd lost all the weight and was taking these antibiotics for my skin – and I couldn't get over the fact that people suddenly changed. People who wouldn't give me the time of day in the first year were now all over me like a rash. I didn't feel like anyone was real. I hated it.'

the recycling box

Monday morning began with a double period of David's A-level group, where he distributed his printouts and they discussed the symbolism of 'The Pardoner's Tale'. Lunchtime brought no respite.

Aside from occasionally letting a student borrow his cigarette lighter at the steps by the side entrance, PMP's debating society was David's only extra-curricular activity, and since the teacher who ran it had gone on maternity leave, he was now required to attend every weekly meeting. *This House Believes that America No Longer Leads the Free World.*

The in-house genius in the debating society was little Faizul, the Egyptian. He proposed the motion, voice fluttering between outrage and plea, hands frantic as shadow puppets. The rebuttal was provided by myopic, ungrammatical Clare, Queen of the Home Counties, and David watched the fifty golden minutes of his lunchtime tick away.

Before afternoon class he checked his email in the computer lab and found Ruth had replied to his message thanking her for the trip to the gallery. He'd also asked her if she fancied catching the latest ridiculous Hollywood remake – she'd mentioned her inexplicable weakness for blockbusters – and she suggested Wednesday night. And did he want to ask Glover, since he'd said he wanted to see it as well?

The movie was exceptionally poor, David thought, though Ruth claimed to agree with Glover's verdict of 'silly but fun'. As David walked out onto the pavement ahead of them he was already writing The Damp Review's post in his head: *Never remake monster movies. It's always a mistake. One can upgrade certain things – special effects, sets, costumes, even the actors – but one cannot get the better of nostalgia. One can't improve on memory: that subtle, slanted light.*

Ruth and David lunched the next week, and he met her for a drink after she'd been to a gallery opening. And so it continued. He would sit opposite and watch the internal weather of her emotions play on her beautiful face. She lived at the surface of her life. Nothing yet had happened between them but David felt the sheer intensity of their interactions precluded his role from being the usual one of confidant. Sometimes she held his look for a second or two longer than necessary, and sometimes she smiled in an impudent, daring way that David would think about later. In the meantime she was laden with a great deal of emotional baggage – this dancer called Paolo, still calling from America.

One chill November night the three of them saw *Othello* at the Globe and, after hailing a cab on Blackfriars Bridge for Ruth, the flatmates began the footslog back to Borough. The streets were almost deserted, plucked clean by the cold, and the icy pavements glinted like quartz. The play had not been good and David was extemporizing. After a pause, occasioned by his comparing the director to a back-alley abortionist, Glover said, 'How do you *really* feel about Ruth? I mean honestly.'

'I *really* like her,' David said, mimicking his emphasis. 'Why, don't you?'

'Of course, but I was wondering if you were going to do anything about it.'

David knew what he meant immediately, but something in his tone – some hint of irritation – offended him. Glover was always trying to push him into the world, offering to try internet dating with him, suggesting they reply to the newspaper personals, telling David to walk up to girls in pubs. He thought Glover considered him inert, as if he just needed a shove in the back to start rolling forward, but David was acquainted with rejection. He could only proceed at his own pace.

'We're old friends, you know? Really old friends.'

A crisp packet scraped along the pavement, worried by the wind, and Glover kicked at it. It flipped up over his track shoe and settled back, face down.

'I suppose the question is whether you're attracted to her.'

David bristled again and sighed with impatience. 'Anyone can see she's attractive.'

'Yeah, I think so.'

He didn't reply. What was it to Glover? They'd reached the front steps of their flat and the conversation was parked there, by the wheelie bins and the recycling box in which someone had dropped a half-eaten kebab.

like road maps, abandoned

On a wet, dark, interminable Wednesday, one of those winter days that lacks an afternoon, Ruth emailed to invite David to dinner. He'd never been asked to her flat before, to the Barbican, and Glover's email address didn't feature in the recipients' section. Her note was casual and he matched the tone, replying with one line: *Sure, that'd be nice.* Probably nothing would happen, but the night before he was due for dinner, he ironed his sky-blue shirt. This action carried a certain evidential weight: he loathed ironing, its peculiar blend of fussiness and tedium, and got away with wearing round-neck jumpers at school. However, that particular shirt, according to his mother, brought out his eyes. He was childishly excited to see Ruth's natural habitat. He'd never known her to cook before and was envisaging something plain, unfussy. Italian perhaps. Zucchini. Basil. Pecorino. Fruit to finish.

The day itself was a write-off. The only thing achieved was managed after hours when David, on the rota to supervise study group from 4 to 6 p.m., helped Susan Chang, who smelt of vanilla ice cream, remove a paper jam from the photocopier. He felt delighted by his small victory, and to celebrate, and in preparation for the evening, he decided to smoke some of the emergency weed he kept hidden in the locked drawer of his desk. He visited the staff toilet, perched on the edge on the flipped-down lid and skinned up. The joint was small, heavy on green, pointy as a golf tee, and would take the edge off the nervousness he was feeling. It was not beyond reason that it might be tonight. Ruth was unaccustomed to being alone.

He slipped the joint inside the pocket of his jacket and, at six o'clock exactly, headed up the ribbed linoleum stairs, wedging the fire-door ajar with an empty Coke can. Out on the roof of the school the evening sky was enormous. Tidal night was rolling in across the rooftops and the horizon was stacked with sinking bands of oranges and reds and pinks.

Sometimes David saw things and wanted to tell someone about them, face to face, eye to eye. He had had a girlfriend once, Sarah, years ago. They'd met in the students' union in their last term at Goldsmiths: she'd spilt his beer and then insisted that he buy them both another. Over the next four months it happened that nothing became real to him until he'd told her about it. If they weren't together, they rang each other in the afternoon to describe what they'd done in the morning, then spent the evening recounting their afternoons.

Back then David still had hair, and one stoned lunchtime Sarah had used her flatmate's clippers to shave it off. David saw what he would look like bald: insane and shiny, a spoon with eyes. In her bedsit, above a fried-chicken takeaway in Turnpike Lane, they watched a lot of New German Cinema, lit joss sticks and had clumsy, vehement sex. In the moment he'd once accidentally caught her fish-shaped earring and her ear had bled on the sheet. She hadn't cried but had squirmed below him faster, panting, and then slapped him on the shoulder hard, saying, 'Now hold me down. Now put your hand across my mouth. Now hurt me, hurt me.' When she went to India for six months, she wrote to tell him it was over. It did not escape his notice that the letter had been posted, presumably from Heathrow, on the same day that she left. He had only been in love once, and it wasn't her.

Queuing in the student cafeteria, in his first week at Goldsmiths, he had reached the checkout before discovering, in a hot flush of shame, that he'd forgotten his wallet. The girl in the line behind him had tapped him on the back, and when he turned had pressed a five-pound note into his hand, saying, 'Take it, really, it's fine.' He had never seen anyone be so kind. She didn't know him at all. He ate his lunch directly behind her and couldn't take his eyes off her hair. Thick and dark and shiny as an Eskimo's. Natalie was a third-year, he found out, and when he met her the next day to pay her back, they'd ended up eating lunch together and he'd made her clear green eyes close repeatedly with laughter.

David leaned against the red-brick chimney stack and lit his spliff. He thought how he was growing old and odd, how he was falling prey to calcified and strange routines. The thick unfiltered smoke began to spread its anaesthetic chill throughout his head. Two pigeons sat on the bitumen lid of a water tank, cooing and soothing the traffic below. He moved towards them and they fluttered off, settling on a lower ledge. In the distance the British Telecom minaret rose above the hum, and the satellite dishes on the roofs stood out like white carnations fixed in buttonholes. He stubbed what was left on the lid of the tank and was halted for a second by the presence of the moon. It was cinematic, scaly and yellow, and had crept up silently behind him as if it meant to do him harm.

On the pavement, foggy but relaxed, he put on Elgar's *Sea Pictures* and caught a 38 on Oxford Street up into the City. The Christmas lights had been erected, but were not yet switched on. He was going to be early, so he got off by Turnmill Street to walk. This was the hour before the evening started, the hour when anything might happen. It was the hour when the newspapers were skimmed and ineptly refolded like road maps, abandoned on the vacant seats of tubes and trains and buses. It was the hour when the smell of cumin and curry would waft across his parents' garden in Hendon. It was heaven. It was the dog-walking hour. It was the hour of a million heating systems clicking on and thrumming into life, the hour of a blue plastic bag whipping above the building site on Clerkenwell Road in spasms of desire. Would Ruth be wondering, right now, about tonight? Would she be looking down at London in transition, and thinking anything could happen? This hour must once have been the kingdom of the lamplighters, and subject to their piece-meal, point-by-point illumination, but now the street lights all came on in a single instant pulse, a blink, as David stopped by Smithfield meat market to spark his Marlboro Light, where the floors had been hosed down and water ran in rivulets out into the street, creating tiny eddies round his sensible brown loafers.

Natalie had graduated a few weeks after the incident in the cafeteria. She'd found work in a graphic designers in Ascot, though she came back to London at weekends to stay with her boyfriend in Clapham. Every so often she spoke to David on the phone but was always too busy to meet. So on Friday evenings and Monday mornings David took to hanging around in Waterloo station – along the route where she'd have to walk from the overground train from Sunningdale down into the Underground to catch the Northern Line, and back. He did that for two months and never saw her, not once. He had wanted her so much he could barely think straight. He wrote her hundreds of poems and letters that he never sent, and a few that he did. He wanted her in his arms, in his eyes, in his kidney and spleen and heart. He wanted to unbutton her white shirt and slide the snakeskin belt out of the loops of her Levi 503s. Jittery with excitement in the station, he would take up his position by the ticket machines and scrutinize for an hour or so the unknown faces passing through the barriers until, eventually, he would give up, and move off with a grimace and a heavy gait, as if some part of him ached when he took a step.

As the lift ascended the twenty-three floors to Ruth's flat David stared at himself in the mirror. Here was the elliptic face.

The joint had left his eyes watery and the walk had taken it out of him. His sweaty head shone like a conker, and his cheeks were watermelon-pink. He pulled a tissue from his pocket and blotted himself. At the second knock, he heard Ruth shout from inside, 'It's open.' He tried the door and here she was, walking towards him in dark skinny jeans and a black kimono jacket. Her hair was still damp, swept neatly into a side parting, and such unfussiness lent her face a new authority.

'Hey hey hey,' David said, for no good reason he could think of, lifting his arms like some favourite uncle.

'Wonderful to see you.' She offered her cheekbones to kiss in turn and then presented a cordless telephone, the mouthpiece covered by one of her palms. 'I'm just in the middle of something.' He mouthed *Sure* and she said, 'The living room's through there,' nodding up the corridor, before pushing the door shut with a naked foot. David noticed that her toes were not beautiful – misshapen as pebbles – but the nails were painted electric blue.

He propped himself on the arm of a massive maroon sofa. It ran the entire length of one glass wall – the exterior walls of the living room were ceiling-to-floor windows, and an outside walkway ran along them, enclosed by a chest-high barrier of hammered concrete. In the corner of the living room there was a huge battered travelling trunk – the kind of thing a seven-year-old in a peaked cap and uniform, going back for Michaelmas term, might sit on in a railway station in the 1950s. There was an armchair that matched the sofa and was functioning as a filing cabinet of sorts – papers were divided by being stuck behind, or to one of the sides of, the seat cushion. Ruth was at the other end of the hallway – in the bedroom he assumed – talking loudly.

'Look, all I'm saying is you can do all of that stuff after you've graduated ... No, no, I think it's incredibly important that you do it, you *have* to do it, but after you've graduated ... Honey, I understand that completely. But you've spent three years working towards this thing ... I don't care *what* he says.'

David shrugged to let his satchel fall from his shoulder. It landed on the oatmeal carpet with a jangle of the keys inside.

'He did *not* pay for your education. Did he say that? Who paid the fees at Wellsprings? Who pays for your apartment? ... No, all I care about is you making a mistake now that in ten years or ten days, you might regret ...'

David stepped into the galley kitchen. It was pristine and impersonal as a show house, except for invitations to art events that patched a cork noticeboard. How could she already have received so many? A door shut at the far end of the corridor but no footsteps approached. He slipped outside to the balcony; he could then at least pretend not to have been listening. London laid out like a postcard, like its own advertisement. The Millennium Wheel, Big Ben, Tower Bridge. A light blinked on the pyramid top of Canary Wharf to warn migrating birds and gazillionaires in helicopters not to come too close. He sat down on a plastic folding chair that dug into his back. From this level he could only see the sky, its baggy cloudlets and scatter of stars. He fastened his duffel coat and retrieved his satchel from the living room, skinned up again and smoked, and waited. He listened to a few Leonard Cohen tracks on the iPod, then some early Sinatra to lighten his mood. When he went back in again to get a glass of water, according to the wooden sun-clock hanging above the sideboard, twenty-two minutes had passed. The flat was silent. Down the hallway the bedroom door was open and inside the bed was huge and white, the tangled sheets and duvet ski runs, snowdrifts, ice crevasses. He faked a little cough to warn of his approach, but it dislodged something solid in his throat and by the time he reached the closed door of the bathroom he was hacking noisily. He knocked, needlessly gently now – a tap was running within.

'Ruth, everything all right?'

'Oh no, fine. *Sorry*. I'll be out in two minutes. Sorry.'

He turned to pad up the corridor but the lock snapped back and she appeared. She'd taken her jacket off and was wearing a yellow vest that showed her shoulders, freckled and thin but tanned, un-English. Her eyes were just cuts now in marshmallow puffiness. She'd been crying and had washed her face; she still gripped a small black towel.

'I'm so sorry, David. This is sort of embarrassing for me, and probably for you too. Bridget is being so difficult and her father …'

She began to cry again and then moved towards him. The actual contact came as a shock. He'd kissed her cheek many times, and even once lightly pressed his fingers on her shoulder as they parted. But now they embraced, and he arranged himself in it, and felt her shoulder blades sharp on his forearms. Things were changing. He knew he would never see her in quite the same way again. In an instant she had grown beyond the abstract; desire was no longer theoretical. Touch is much more dangerous than sight, or little smiles, or honest conversations, or whispers about pictures in a gallery. Touch is how the real thing starts. He felt an overwhelming urge to protect her, to gather her up and keep her safe. Her slender body shivered as she exhaled a long sigh, and he gripped her tighter. She was so light. He could lift her so easily. The smell of coconut soap came off her hair and he breathed it in deeply, willing it to fill every cell within him.

When she straightened up and stepped away he was almost surprised to find his body hadn't retained the indentation of her form. Immediately she busied herself – arranging the towel on its rail, tugging off the bathroom light. She walked quickly and he followed. When she pulled a bottle of Pinot Grigio from the fridge he leant against the kitchen counter, watching. It seemed to him then that leaning against a kitchen counter was obviously the embodiment of style. He felt enormously powerful. If he so desired he could run a marathon or lift that fridge and throw it. Instead he handed her the corkscrew, the only visible utensil in the room, with a courtly flourish of his wrist. A hypnotic spell of domestic familiarity had been cast between them, then she broke it.

'God, I'm sorry, David. I hope I didn't make you feel …
awkward.'

Did he look awkward? It wasn't awkwardness he felt. She gave
a sad laugh, took a sheet of kitchen paper from a roll hanging
on the wall and blew her nose loudly. This depressed him. He
disliked hearing a nose being blown; he always attended to his
own in private. A little of her mystique disappeared into that
piece of kitchen roll, and it annoyed him that she didn't care. He
tucked his blue shirt back into his waistband where her hug had
pulled it out, realized he had pushed it inside his underpants and
rearranged it.

'Oh shit, I've got mascara on your shirt.' She raised a hand to
brush at it and he stepped back, aware suddenly of the softness
of his chest.

'No, no, it's pen, I think, it's fine.'

'Let's get some glasses, sit down. Do you have cigarettes? Oh
poor Bridge … She's such a wonderful girl. But sometimes …'
She sighed and clinked the bottle down onto the coffee table,
then turned back to the kitchen.

'Teenagers!' David half-shouted after her, and then regretted
his banality.

'Christ – she's twenty. I think this is the way she's going to be.
Headstrong. Like her mother.' She allowed herself an indulgent
half-smile as she reappeared in the room, holding filled glasses.

'What's the actual issue?' David said professionally, taking one
from her and settling back in the sofa.

'She wants to drop out of her acting course. Well, change to a
teaching programme. And I don't think it's the *best* idea she's had.'

'You know, *I* came to see you once when I wanted to change
courses. I stayed behind after a lecture. I'm sure you don't
remember.'

David had always wondered if she recalled their conversation,
and now he saw she didn't, although she wasn't going to admit
it. She walked to the balcony door and looked out.

'Of course I remember. You were going to switch courses …'

'You were very supportive. You said I should do the thing I thought was right for—'

'Oh, I know but, David, this is my daughter. You were some …'

She couldn't choose a noun and her indecision seemed to spark something unpleasant in her: she cried, 'Oh, be realistic!' and waved a hand at the window, the walls, anything that might be secretly encroaching on her life. David, mortified, stared hard at the arm of the sofa. He had become Bridget's surrogate in the argument. Ruth sighed, then added softly, as if it should be a comfort, 'I wouldn't have cared what you did. I didn't even know you.'

She was upset. And even though he hadn't for a moment thought her version of their chat would coincide with his, he felt her admission as humiliation. Here was his pedigree, here was his rating. He could go ahead and fuck his talent in the ear, he could give up art, teach English, but the meagre flame of Bridget's gift should be somehow sheltered from the buffetings of salaries and standardizing test results, from buses and marking papers and the merciless alarm clock. A still, clear moment in his life. A kind of emotional vertigo – becoming suddenly aware of someone's real opinion. Unsteadily, he set his glass on the carpet and stood up. Ruth was staring out of the window as he walked over to the shelving unit with its untidy stacks of books, piles of prints and photographs. As lightly as he could, he said, 'I know *that*, of course. I just mean that maybe, you know, you should listen to her arguments and then—'

'Her *arguments* consist of telling me I don't know what the world is like. Look, David, I didn't mean I didn't care. I just meant—'

'No, of course, I understand. It's fine.' He grinned enthusiastically, multiplying chins.

'She has this thing,' Ruth continued, swerving back to her own road, 'that she wants to teach inner-city kids and change to an education major – she's just spent the last three years in drama.'

'Is this her?' He'd lifted a small photograph off a pile of four or five of them on the top shelf. A stringy girl with long chestnut-coloured centre-parted hair. She had her hands in the praying position and was sitting cross-legged on top of a picnic table. Behind her, the columnar trunks of vast redwoods formed a solid backdrop.

'God, no. That's about twenty-five years old. Those are flares, David. That's Jessica. You remember. She lives in New York. Her partner Ginny edits that journal – you should send some reviews there.'

'She was very pretty.'

He set it back on the pile. She had told him once about sharing a flat in the Latin Quarter with a girl named Jess.

'Oh, she still is. Bridge is too, but even darker, like her father. Dark and mean.'

She sat down neatly on the sofa and pulled her legs up, hugging her knees to her chest. David had just realized that there was no sign of food preparation, no preheating oven, nothing. He felt his stomach tense. It was listening very carefully as he asked, 'What about dinner?'

'Ah, that's the other thing. Can we cut out and grab something?'

the first person plural

Ruth had seen a little Chinese place, the Peking Express, not far from her flat and wanted to try it. That they were the sole customers became apparent only after entering. David wanted to leave but Ruth had already settled on a table in the corner, beside the aquarium. The tank was coffin-long and faintly stagnant-looking, and as various fish twisted their sad eyes to David, he got the definite impression that he was there for their entertainment and not the other way round. In greeting he parted and closed his lips at the glass. A scarlet fantail jerked away, billowing flamenco skirts.

Just as the waitress arrived at their table Ruth was telling David about Bridget's mad plan to marry her boyfriend, Rolf, and she lifted the palm of her hand to ensure quiet until she'd finished. The waitress, a Chinese girl of about seventeen, dutifully stood there, head down, as David tried to shoot her a pleading, apologetic look. When Ruth delivered the kicker – *And I said, darling, I* remember *what it's like to be twenty, but* no *feeling's for ever* – the waitress palmed a small gold lighter from a pocket in her skirt and lit the stubby candle, then gave a neutral lethal smile.

'I think we need another minute.'

Ruth had a knack for touching on questions that encouraged self-examination, and over dinner she asked about David's relationship with his parents. He found himself talking about rejection, about disappointment and resentment. Ruth interrogated softly, and as he was speaking he realized he was actually learning certain things about his life.

He didn't think her interest was compensation for her earlier, peremptory response. Unlike David, she couldn't feign successfully, or not for long. She was not *nice*, that damning adjective, and her curiosity, when it came, was undiluted by politeness. Instructed since birth in the cardinal virtues by a joyless Calvinist mother, David barely knew what interested him any more. He was sure of how he should behave, of the questions he should ask, of suitable responses. But he'd had enough of that. At least if Ruth appeared intrigued by something, it was simply because she found it intriguing. She might be a slave to her id, to insistent desires, but she wasn't boring. There was no ritual in her conversation and no taboo. Nothing was beyond analysis and articulation – over dinner she told him that she thought his mother probably hated him on some subconscious level because he tied her to his father. David felt Ruth and he were pulling close, aligning themselves, and the fit was remarkably good.

This was why men went mad for her. She looked at David with such intensity that he could believe he was the centre of her universe. It was not need: that would have been off-putting. But she gifted him the rare belief that he was special. He was the millionth visitor. He was the only one who understood, the only one she wanted, the only one to save her.

Her continuous low-level anxiety was brought to the surface by the usual liberal flashpoints. The environment. Her own ageing and death. American foreign policy. She assumed his politics, of course, as she assumed most things, but he didn't mind. The waitress appeared with more wine and her assassin's smile. David watched two tiny neon-blue fish dart like courtiers around a large black catfish. It slowly turned its ribbed underbelly towards their table and began grubbing on the dirt that clouded the glass.

As they left the restaurant, the two waiting staff and three chefs lined up like the hosts at a wedding ('Goodbye, we see you soon'). Ruth had insisted on leaving the change from her fifty, which meant the staff got a tip of fourteen pounds eighty. The food was completely average, but if the mood took her, she could be crazily generous – although her absent-mindedness, more often than not, left a wake of insulted and unthanked, the doored-in-the-face. She may have lacked intent, but culpability resides also in neglect: David was sure of that. He felt several things about her simultaneously. Her worries and concerns were all near the brim, so he found he forgot how fucked up and desirous, how petty and distraught he himself usually was. She let him know that he was not abnormal, by which she meant alone. The two of them were in this thing together. It was seductive, that, to be appropriated to someone's side. He could imagine that his interests tied in entirely with hers. As to what she saw in him, he wasn't sure. He knew she thought him entertaining. He was one of the amusingly crucified, and plainly devoted to her. He figured that she might enjoy his obvious delight when the conversation turned to art, to books, to anything that might broaden and sustain the mind. And maybe she was lonely too.

Out on the street she slid her arm into his. He squared his shoulders and straightened his back, possessive of this creature by his side. A cairn of black bags was heaped on the pavement by an overflowing litter bin and they swerved to avoid it. The last few yards had passed without speech. David was in a small reverie of contentment, thinking how he had, belatedly at thirty-five, met someone he found interesting, met someone who was *doing* something. His life had turned a corner. Their footsteps made a pleasing beat, which he was about to mention when she drew his arm a little tighter and said, 'I need to say something. I know you're going to think it's crazy, and I do too … believe me …'

Her tender tone and the wished-for words accelerated regions in his heart. He squeezed her arm back as she whispered, 'Do you think ... I mean *I* think there might be something ...'

She paused and David felt the shiver rise within him. He lifted a hand to his chest as if that might be enough to keep the blood pumping and the whole thing in place.

'Something between James and me ...' She stopped walking then, pulling him to a stop, and looked up into his face to examine his reaction. He yanked a fierce smile from somewhere. He felt cold, distant from himself: the real David was a many-legged scuttling thing, climbing up inside his body and now peering out with sad despair through the windows of his eyes.

'Oh God, you're outraged, right? Is it outrageous? I know it's a little crazy, but ...'

'The thing is ...' He started walking again, looking forward, almost dragging her down the street. 'And I know, because we've talked a lot, he finds it hard to trust ...' David made a preposterous gesture of holding a weight in his open hand. It might have been his ousted heart.

'Yes. He's told me about that, about college.'

Had he? When? Each time David left the room did they change gear to intimacy, then slow up again to casual acquaintances when he returned? Were they telepathic? Email. They were chatting on email. How nice for them.

'He's such a sweet man. He's so ... *sincere*.'

'Earnest, you mean? Yeah ... not like us.'

She turned her head and gave David a curious look – it was almost a flinch of injured pride; but then she saw the vanity of that move and turned the thing into a joke on herself.

'No, exactly, not like us. We're cynical old things.'

David wanted to disentangle his arm from hers but thought that might reveal too much. He succeeded in jollying himself along, but all he wanted was to be out of her presence, to get home and climb into bed with a pint of wine and a spliff. Things began to draw clear. She had asked questions about the two of them living together, about how David had met him, about where Glover was from, but stupidly, idiotically, shamefully, he had thought he was the focus. She chattered on emptily now about how ridiculous it was, and she was sure that nothing would transpire but she just wanted to say something, she needed to say something, she felt something between them, and what did he think? Over and over. And then the childish denouement: he was sworn to secrecy. Then they were standing at the bottom of the rock face of her apartment block, and over-eager to prove himself unfazed by the news, David found he had asked her round for dinner next week. When they had settled on Thursday, he added, 'And I actually *will* cook for us.'

Ruth laughed and then there was an elongated pause, as the first person plural hung in the air and both of them wondered if it might include Glover.

two in the afternoon

Buddha's bogus smile

David decided not to tell James about dinner, but it made no difference. Maybe she emailed him and mentioned it, or maybe Fortuna, in the earthly guise of the Bell and Crown rota, decided to give him the night off. David didn't know and never asked. By the time he'd dragged the shopping home on the Thursday evening, he was sweating and tired and dejected. The shower was running and a few minutes later Glover appeared in the kitchen doorway. Relaxed, barefoot in jeans and a T-shirt, he seemed fresh and new, the hair glossy and spiky, and he watched as David unpacked the groceries. On hearing that Ruth was coming for dinner, he acted neither surprised nor especially pleased, rubbing a palm up and down the door frame as if sanding it. He offered to help with the cooking but David said no, he was fine, and the TV went on. When the intercom gave its buzz of static David ignored it and Glover took the stairs down one by one, in no particular hurry.

He was listening hard as they ascended but heard nothing until they entered the flat. The dynamic felt immediately different. When he came out from the kitchen Glover had already taken her coat. Her perfume seemed stronger, a pleasant, singed citrus, her hair was newly cut and dyed, and he was sure her make-up was more pronounced. Black form-fitting satin trousers showed off her trim behind. Leather stack-heeled boots added an inch or two of height. A large tiger-stone pendant drew the eyes to the V of her grey cashmere V-neck, and its deep cut of tanned cleavage. Time had been taken. Money had been spent. It was premeditated, David thought, like the worst kind of crime, but she did look good, and she did smell good, and when he kissed her hello and gave her a hug, platonically quick, she felt wonderful too.

As he finally slotted the casserole dish in the hot yawn of the oven, David thought that this was easily the nadir of his year so far. He had another month for it to get worse, of course, but tonight he was on a date, as the chaperon, in his own living room. He was about to watch the only woman he'd been even vaguely interested in for years make a play for his flatmate. And he was cooking for them. He downed a glass of Something Blanc and reluctantly went in. The conversation was about Suffolk. Ruth tended to talk, David knew, to one person. When you were chosen you became her solace, her intimate confrère in some subtle plot against the whole thick-witted world. She watched you and read you, responded only to you. Such was the exclusive nature of her consciousness, operating in daily life through a series of mini-love affairs. David knew the intense joy of being concentrated on like that! Together they would sit and worry at a subject until something, however small, was clarified, but if you weren't elected, if you were secondary, then it meant you had to sit and wait, woebegone, and watch, and throw remarks like popcorn at the principals.

He flopped down by the stereo and scanned his eyes up and down the stacked CDs. They were so taken with their conversation they hadn't even turned the music on.

'But when you were growing up, did you think the town was dying?'

Glover noticed David looking at the CDs and said, 'My *Blood on the Tracks* is there somewhere.'

'Oh yes, play that,' Ruth said. 'It's his best.' A male thing to say, so definitive and presumptuous. David saw she was taking charge with Glover. Whatever would happen would happen tonight. As she plucked at the stitching of the red cushion on her lap, she was scrutinizing Glover's profile from beneath her calculated lashes. David found the CD and set it in the stereo's extruded tray, intruded it, pressed play. The opening chords of 'Tangled Up in Blue' came through the speakers.

The evening went slowly. David found himself irritated when Glover cracked some joke that made her laugh, and laugh excessively, or when she asked him yet another question. He was too familiar with the sense of being overlooked not to feel it keenly. When he went to check on dinner, he unzipped his hooded top and took it off, and wished emotions were like clothes, that he could remove them, fold them, set them somewhere. He laid the table and stood at the sink, then pressed his hand on the steam of the windowpane, where it left a perfect print. He went back in and downed a lot of wine and smiled.

It was true enough: Glover was handsome. His physique was nothing but tendon and muscle, and he fitted it entirely. He couldn't imagine the ugly-duckling version, fat and acned, though there was no doubt he was a swan now. David had been an ugly duckling too, and had then grown into a penguin. Or a dodo. A booby. He had never seen Glover drop or fumble or break anything, and that capability could be seen in his hands: they were large, graceful, lightly veined. His movements had an easiness, and because he was not physically false, he also seemed not *personally* so. His body was honest; it showed its workings and let him interact 'naturally' with others, David felt. His own mechanisms lacked transparency. His body was growing into Buddha's, and beginning to conceal its mysteries, and he must make do with Buddha's sexlessness, with Buddha's bogus smile.

He'd made a chicken and broccoli pie, and before the others had even finished their portions he'd eaten two-thirds of the entire thing. He needed to slow down, so he spooned a few new potatoes, slippy with butter, onto his plate. These he ate deliberately, cutting each in half to expose the soapy moon flesh before spearing it, sending it home. Afterwards, he wouldn't let them help him clean up, and though he recognized the gesture as passive-aggressive, part of him wanted solitude. Who wants to be entangled in the nets of other people's sexual tension? And this was everywhere; it was tinnitus; he couldn't block it out.

After washing up and wiping down the work surfaces, listening to them whispering and laughing, he came back to the living room and Glover thanked him for cooking. Ruth said it was just right for a wintry evening, then added, 'You know, David, I thought we could talk about the project. I had some ideas about the conception of it . . .'

Despite himself, David smiled. In Larry's club they'd talked for ages, drunk, about doing a joint project. And best of all, Glover was not involved, although she looked at him as she explained, 'I've always wanted to do something words-based, something very clean and plain, like signs that don't read like you'd expect them to. Though not that.'

The problem with the project, nascent as it was, already lay with her phrase, 'Though not that.' The few times they'd discussed what they might do, her words had seemed to drift towards what she meant, and David would think they were on the right track, but then she'd finish with that bewildering and unequivocal disqualification: *Though not that.*

Glover nodded gravely – the usual prelude to a one-liner – and said, 'Yeah, with his looks and your brains you could really come up with something amazing.'

Ruth giggled and play-slapped him on the arm – so this was her in fifth gear. David felt a little tremor of disgust and took a sip of wine to cover it. At any moment she might draw a fan from her sleeve and start fluttering it under her eyes. *Oh sir, I beg you . . .* To tamp the conversation down, he said, 'I could come in this week and see you, actually. I've been writing bits and pieces. Thinking about the temperature of the thing.'

Glover cut his eyes at him to say *The temperature of the thing?* Ruth was bobbing her chin intently, and staring at a point above the coffee table. When she talked about art she tended to peer, David had noticed, into the middle distance, as if to keep her mind unsullied by the grubby objects of this world.

'I think it should be about replicating surfaces that are usually graffitied, but with the actual writing being arresting, counter-intuitive,' Ruth said, sitting back on the sofa so it rocked slightly.

Glover, warming to the game, clicked his fingers and pointed at nothing. 'You could make an instruction manual, and then have it cover something completely different.'

'Insert the digital cable into your anger,' David said quickly; he would not be outdone by Glover.

'Exactly,' Ruth murmured. 'But not quite that.'

'Or a street sign that says "Despair 8 miles, Contentment 26".'

'I once saw a guy begging with a sign that said "Blah blah blah …" What about toilet graffiti that instead of being something sexual said, um, "I really like what you've done with your hair"?'

David snorted with laughter. Glover could always make him laugh. They were specialists at this kind of baton-passing and bar-raising. Ruth was not; she adjudicated.

'Yes, that's funny, though maybe not that exactly.'

David drifted on a sea of wine from tragedy to comedy; he was starting to find it compelling. Here was a 45-year-old woman hitting on a 23-year-old man, and he couldn't tell which way it would go. When the third bottle, the last, was almost empty (a little moat of red surrounded the glass fort in the middle) Glover left the living room and came back ready to hike up Scafell Pike, tugging a black beanie down over his ears.

'I'll nip down and get another bottle.'

'Maybe two,' David said, pushing his hand into the pocket of his jeans.

Glover shook his head. 'No, you're all right, I've got money.'

When the door closed on Glover's exit David attempted to marshal some salient facts. Everyone was a bit drunk, and had spent the last hour in different postures of swoon. He himself was almost horizontal on the floor by the armchair; Glover and Ruth had been sharing the sofa.

'Ruth, should I go to bed? Leave the pair of you to it?'

He hated himself for talking like this, for giving in. No one else might have noticed, but it was still his flat.

'No, don't be ridiculous. But what do you think?'

'About James? I didn't ask him. Should I have said something?'

It was like having toothache, David thought, and not being able to stop one's tongue making its testing, hurtful probes against the problem. He should go to bed.

'No, God no. That would be embarrassing ...'

She pulled a small silver mirror out of a side pocket of her bag and flipped it open, then drew back her top lip in a distressing way, like a horse. Her teeth were long and high-gummed. He said nothing as she started to reapply her lipstick, then he looked away from her, over at the play of shadows on the window. Witnessing the prep and effort was too intimate. Something soft, like pity, rose within him, and the experience made him uncomfortable. He tried to stabilize the mood.

'It's going to be great to be working on this project together. I thought some of the ideas about the graffiti were really interesting.'

Ruth tipped her head a few inches back from the mirror and smiled unconvincingly, her mouth staying closed. He realized she was buying him off. She pitied him enough to gift him this preoccupation, this little enterprise, in order that she might stay in his flat and, without guilt, have sex with Glover. He kept silent and a calm descended on them as she put away her make-up.

David remembered some graffiti he'd seen on the wall of a beer garden in Kennington. It said *Fuck you if you're reading this.*

Glover returned and David slid into a blue funk of drinking and observing. Both Ruth and Glover tried to deflect some things to him but he was too tired to play. Then it became one of those evenings where he drank and was fine and drank and was fine and drank and smoked a cigarette and suddenly was not fine at all. He was suddenly very, very far from fine. He struggled to his feet and whispered, 'I have to go to bed.'

On top of his duvet, in the dark, fully clothed, on his back. If he didn't keep absolutely still, the room was sucked into a whirlpool, at the centre of which was his head. Ruth was squealing about something and then someone put his Carole King CD on the stereo. He heard the start of 'It's Too Late', then fumbled for his earplugs on the bedside table, squashed them in and passed out.

When David's radio alarm went the next morning he groped for it, turned it off, dropped it and then opened his eyes very slowly, testing the vigour of his hangover. It was strong, say three stars, maybe four. At some point in the night he had climbed under the duvet and removed his socks, but was otherwise still dressed. Getting vertical was a lengthy process, akin to dry-docking a ship. Carefully he stripped and manoeuvred himself into the shower of his tiny en-suite, working mostly by touch. He sat down in the scald, propping his back against the cold tiles, and let the water relentlessly batter his downcast head. This must be what exhumation is like. He was a revenant come back, reluctantly, to light. His hangovers came in different brands of mental anguish, and this one, he could already tell, was a specialist in self-loathing. He hugged himself in despair. The blank metal mouth of the drain was segmented, as if it wore braces. It imbibed and ingested; it guzzled and swilled. As he watched water pool in his indentations and run off his blossoming gut, his pubertal breasts, he wondered about Ruth and Glover. For twenty minutes he sat there, his naked head bowed, fingers and toes crinkling and crinkling, wanting the water to wash him away, to dissolve him and send him in strands down into the city's sewers, where he belonged. Were they ten feet away? In one another's arms? Asleep or making love? He was a negligible thing, an invisible man.

sixties fittings

He didn't see Glover again until Sunday, when he arrived back whistling from church. They were heading up to David's parents' in Hendon, and James was cradling some white lilies he'd bought on the High Street. Their scent, filtered through David's hangover, was sickly. He told him they'd have to go in the boot. Glover laughed and began whistling again. David recognized the hymn. Something about a rock. If this was what it did, he needed some of that old-time religion. They trooped downstairs to the street, where two young Arabs were pushing a knackered Volvo estate past the flat. Another sat in the driver's seat. One pusher gave a theatrical grunt and the other mimicked it, louder. They laughed.

'Shall we give them a hand?'

'We're late as it is, and you know my mum's roast is all about the timing. The window of edibility's small on a good day—'

Glover thrust the lilies at David and jogged across. 'Can I help?' He didn't wait for an answer. The Volvo picked up momentum and the driver gunned the ignition; a couple of coughs and it woke into life. He revved the engine hard and waved out of the window, beckoning the men to get in. One of them – moustache, baseball cap – clapped Glover on the shoulder, and the car gave a long toot on the horn as it took off.

'We're going to be late now.'

'Don't be such a miserable bastard.'

The heater of David's Volkswagen Polo was broken and there was no parcel shelf, and the smell of the lilies in the boot was strong, almost bodily. David was cold and nauseous but – the toothache again, that wish to feel some new sensation, even if it happened to be pain – he couldn't help but ask about Ruth. He'd tried to speak to them on Friday and Saturday but both their mobiles had been turned off. Glover recounted their day very factually: after the Tate Modern they'd bought tickets for Haneke's *Caché*, but in the end they passed on the screening and instead sat in a pub round the corner. David had reviewed it on his blog, and told him he'd missed a rather fine movie.

'So you're definitely seeing each other?'

'Not really sure, to be honest. Though I went to hers last night after work.'

David had a shocking single image of Ruth lying naked on the bed, her body spread-eagled, sated, then Glover strolling out of her flat, whistling that fucking hymn again, work done. He was going on about how great her place was, how the view was amazing, how the kitchen had 'all its original sixties fittings'.

'That works.'

'Huh?'

'Child of the sixties.'

'Barely. Forty?'

'Closer to fifty.'

Glover snorted. David idled the car in first, waiting to filter into the right lane.

'She's twelve years older than me. She's forty-five, maybe even forty-six.'

'No way.'

Glover was silent. David could have tooted his horn in triumph. He chuckled and glanced over at James, who said, 'Huh.'

'Almost twice your age. Well preserved, of course. What age is your mother?'

'Fuck off ... She's fifty-two.'

'Well, that's something. Did Ruth tell you she was forty?'

'No, I just ... She said she was like all women, that she wanted to stay forty for ever or something. I thought that meant she *was* forty...' Glover gave a laugh then too, though it wasn't quite real.

'Well, whatever.'

He was subdued for a couple of miles and then, as the Polo whinnied round Staples Corner, David turned the radio down.

'So how was it?'

'I'm not discussing that,' Glover said immediately, humourlessly. It appeared that Glover, that fine appraiser of the female form, would only talk about women in the abstract.

'It's not my fault she's old.'

'I don't care what age she is. It's just numbers. It's totally irrelevant.'

'Oh come on. It's not *totally* irrelevant. And I need details, man. You're among friends.'

Glover's face twisted in distaste and then becalmed itself; he made the decision to be honest.

'We didn't do it, if that's what you're asking.'

David kept his eyes on the cavernous nostrils of the Benetton model on the back window of the bus ahead: her head was thrown back and she was cackling at the endless hilarity of life. He felt, strangely, a little ashamed. Glover's attitude struck him as puritan and silly, but also exposed him – unfairly – as somehow voyeuristic. Still, he was used to shame. Since Ruth had told him that she fancied Glover, a wave of it kept breaking over him, out of nowhere, like some menopausal flush, leaving him dizzy and uncomfortably hot.

Another image of them surfaced in his mind. She was sitting astride him, naked from the waist up and Glover's open mouth advanced on a low round breast, on a nipple dark and crinkled as a raisin. He felt a prickle of sweat between his shoulder blades and pressed hard into the car seat to stop it trickling down his back. It wasn't just shame. There was room for anger too. They'd made a fool of him. Screw Glover's new-found propriety; he pressed on. 'Really? How come?'

'This feels a bit weird, to be honest. You're a friend to both of us. I don't know that I should talk about this stuff with you.'

David sighed, then wrenched the steering wheel round and slammed the car into an oncoming juggernaut. No, he didn't. But he was pissed off. Glover dictated the terms of their friendship. Everything was done to suit *him*. Ruth would be more forthcoming. David let the silence build. London heaved and wallowed. He was not often directly insulted, but he could recognize it when it occurred. Glover should apologize. He wouldn't be treated like this.

When Glover spoke again, though, a few minutes later, he'd drifted far from their conversation. 'She's different, isn't she? Ruth.'

It was one of those unanswerable statements you can do nothing with – that you must just try to outlive. David noticed that someone had knocked against the wing mirror. He could only see the reflection of his car door, its stagnant avocado green.

'She'll be going back to New York, of course ...'

'Oh no, I know that. I'm not thinking about it as some big romance. And it doesn't matter, but I didn't know she was quite so ... That there was such a big age gap. I'm just saying she's very different to most people I've met. When we went round the Tate she knew about everything, and was *excited* about everything ... She's had this whole *other* life.'

David was silent as Glover chased his own thought down its rabbit hole.

'About a month ago this guy started coming into the Bell almost every evening. Never talked to anyone. About your age but smartly dressed, suit, tie, wedding ring. He comes in at six on the dot and stands at the bar, orders a large white wine, downs it in one and goes. And that's it. Takes a minute, ninety seconds.'

There was a Border collie pup in the boot of the estate car in front. Each time the traffic stopped it appeared, pressing two out-sized paws against the back window and staring mournfully out.

'I don't get it.'

'Just ... this guy's obviously steeling himself to go home to someone he doesn't want to go home to. I don't think there can be anything worse than that.'

'Ri-ight ...' The traffic moved: the pup's paws slid off the glass.

'I suppose I was just thinking that I can't imagine ever again meeting anyone like Ruth. She wouldn't ever feel oppressive. She's got too much going on in her own life. She's too cool ...'

'Jesus Christ, James, you've just met her.'

'I know, I know that.'

The indicator ticked to turn left. The dog in front was watching them attentively with its moist sad eyes and David looked away, finding it unnerving. The huge billboard to the right was an advertisement for chocolate or washing powder; or perhaps the brilliant whiteness was the beginning of some subtle teaser campaign. Then, with a small embarrassed shock, David realized the billboard wasn't postered white; it was blank.

what all these people did

He heard from Ruth, finally, on Monday morning, during his A-level class on Chaucer's *Troilus and Criseyde*. At the start of term in September he'd made the mistake of reciting some of the prologue aloud and now had to pretend to a working knowledge of Middle English; this involved him reading a few lines in a kind of strangulated Glaswegian lisp at the start of each lesson. He had just begun this charade when his mobile beeped. No one had noticed, he thought, until he finished declaiming and Clare murmured something about *inconsistency in phone policy*. He sighed sadly and said he was waiting for news from her probation officer, which got enough of a laugh to shut her up. After giving them a gobbet to paraphrase and parse, he opened Ruth's text. He could feel the sweep of twelve sets of eyes over him and adjusted his face to its death-mask setting, breathing through his nostrils and biting his cheeks. The message, in its entirety, read:

Thanks for Thursday! We must talk. X

Big deal. Big sodding deal. He was her Pandarus, her pimp, and at the end of his usefulness. When the lesson finished he rang her, and discovered there were new ways in which he could serve her. She wanted details: what had James and David discussed, what had James been doing? He knew his replies sounded slightly short and explained that he was hurrying, that another class was arriving. How well he managed to disguise his real feelings he didn't know, but she was probably fizzing too much to notice anyway.

By the time David and Ruth met the following night in a wine bar in Old Street, Glover had rung her and she was playing everything cooler. When he asked whether she thought they were actually going to have a relationship, she angled one eyebrow and said, 'Oh, David, don't be silly, he's a child. He's practically the same age as Bridge! It's just *fun*. I'm entitled, aren't I? Isn't everyone?'

Then a grin rushed her face as if she'd remembered something and she sipped from her wine. David necked two glasses to her one and they left for an opening nearby.

It was a German artist living in London. He'd photographed passers-by in the street and then followed them, without their knowledge, to their homes. The snatched portraits were displayed alongside the shots of the dwellings. Scores of these pairings covered the walls of the small gallery.

'This is *very* interesting,' David said as they stood and looked at a young Asian boy in a school uniform coupled with a graffitied blue door beside a dry-cleaner's. Ruth didn't reply. When David was very young and his family drove anywhere, he'd grow overwhelmed by the sheer quantity of people in London. He'd ask his parents what all these people did, all these people who lived in all these flats and houses, all these people on the pavement, all these people in the cars and buses. His father would look at his mother and then give a terse assertion that people did everything and anything, that they were teachers and chippies and dentists or worked in shops or were on the dole. It didn't answer the questions David's emergent consciousness was really asking: *How can these people, who aren't me, exist at all? Who are they? What are they for?* The exhibition reminded him of that astonishment he'd felt. Here were hermetic lives unsealed, here was offered proof of other people. He stared for a long time at a photograph of a Jamaican pensioner in a large green felt hat, and the entrance sign to her estate, Brookville Gardens. Ruth joined him, peered at the picture doubtfully.

'Garish. One trick repeated.'

David walked her back to the Barbican afterwards, disappointed that she hadn't found the photographs as moving as him. They were passing a closed department store and he was shocked at the disparity of their reflections. He hulked along, shapeless in duffel, whereas Ruth was fawn-like, her legs elegant and particularized in tight black trousers, the heels of her ankle boots forcing a graceful, straight-backed stride.

'Do you know how sweet James is? He's like something from before colour TV.'

She was a child, a child who'd been given a present, and he wondered how soon it would be before she was bored with it.

'I would say that he's as sweet as ... as sweet as one of those mai tais.' They'd been serving three different cocktails at the opening, all of them astonishingly saccharine.

'Oh, much, much sweeter. He told me that he wants to *wait*, before we have sex. He said, "It's important to get to know each other." Why didn't you tell me he was a virgin?' She clutched David's hand and swung it. Then she took the time to look at him, and realized his shock and her error. Immediately, David released her from any obligation, doing the stupid mime with the pursed lips and invisible key.

'Please – yes. I didn't realize that he hadn't ... He's had a difficult time. His father was very religious and cold, I think. And he was an unhappy child, very overweight. He has no idea how gorgeous he is now. When he finds out he's going to be ... Well, maybe less of a romantic.'

David was wondering how he hadn't realized it before. Glover was as dissembling as the rest of them. He'd never actually talked about ex-girlfriends but he always left the impression that he possessed at least a minimum of knowledge. He didn't lack for attention. They were at a crossroads where the bulb in the lamp-post flickered and crackled, and Ruth said, as if to let David share in her joy, 'You know, my studio's just up there. Would you like to see it? Shall we drop in?'

Street led on to narrow street and they reached a large steel padlocked gate. Ruth drew a single key from the hip pocket of her jeans and, after some expert wiggling, the padlock's jaw dropped open. The gate swung out with a rattling scrape – David looked down to see a perfect sunken arc in the pavement, engraved over years by the bottom bolt – and they entered an unexpected cobbled courtyard, with several glass-panelled doors leading off it. The visit felt somehow illicit and David was wait-ing for a torch to shine, a voice to boom. Ruth strode to one of the doors and unlocked it; it opened inwards and she tapped at the wall until strip lights, resentful of the late hour, came on with a whine. The roof was at least five metres away and three Veluxes showed the city sky outside to be a formless black, bruised in one window's corner by clouds. Crates and boxes were piled everywhere. Three trestle tables were erected against the far walls, and in the middle of the floor was a yellow easel.

There is something about two people in a large space that makes the experience oddly intimate. It works on a reverse scale to the size of the venue: in a lift, two people, even if they're talk-ing, face forward and avoid eye contact; in a room, the people tend to remain relatively stationary, catch each other's eye occa-sionally but still focus on something else, the television, say, or the dog; in an empty warehouse, though, or a studio, two people revolve around each other.

'I almost started to put this on.' She held an apron, white orig-inally but splattered dark with colours, and hooked its string back on a nail by the light switch.

'I spent the last three days sorting those pieces into size ...' Ruth gestured to one of the tables, where hundreds of glass shards were spread over plastic sheeting. What David assumed was a polishing machine – two buffing wheels, protective shield – sat alongside them.

'Amazing place,' he said, and was irritated by the false note his voice struck. He *was* interested. He tried again. 'What are they for?'

'A glass heart. I made one last year in bottle-green but this one's going to be clear glass and a lot larger.' She trailed a finger through the stones, leaving a wake of polythene. 'I found them along the banks of the Hudson. They'd been smoothed down by the water. There's something harmonious about found objects. Look.'

From a shoebox padded with newspaper, Ruth lifted out a misshapen frosted lump, which, as she gently turned it, resolved itself into half of a glass heart. It was a beautiful thing, far from cliché. It was constructed from dozens of tiny polished pieces, soldered together in spidery, vein-like seams. It was the proper shape, bulky and lopsided like the pig and cow hearts David's dad would get in the shop. But though the shape was real, the material was metaphor. This heart screamed, *I am brittle; I will break; I was put together tenderly with the utmost care.* She laid it back in its box. It left David strangely breathless. She saw he was still staring at the heart and said, tracing a hole in the crystalline latticework, 'Just here's where the aorta'll go. It'll come out for a few inches and then down here ...' She tried to pick a speck of something off a panel of the heart, then bent over and blew at it. Her blonde fringe swayed with her breath and separated into strands. As her jacket rode up, a raised freckle came into view on the pale skin above the red patent belt of her jeans. David was tingling. He had an urge to reach out and place a fingertip on it. He was Aladdin in the cave. *Look all you want but touch nothing.*

There was a sink in the corner and a kettle on the sill of one of the long windows that faced into the courtyard. Just as he was about to suggest having a cup of tea here, while looking at her work, maybe even talking about their project, Ruth glanced at her ancient black Casio and tapped its face, saying, 'Oh, we've gotta scoot. I don't want James to arrive back before us.'

Was this to be the routine? He would spend the evening entertaining, like a eunuch, and then Glover the Sultan would arrive to take over, and take Ruth and her body to bed. Half an hour later the buzzer of her flat went, and he appeared in the living room, tired, unshaven, swinging a bottle of wine by the neck. He gave her a slow sideways look and then kissed her hello. David watched as she inclined the other cheek upwards but by then he'd turned away from her. The flatmates shook hands with an odd formality while Glover scratched at his stubble sheepishly. Ruth carried on talking about an exhibition that she'd visited in Amsterdam last year.

'And I went in having seen most of the paintings before, and having loved Rembrandt all my life, but honestly I left convinced that Caravaggio was the greater artist. In comparison his pictures seemed so stringent, so sharp-edged and distinct ...'

'James might not agree with you there. He's still very much a Rembrandt man, thinks Caravaggio's use of light's a little obvious.' David was smiling broadly. Glover gave him the look he deserved.

'Piss off, David. I know who Rembrandt is.'

'He doesn't *just* make toothpaste.'

Ruth put on a pained expression. 'Don't be so mean, David. James has plenty of time to find out about—'

'Fucking hell,' Glover said evenly, 'I *know* who Rembrandt is. All the self-portraits. Big potato face.'

'There, so we all know. You want me to open this? We have a bottle of Chianti on the go.'

Glover connived a smile and nodded to the bottle of white in her hand.

He left them half an hour later. Ruth said she had to get up early, so David gathered up his satchel and duffel coat and caught the tube. They weren't exactly finishing one another's sentences, but still he was surprised by how relaxed they seemed around each other. At one point Glover mentioned his mother breaking her wrist, and Ruth interrupted him to say, 'This was before you moved to Felixstowe.'

'Yeah, just before.'

Ruth nodded seriously, filing the information somewhere. As David waited for the lift to sigh into the ground floor, he imagined they'd already stripped off and were having sex on the carpet or the sofa or the dining table. Why would they wait, feeling as they did?

all about frustration

Glover lay in his default position, horizontal on the sofa. Midday winter sun poured through the window, filming him sleeping. One of his hands was tucked up inside his T-shirt, across his chest, exposing his level stomach; a line of black cedilla hairs ran from his waistband to his navel. Newspaper supplements were spread round the room, covering the available surfaces so thoroughly he might have been prepping the room for decoration. Glover seemed so at home in the world, so *placed*, that David felt he'd intruded into his own flat. Then the sleeping body shifted, taking an imaginary step, and squinted at him.

'Hey.'

'Hello.'

David had grown a little awkward round him.

'Everything cool? Haven't seen you for a few days.'

A magazine slid off his leg and landed on the floor.

'Since Monday. Yeah, everything's fine.' David hoisted a bag. 'Got some things for the house. Toilet roll, tinfoil, disinfectant.'

'Superb,' Glover said, making no move to get up and help him.

'So, how's things? How's Ruth?'

'She's great. She said to say that maybe you two could do some work together this week.'

'Sure. I'll text her or something.'

He went through to the kitchen and Glover shouted after, 'I'll be seeing her later, so I could tell her when suits.'

'No, it's fine. I'll need to check ...'

What? Nasdaq? The weather forecast? David didn't want Glover as his intermediary. He'd ring her himself. James padded into the kitchen, rubbing his eyelid so hard it made a ticking sound. He stood there and watched David unpack the bags.

'And your mum rang. Wanted to know whether I was still coming over. She said' – he adopted a high-pitched Scottish burr – '"Will you still be gracing us with your presence on Christmas Day, Jamesss?" I said *I'd* definitely go, even if you were too busy. She loved that. "Och, James, sure you'd be *more* than welcome to come on your own."'

'I can see your face if I didn't ...'

'What are you talking about? I'd love it. I could hear about your difficult adolescence again.'

David stepped round him and slid a new kitchen roll onto the holder. 'It might help you get through yours.'

■ ■ ■

David was concentrating. It was birdsong at dawn; then a door slammed in his face. It was the tinkling of tea into china; then an engine starting, a farmer's shout. The pattern was repeated ad infinitum: plinkety-plink high notes tickled by the right hand; then a span of keys thumped in the lower register. He noted from the programme that the piece was entitled *Disinhabited*. Both Glover and Ruth had shut their eyes, so he did too, just in time for the piece to conclude. The composer, a tuxedoed Chinese-American with a black mohican like a circular saw, strode slowly to the front to take a deep, pensive bow. David was at his first piano recital, the night before Ruth left for Christmas.

The three of them sat in a shabby, high-ceilinged room in the Canadian embassy, in the third row of orange plastic chairs. No one had mentioned to David that it wasn't classical music they'd be listening to, and when a brawny Nordic in a black collarless shirt swaggered up to the shiny grand piano, sat down and started banging the ivories at random, he'd almost laughed. It was funny. He could have done it himself. With one diving flipper and a wooden spoon. He glanced behind to see if anyone had notified security, but the rest of the audience was pretending to be rapt. *This* was the recital. David watched the pianist's anvil jaw jerk above the keys for the next forty minutes, and he tried. He really did. He even quite liked some of it, particularly a kind of shunting jaunt that couldn't have been written before the industrial revolution. That was followed by *Six Preludes* – which each seemed to David the spasmodic and overlong death throes of a trapped animal. The problem was each piece strove for profundity but at its best brought to mind the incidental music from a Hitchcock movie. A wardrobe slowly swinging open. A chase scene. Ratcheting of tension and shrill revelation.

Still, the emotion must go somewhere, must take on *some* colour, and David knew the argument that the music was about disharmonic tension, about disjunction, about mechanization. The repetitive commute and dialling tone and automatic doors. At the end, to show he could, the Nazi lumberjack played the 'Maple Leaf Rag' and the quality of the clapping changed, grew gleeful and relaxed. It was over. Even though David thought a tiny part of each of them had changed, had *been* changed, he couldn't quite stop himself. It was too easy to disparage. As soon as they stepped outside, onto Westminster Council's pavement, he turned to Glover and winked and whispered, 'That was one long hour.'

He should have known better. The days of solidarity were past. Glover's face was joyfully apologetic. 'I have to say I loved it, actually.'

'Oh, you *have* to say that, do you?'

'I'm not doing it to annoy you, David. I really thought it was great.'

Ruth appeared beside them, winding a stone-grey silk scarf round her neck. 'I loved *Ease* by David Jermann. Wasn't it graceful? The dropnotes.'

'I liked that one too,' Glover said.

'I'm so glad we came. I'd no idea the music would be so interesting.'

'May you listen to interesting music. It's like a Chinese curse.'

'Oh David, didn't you like it at all?'

'No, I did. I did. I just missed melody.'

'But modern music – I mean what about Glass – surely you get an affective response to him – you must feel *something* . . .'

David couldn't face a discussion. 'I feel like I could eat something large and dead. Any thoughts about dinner? I'm too tired to walk into—'

Ruth caught his wrist. He felt his pulse pass under her thumb. 'No, go on. Say what you felt about the music . . .'

David let himself sigh heavily. 'I suppose I missed the lack of progress. I found it frustrating.'

'It was all about frustration. That was kind of the point,' she said, smiling sadly.

'*You* should get that,' Glover chipped in.

Ruth threw him a sharp look.

Over the last month David had felt them both pulling away from him. His texts and messages seldom elicited replies. Glover stayed at Ruth's almost all the time. David would leave notes on the kitchen table and they'd still be there when he got home from work. It was obvious: he was otiose. And Glover's manner was very brusque if he appeared to be asking anything of him. Added to that, David heard a hint of superiority in everything Glover said, and if he smiled or laughed it was code for *Oh my friend, you didn't really . . . you didn't really think you had a chance?*

Admittedly, he had invited himself along to the recital. He'd emailed them about going to see a movie which it turned out they'd already seen, without him, and then he asked Ruth if he could come out with them. He felt entitled. It was normal that they'd want to spend time together alone: they were at the start of their relationship, infatuated, in love, lust, whatever, but they could have handled it better. He had his own things going on, of course, teaching and reading and blogging. The Damp Review was getting several dozen hits a day, and he'd begun chatting to another blogger who'd left comments. 'Singleton' lived in SW9. She *lol*-ed a lot and had recently posted a review on her own site of the same Wong Kar-Wai movie that David had written about. Like David, she displayed no photographs of herself, though she had a slinky cartoon avatar, who wore a silver miniskirt and had masses of black curly hair and huge violet eyes.

The Damp Review was anonymous, though David signed his posts 'The Dampener'. His alter ego was unafraid, hard-boiled, outrageous. David's blog was his counter-plot, and everything was up for judgement and redressal. If he watched TV or read a book, was delayed by roadworks or bought a sandwich, he'd blog about it. Then the comments from others might appear. It was peculiar what brought people to his site. Anything and everything. And when they arrived they'd look around, then join in. People take so much shit that they'll jump at a chance to give some back. And David's rancour was applauded. He was permitted. He felt fine. He didn't need to justify, but on occasion, late at night, adrenalized with vitriol, some cobwebby corner of him almost understood the problem: he was searching not for things to love but a place to put his rage.

Glover led them from the embassy through the alien streets of Victoria. Christmas had arrived as advertised. The streets were full of work outings, of drunks and shoppers. They came to a Thai place, Luxuriance, which Tom had apparently recommended. David was not really speaking to his flatmate. Glover took any opportunity now to differentiate himself from David, and his reaction to the piano recital was a case in point. David stared at the menu. For weeks all he had done was eat, laying down reserves for some coming hibernation, and now he found it almost impossible to pick a main course. Each choice was too freighted with corollary loss.

When Ruth slipped off to the bathroom, the men were left facing each other across a gold elephant-shaped candleholder. Glover's hair had been cut slightly differently, shorter at the sides, and he'd shaved, so his face looked very soft. He could have been seventeen, about to be sent off to war. He tipped forward and propped both elbows on the table; two light indentations appeared on his brow above the neat nose.

'How exactly have I annoyed you? What have I actually *done*?'

'No, it's nothing. It's fine.' David looked down at the tablecloth.

'What's fine? What are you forgiving me *for*?'

'I don't see why you had to be so pissy about the concert. It's like every time I say something you have to disagree, and it's not like we even see each other any more ...'

Glover gave a patient sigh, tried to smile.

'I *genuinely* enjoyed it. I don't know why that should upset you ... I'm sorry if you feel a bit neglected.'

David poured himself another large dose of Sauvignon Blanc and set the bottle back down without refilling Glover's glass.

'Well, that's one of the unpleasant side effects of neglect.'

'You want every relationship in life to be all-consuming. I sometimes think you have problems understanding that you're my *flatmate* and not my boyfriend.'

'Oh, go fuck yourself.'

'All right, all right,' Glover said tightly. 'Sorry, let's take it down a notch.' He had exhausted his verbal scope, and now he play-punched David on the shoulder.

'It's fine, really.'

'Come on. I've got Christmas Day off. I'm still coming to your folks' for lunch. We'll have a few pints this week and go to the pitch-and-putt.'

'It's winter. The course will be closed.'

'We'll climb the fence.'

'In tam-o'-shanters.'

'And plus fours.' Glover gave his baggy smile, and shrugged. 'I didn't mean to be a prick. This is all pretty fucking strange for me.'

'And for me too.'

Glover stood up then to go to the toilet, and pretended to essay a putt into Ruth's handbag.

David hated sitting in public by himself and took out his phone to check for messages. When Ruth returned, he was in the middle of giving a tentative bite to the flower carrot that decorated his satay plate. It seemed to have been somehow vulcanized.

Ruth watched him set it back down. 'I'm sorry it's been awkward tonight.'

'Oh, it's not your fault. I think James has been really busy at work. He's just tired.'

The fact that David was defending Glover seemed to irritate her, and he wasn't sure why he'd even bothered. She pushed her tongue up over her top teeth, as if checking for one of the two butterfly prawns he'd seen her eat that evening, then added with a certain triumphant brutality, 'Hmmm, I know it's not *my* fault. He's pissed because *you're* here.'

She was daring him in some way and met his astonished stare, for a moment, with defiance. David felt humiliation single him out like a spotlight.

'I didn't realize ... I shouldn't have come.'

She blinked and smiled sympathetically, though the dark pools of her eyes were still backlit with mischief. 'Oh no, he's not *really* angry. It's my fault. I should've asked him before I said you could come this evening. I think he wanted it to be just the *two* of us. He says he's going to miss me this week' – she flashed her eyebrows at such a sweet absurdity – 'and he wanted to say goodbye properly.'

Glover managed to say goodbye properly for about an hour later that night. He was certainly not a virgin any more, and David couldn't help but think that he was doing it on purpose. After the dinner, he had made a show of insisting they spend the night in Borough and David felt it was for his benefit, to demonstrate the power he now wielded over Ruth. To be accommodating, David had gone straight to bed, pleading a headache and general exhaustion, not that they pushed him for reasons. He left them on the sofa, her bare feet across his lap, the toenails still electric blue, Joni Mitchell on the stereo. When he heard them enter Glover's bedroom he was listening to the shipping forecast, feeling as utterly remote as a trawler rounding Cromarty or Malin Head or FitzRoy. He turned off the radio and listened. After a few minutes the faintest creaking of the bed could be discerned. When it speeded up, someone seemed to slow it again. A couple of times the headboard gently knocked against the wall.

David lay very still, with his eyes closed, and saw the machine with no face, white and entire, rocking and working itself to the edge, and over the edge, to the weightless fall. His head could only be the distance of an outstretched arm from theirs. When he woke she had left for New York.

reconciling everything

Two days later, Glover was still in bed when David sloped out into the living room at 8 a.m. It was Christmas morning. David's body clock was on school time. Glover had left the heat on overnight and the whole flat had the stifled atmosphere of an airing cupboard. He swooshed the curtains open in the living room and let the grey light fall in on a classic Yuletide scene: crumpled Stella cans on the coffee table, an ashtray cluttered with butts, and the *Radio Times* draped like an antimacassar over the back of the armchair. Outside, the street was just as dead. Windscreens and bonnets glinted with frost. All the houses were sealed up with curtains or shutters or blinds. David watched the neighbours' baleful white cat trot into view on the opposite pavement and then out of shot again. Welcome to the bleak midwinter.

Glover's parents had gone away for the holidays, to stay with his father's brother Geoff, who'd retired to Malaga to lay-preach to tourists, play golf and occasionally return to Suffolk with a tan the colour, Glover said, of peanut butter. His sister was a social worker in Durham, married with two children, and had asked him up to stay for the holidays. David had listened to him on the phone, pleading prior commitments, of which the main one, he could now see, was drinking Belgian lager.

By the time David emerged from the shower Glover had cleared the coffee table and sat slouched in the armchair in his dressing gown, drinking tea and watching a cartoon. Two bow-tied bears on-screen were driving a car constructed from tree trunks and boulders.

'Merry Christmas, then,' he said flatly, raising his mug in salutation but not looking up.

'And to you.' David sat down heavily on the sofa. 'Sooooo. Are you ready for the Pinner Christmas?'

'I'll tell you what I *am* looking forward to, is a proper spread. I had cheese on toast for lunch yesterday.'

'Was that it?' David's stomach, his most compassionate organ, contracted involuntarily with sympathy.

'With a dash of Worcestershire sauce.'

'You poor, malnourished fool. Did you speak to Ruth? How's New York?'

'Under three feet of snow but she's good. Missing me apparently.' He looked up and raised his eyebrows, meaning *Women! What can you do?* 'She's going to her friend Jess's for dinner, and seeing Bridget and her boyfriend in the morning.'

'Lovely. Shall we leave about twelve?'

'I've church at ten and I need a bath.'

'Don't make it an epic.'

The Polo had frozen up. David sprayed his initials on the patinated windows with the anti-freeze and they climbed in and waited, watching in silence as the liquid ploughed transparent rills down through the ice and revealed the street in strips.

In Hendon, David's father was sitting on a wicker stool in the porch, wearing a yellow scarf and a new navy duffel coat very similar to David's. The porch was now the only place where Hilda allowed him to smoke, and he sat there at all hours, diligently filling the glass box with wispy clouds and silky filaments. As they crunched across the verge towards him David was reminded of a physics experiment at school which sought to demonstrate atomic theory by Brownian motion: one observed smoke particles, then deduced that their random movement was due to being pinged hither and thither by the air's invisible molecules. Ken got to his feet slowly, and David had to dismiss the thought that someday his father would die.

'David, James, welcome. Merry Christmas.'

'Merry Christmas, Ken.'

'Merry Christmas, Dad.'

Glover handed over two bottles of mulled wine from the corner shop.

'Merry Christmas indeed,' Ken declared with an off-putting chuckle. David looked down at the little wicker plant table to see a half-empty bottle of Sandemans port, a used glass and several cigar butts. He was in hiding and, at one o'clock, already a bit drunk.

'I like the Paddington Bear get-up,' Glover said, giving a little tug on the hood of the duffel coat.

'Christmas present from Hilda – so I can stay out here longer.'

Lunch was a buffet. Ken didn't like turkey and Hilda wrongly assumed that choice equated to quality. She had put on perfume, a purple pleated skirt and a cream silk blouse, along with an expression of radiant mania. She loved Christmas. So much could go wrong! Normally when someone entered their household the three of them behaved as if it were a gala performance, but today David couldn't rouse himself. When he stood with his back to the white marble fireplace, where a pyramid of smokeless fuel produced a flameless, heatless fire, he wanted to lie down on the rug and sleep.

Across the living room, in front of the closed venetian blind, his mother had set the small plastic tree on the magnified snowflake of a lace doily, atop the tallest of the three nesting tables. Since some of the branches had been slotted in wrongly to the metal trunk and were now stuck, it was bush-shaped rather than conical, and bare of decoration but for a single strand of silver tinsel that snaked around it, and an angel David had made at school from yellowed card and pipe cleaners, with a polystyrene ball for a head. The angel had had a cardboard wand once, and over the years Hilda had replaced it with a toothpick, a paperclip and now, rather ominously, a red-headed match. Ken, Glover and David sat obediently at the tablecloth embroidered with cartoon reindeer. On the sideboard knives and forks poked from a tumbler, and David thought how it looked like a modernist posy. Art was addictive, he realized, because analogy was a technique of integration, and thus gave endless, untrue hope for reconciling everything.

The day passed, however, without argument. David mined a tin of Roses for the hard centres. Relatives rang and the phone was passed round with dumbshows of refusal followed by enthusiastic words of greeting. Glover laughed at each mime in turn, conferring upon the Pinners membership of their own family.

Ken washed up; Glover dried; David made the tea. Hilda had been exiled to the living room and they could hear her pummelling the cushions to reshape them, then aligning the slate coasters with the edge of the coffee table. Ken asked Glover what he thought of QPR's new manager. Outside an antic blue tit alighted and clung and pecked at the feeder that hung on a nail in the fence post. Ken stood very still, watching the bird, letting only his hands move beneath the waterline of suds.

'Where do these go?'

Glover held four plates in a stack. David nodded at the wooden cupboard by Glover's head. 'Can you get me mugs when you're in there?'

As David poured milk from the carton into the Royal Doulton jug and set it on the floral tray, Glover clattered the mugs down beside it. David saw his dad glance at them and waited for him to speak. When he didn't, David said, 'No, not that red one.'

'What's wrong with it?'

Ken was looking straight ahead, out of the window. The bird had flitted off. All at once David could feel the heat of his father's tiredness. David said, 'That's the workman's mug.'

'Which workman?' Glover was grinning with disbelief, one eyebrow raised.

'Any of them. Mum has a thing about it not being used by family.'

'Should I take it? I work.'

David lifted the red mug and set it back in the cupboard. Ken, choosing deafness, continued staring into the garden, his hand moving a sponge inside a saucepan with a circular, meditative motion.

Glover and Ken sat at either ends of the new huge Land-of-Leather sofa, working industriously through a box of orange Matchmakers and a case of Guinness, amiably taking turns to retrieve cold cans from the garage. The sofa had arrived two weeks before and was an all-white, deep-backed, six-hide thing, which slumped against one wall like a snowdrift. Glover called it very bling-bling, and then had to explain what that meant. Hilda smiled but gave a tiny wounded sniff, so he began stroking the leather and saying, 'You know, this *really* is soft.' As for David, he was too old to sneer at anything in his parents' house. Taste, after all, was just taste. Refinement in such matters meant nothing but the smallest aspirational adjustment. Everyone needs something to lie on.

He sat at the dining table and flicked through one of his mother's magazines. He wasn't reading it exactly, but he found that looking at the airbrushed and the collagened, the perma-tanned and siliconed, made him strangely angry, and he lifted a biro from the sideboard and began doodling the obscenities of real life on them: double chins and buck teeth, spectacles and birthmarks, facial hair and frowns. Hilda announced herself with a sigh and settled in on the other side. Between mother and son the embroidered reindeer raced among the crumbs and spills. Her hair had been redone for Christmas and she lifted a hand to it now, patting to check that everything was in place.

'Are you having a nice Christmas, darling?'

'Of course. It's been great.'

She shifted in her seat a little, and raised her wine glass. Her lipstick had imprinted a cerise half-moon on the rim and she picked a white serviette from the pile on the table and wiped it off. He was reminded of taking Communion, kneeling between his parents at the rail, and watching the insipid verger wipe the silver cup before it came, disgustingly, to his own lips.

'I'm sorry the ham was tough. You never know until it's cooked. Even your dad can't choose one that—'

'It was fine. It was lovely.'

'So, are you going to tell me about your new friend, about this Ruth?'

He'd been stupid enough to mention her name on the phone to his mother once, though it had been so long ago that he thought she had forgotten. In general his mother was not a great listener, appearing to be counting seconds until she could speak again.

'Oh, she's well, as far as I know. She's off to New York for Christmas, actually.'

Hilda gave a cautious little smile, and pulled sharply at a loose brown thread attached to Rudolph's antler.

'Because your father and I wouldn't be ... we wouldn't object to meeting her at some point, you know.'

'Well, she's *just* a friend.'

Hilda nodded solemnly, entrusted with some vast and confidential responsibility. David was aware that Glover could probably hear, though Ken had found some goal-of-the-year programme on Sky Sports and was loudly disputing the findings. He lowered his voice.

'Actually, as it happens, she's started seeing James.'

His mother wilted. She drew her hands in off the table and set them in her lap, and looked much smaller suddenly, and old.

'Oh? I didn't realize that James and ... I didn't know.'

David was willing her to pretend that it was fine, that she wasn't upset, but she couldn't, or anyway didn't. Her face congealed into its pained expression, the very particular grimace that appeared when she watched the news or surveyed her neighbours' gardens from the back bedroom – his room when he stayed. Her weak chin elided into her neck, her eyes seemed to retract: every part of her tried to get as far away as possible from this repellent earth. David returned to looking at a wedding spread in the magazine and focused on the pictures. This happy couple's taste was refined as far as a three-year-old's fairy tale. Everything on their special day was gold and pink and white. David wanted his mother to get up and cross the room, to go back to the kitchen, but she started talking again, slowly now, in her dumb, tender voice.

'It's just we thought, when you talked about her on the phone ...'

He took up the biro again and started scribbling a moustache onto the bride, scoring bristles across her pointy little chin, her piscine pout. The pen broke through the page and ripped it. He knew Hilda was watching him with awkward, misplaced compassion and he said sternly, 'There's really nothing to talk about ... It's great. They're really happy together. *I'm* really happy for them.'

The grimace came again.

'All right, darling, all right. Shall I make some tea? I'll make some tea.'

jeroboam or something

David spent nearly all of the week after Christmas online. Singleton, it turned out, was nicely sarcastic, with good taste in movies and books, and she was also, like David himself, a truth-teller. She could see past the hype. Things between them were still in the abstract. They hadn't broached the topic of meeting yet, and neither had offered any real facts about themselves. They knew each other only by the soft individuating detail of their lives, their preferences and references and wit. He found himself thinking a lot about what she might look like. She had mentioned her 'untameable hair' but would only send a photo if he sent one first, and so far he hadn't. She had even begun to sign off with an X, sometimes two.

Glover's mobile curtly buzzed while *Zulu* was on telly after lunch on Wednesday, and the flatmates were in the middle of a game of Scrabble. He looked up from its screen to announce that Ruth was hosting a New Year's Eve dinner, and David was invited. The way he said it was particularly annoying, as if his own presence was a given, whereas David's was a gift. Instead of smiling, David simply nodded, not raising his stare from his rack of tiles.

'Yeah maybe, I'll need to speak to some people.'

His relationship with New Year's Eve parties was deeply unhealthy. They abused him, humiliated him, and he came back begging for more. He would spend the evening leaning in some stranger's kitchen doorway, getting snubbed and drunk, then queue for hours to use the single toilet, which would normally be blocked. The other thing was worse. He did it once. New Year's Eve alone.

David spent the tail end of the week reading Fowler's *The King's English*, having been asked a question in the week before Christmas about tenses, and having been stumped. He'd been standing at the whiteboard listing subordinate clauses in a monologue of Browning's when Clare, the Home Counties Queen, raised her hand and asked whether a certain phrase was in the pluperfect. David was flustered and avoided answering directly – saying, 'Well, what do *you* think?' – and she made a snotty little comeback about not being paid to know. At her intervention the entire class perked up, witnessed David's blushing, then lowered their embarrassed gazes, along with their expectations.

On Friday, New Year's Eve, he faced the horror of his wardrobe. Firstly, he ruled out what he wore for school – cords and chinos, the round-neck jumpers – and examined the rest. If what one wears says who one is, David decided he was either a lumberjack (three plaid shirts) or a slovenly undertaker (one black suit with a crusty stain on the sleeve). He stood in front of his wardrobe mirror in a pair of checked boxer shorts, and then in the bathroom stepped tentatively onto the scales. The needle swung and vacillated with his heart. Fourteen stone seven pounds. He used to weigh – when he started at Goldsmiths – twelve stone three. According to his mother, he once came in at seven pounds and six ounces of blessing and trouble.

Women tottered on and off the carriage, clutching each other and laughing, while the men grinned and cracked gags and clinked bags of drink. There was a determination to have fun, and even David succumbed to the microclimate, detecting a bounce in his step as he walked from the station to Ruth's tower, arriving at eight exactly. In his satchel the dark wet weight of chilled champagne and a shrink-wrapped box of chocolates waited, and as he stood in the foyer, watching the illuminated countdown of the lift descending to him, he came to a decision: tonight he would have fun.

Glover opened the door of the flat in a new caramel slim-fit shirt and a thin striped coffee-and-cream tie. His hair had been feathered or distressed or something. He looked as if he was the tough one in a boy band, and David told him so.

'Happy New Year to you too.'

In the white glare of the galley kitchen Ruth rushed towards David, her hair freshly dyed and cropped in New York, her eyes panda-ringed by eyeliner. She appeared to be wearing a kind of purple vestal robe. Everyone looked shiny and new, David thought, except him. As he was kissing Ruth hello, Larry appeared behind her.

'We're celebrating. Aside from this tiresome business of New Year's Eve, we just heard yesterday that the Tate are taking two pieces of Ruth's for their permanent collection.'

'The only reason Larry's celebrating is because he thinks he's going to make some money.'

The gallery owner mugged and winked at David, and David grinned obediently. He felt an irrational hatred for Larry's white collarless shirt, for the way his navy slacks were precisely tailored to hang with a single crease above the tips of his glossy brown brogues.

'Have some bubbles. Larry showed up with a nebuchadnezzar or a jeroboam or something.'

Ruth handed him a filled champagne flute, and then kissed him unexpectedly again on the cheek. David took out the chocolates and his ordinary-sized bottle of champagne and set them on the counter, beside Larry's goliath of glass. Ruth skimmed a glance at his offerings.

'Oh lovely, thank you. Let's go through to the living room. You have to meet Walter and Jess.'

■ ■ ■

The small chandelier of wrought-iron foliage had been dimmed, and the three light bulbs glowed like Bartlett pears, ready to be plucked. Neatly, sweetly, without emotion, Ella Fitzgerald tinkled in the background. David had once written a Damp review of tame, smug Ella, the most overrated singer of the last, failed century. Glover knelt by the stereo in the corner, talking to a thickset sixty-something man in a tailored navy suit. Ruth introduced David to Jess, a slender woman who didn't get off the sofa, though her eyes moved quickly up and down him. He felt processed, scanned, appraised. Her handshake was sharp, serrated with chunky rings.

'Jess is here for a shoot. She's working *tomorrow*, on New Year's Day. Isn't that crazy? And so unfair on Ginny.'

David shook his head at this new outrage.

'Are you a photographer?'

'Sometimes, but tomorrow I'm styling for a friend.' She had a slight, nasally voice, with a southern elasticity in the accent. David lowered himself down beside her. There was a pause. Jess was the first *official* lesbian he had ever met. He eyed her again, and smiled, and drank.

'You're kind of difficult to spot in all that black.'

David looked down at his shirt and jumper and jacket, as if he hadn't noticed what he was wearing, then gave Jess a very serious stare. 'I wear black on the outside because black is how I feel on the inside.'

She laughed – David was quoting but she didn't know – and tucked a strand of her grey bob girlishly behind one ear, to keep free her brown, suspicious eyes. David intuited immediately that here, finally, was an ally.

Ruth came back and handed Walter a glass, saying, 'It's such a shame you can't stay for dinner. Especially after I coerced Larry into making risotto.'

Walter gave a snickering laugh. 'I do love to see Larry coerced. No, my driver's waiting. He's listening to his Learn Italian tapes.' Then, as an afterthought, he barked, 'His new girlfriend's Milanese-a!'

The accent was odd, unplaceable, and there was something imperial, anticipatory about the way he sat there. He was waiting to be entertained.

Jess rose from the sofa and swished out after Glover and Ruth, and David saw that she was tall and small-breasted and elegant. Her cream camisole was embroidered with tiny black beads, as though an insect swarm had landed on her. At her neck she'd tied a thin, creased pale-coloured scarf: she could have been sitting beneath a ceiling fan on a veranda overlooking the Nile, awaiting her husband's return from the dig. David was alone with the collector. Walter raised his glass in acknowledgement and David matched the movement, grinning, then hauled himself up and pulled a dining chair over. This was what a man who owned a bank looked like: bald and solid and self-contained, with an old rugby player's leathery face.

'Have you travelled far?'

'Not very. Borough. Just south of the river. I came up on the tube.'

'You're a Londoner?'

'I was at Goldsmiths actually, and Ruth taught me, that's how I know her ... We're working together on a project, or talking about—'

'A project ...' Walter tilted his head back slowly, pouring the thought into his brain. Larry was laughing again; there was a hiss from the kitchen and a sudden smell of seafood.

David said, patiently, 'Yes, an art project ...'

'And what do you hope to *project*?'

Before David could reply, he placed a hand on his thigh and squeezed, hard, saying, 'Sorry – bathroom?'

David nodded in its direction.

Jess appeared with a silver clutch bag tucked under her arm. 'Do you smoke? I think I'll need my coat out there ... Did you remember to bring something warm with you?'

Wrapped in their layers, they smoked on the balcony, twenty-three floors above London. Jess snapped her silver Zippo ablaze in a gesture deft as any pool-room hustler's and proffered the flame to him. Her wedding ring was bulky and silver and square.

Although he was aware it was ridiculous, David had still half-expected Jess to be fierce and angry and dressed like Annie Hall. Instead she had a kind of glamorous exhaustion; had the half-closed, heavy eyelids of a Garbo or a Dietrich, though her skin was not as soft as it had been. She suggested by a slightly brusque and self-neglectful manner that she'd come through the nuisance of her looks, and was glad to have left all that behind her. As David leaned in with his fag, she said, 'So you're James's room-mate? That's quite a romance going on there.'

'Actually Ruth was my tutor at Goldsmiths – I was just telling Walter – and we're working on a project about text in urban settings – graffiti, witness appeals, found notes, that kind of thing ...'

'Ruth's working on a lot of projects ...'

Tenderly, so it seemed to David, Jess slipped her arm through his and steered him the few feet over to the puckered concrete of the balcony wall. They were not scared of physical contact, these people. Before them London was a sunken, bioluminescent world. A black taxi glided far below on Moorgate, shark-like, feeding. The roundabout at Old Street eddied. Headlights shoaled along the Embankment and across Blackfriars Bridge. Jess closed her purse with an immaculate click, and said, 'Very young, isn't he? I mean, I know muses are, generally ...'

David took a long pull on his cigarette.

'A *muse* – really?'

'Sure ... I used to sit for Ruth, you know. A long time ago. It's part of the deal.'

David felt his stubby little heart rouse itself at the thought of these two women, lovers. He betrayed nothing in his manner, but the fact remained – the idea was hopelessly exotic to him.

'She used me for some of the ancestral portraits in the Demand series ...'

David looked up; Jess was watching him, expecting something.

'You know the early work, right? *The Republic of Women, The Gynaeconaut* ...'

'I mean, I've read a bit about them but ... I remember the crockery, with the Greek slave girls and housewives?'

'I was on four of the flags. Or at least my face was on two and my body was on two.' Jess gestured with her cigarette at her shoulders and then her thighs, denoting the cut-off points. '*And* I'd just turned twenty-one. My parents were, well, you can imagine ... Small-town Carolina ...'

David knew a bit about *The Republic of Women*. When Ruth had arrived at Goldsmiths there'd been a special lecture on it by his director of studies, the obese Mr Lawrence Booth, who had evidently loathed the whole thing; indeed had evidently loathed all women, republican or otherwise. Jess was still talking.

'I think it was less about gender, and more about playing with cultural memory, traditions, historicity, domesticity ...'

If Glover had been with them, David would have added *electricity, Kendal, Felicity, the Lovin' Spoonful's Summer in the City* ... but as it was, he nodded with renewed seriousness. He was getting cold. There was one plastic chair on the balcony and he wondered if it would be rude now to sit in it. He said, 'I seem to remember some sort of enormous spaceship in the shape of a teapot.' He smiled; Jess didn't and he stopped. She shook her grey bob.

'That was very late. Eighty-six, eighty-seven. I found most of that collection was a little misconceived, actually. I told Ruth at the time ... But do you remember that exquisite woven rug with a woman weaving a rug on it? Imaging Penelope instead of Odysseus.'

David was wondering about the other lit windows in the Barbican. That, and the fact that *image* was a verb now and no one had told him. The far towers and low-rises of this citadel with disabled access were randomly patched with these glowing squares, the yellow badges of habitation. Here were a thousand variations on the theme of New Year's Eve, occurring just beyond the blinds and curtains. David flicked his cigarette out into the open night. It fell from sight immediately, without spark or significance.

'So has James told you?'

'Told me?'

'Ruth said there was going to be an announcement.'

'Oh my God, she's not ...'

'I think she's a little old for that.'

Amazed, David turned towards the source of his amazement, and saw them in the living room, separated from him by the glass door. Glover, grinning idiotically, had seized Ruth from behind and now kissed her neck. She was holding a complex glass apparatus containing both balsamic vinegar and olive oil but she tilted her face forward in a drowsy motion, so her head was directly under the three lit bulbs: David noticed how the hair was thinning.

They sat at the table as Larry docked a huge plate of risotto in the centre, and gave it one last stir, sweeping it to granulated banks and dunes. Inexplicably, he miaowed at David and everyone laughed. David had to tell himself to look away from Glover's face, then from Ruth's. Both had the same little secretive smile, both added an extra dimension of effort to their glances and their conversation.

They were quorate, and at once Larry, as David knew he would, lifted his glass to make a toast; his pearl-and-silver cufflink hovered six inches from David's face. He wore a large gold ring on his pinkie finger and the nails looked manicured, even and clean. His addiction, his oxygen, was money. He had refined himself as far as he wanted to go, and in doing so had found a steady, solid amount of joy in the world. He held everything at arm's length, where he could see it properly. Jess, noticing the upraised glass, abruptly stopped talking.

'I just wanted to propose a toast to Ruth for allowing me to use the facilities of her kitchen this evening' – Larry turned from Ruth to nod his silver fringe at Walter – 'and to the philanthropist Walter Testa for granting her tenancy of that fine kitchen for six months to bring a little more art into the world, and, not forgetting, a toast to me for persuading Walter to let Ruth escape from New York and general heartbreak' – he paused and swung his glass to Glover – 'and to James, for putting a smile on that lovely face again, and again and again' – Ruth said 'Larry!' and gave a toothy, unattractive giggle – 'to Jess for her wonderful skirt' – the whole table laughed, and David felt stupidly nervous, as though he was going to be picked last, if at all, for the team – 'and her inspired photographs and her wonderfully toned physique, which I have to say is really quite a feat for someone now in the same decade as me' – smiling, Jess said, 'I will throw this champagne over your shirt if you don't ...' – 'and lastly to David, our head cheerleader.' Glover was grinning across the table, almost unable to stand the excitement. He began to push his chair back to stand up.

pyrotechnics

David remembered the small shock of learning that other people didn't sleep in the same posture as him. It had been the first year of some reality TV show, and he got into the habit of turning the portable on when he got into bed. It was company, the rows of sleepers arrayed in that night-vision grey. Some would be lying like saints on their plinths, on their backs, moonbathing. Some would be turned over on their sides, into the recovery position, or frozen mid-leap like fairy-tale characters; and some would have fallen flat on their guts, an ear pressed to the world, listening. Only one or two, like David, would be coiled in a C, a foetal crouch, protecting themselves from what came in their dreams.

So upon waking into a brand-new year, curled in his usual prawn, he was already physically adjusted for the immediate feeling of shame. That sensation sharpened over the next few minutes as the night before came back in shards. He suddenly remembered saying to Jess as he waited for his taxi that she was the nicest person he'd met. She'd patted his cheek as though he were five years old and called him a total sweetheart. He remembered that Glover and Ruth had announced their engagement. He still couldn't quite process that and stored it for later, for when he was less ... dying.

The light in his bedroom struck in round the curtains' edges and turned them a tinned-tuna pink. Gingerly he propped himself up on pillows, like some precious displayed artefact, switched on the laptop and checked his mail, taking great care to move only his fingers. The pop-up blocker was disabled and three windows appeared suddenly telling him that he was the millionth visitor to the website, and that BIG CASH PRIZES awaited him. He shut them down and checked the stats for his blog. Two visitors since yesterday morning. David looked up the IP addresses and checked where they lived. Singleton had been but had left no New Year wishes. He eased himself, inch by inch, back down into the bed. His head felt hollowed out and filled with sandpaper, allergies, hurt, whatever little boys are made of.

His stomach, that dictator, eventually drove him to his dressing gown and kitchen, where he made toast and tea and boiled four identical beige eggs. As they sat in a row before him, in matching yellow china egg cups, he thought of ovals. Recognizing the shapes of things was about all he could manage. The plate was a circle, the knife a tangent. His hangover had begun in earnest, with accidie, nausea and a distinct pain in the frontal lobes each playing competing discordant parts. In the living room the telephone rang plaintively and he decided to ignore it, and that felt good and a little risky.

As soon as he heard Glover's key in the door he jumped up from the table, and spilt the remains of his mug of cold tea. He left it and made for his bedroom. He had assumed he'd see no one all day and had been planning an afternoon of updating The Damp Review, surfing for porn, smoking a spliff and reading Berryman's *Dream Songs*. He was halfway down the hallway when the front door opened, trapping him behind it, and he stood there helplessly. Ruth came through the door first, in a maroon cloche hat and a black pashmina doubled up and wrapped around her neck. Glover's black beanie bobbed behind her. They'd been walking and glowed with vigour and purpose. Glover cradled a bag of croissants and a stack of newspapers.

When she saw David, Ruth started but recovered and cried, 'Darling, Happy New Year!'

David pushed the front door shut to get past them, and kept on for the bedroom, shouting over his shoulder that he'd be out in a minute.

He dressed and sloped into the living room, where Ruth, still standing, handed him the arts section of a newspaper. It was a round-up-of-the-year piece.

'Under the picture of Lucian Freud,' she said, and sat down as he scanned the column:

2005 also saw the arrival of American artist Ruth Marks to these shores. Her gender-led, highly sexualised work attempts to rewrite male orthodoxy and though she sometimes seems hackneyed in content, her formal variety is always of interest. Her Barbican residency brings a welcome addition to the London arts scene. A retrospective runs from 20 January to 18 March.

A pack of his Marlboro Lights was on the coffee table and she slipped one from its box, pinched it in half.

'Ouch,' David offered.

She grimaced and lit the demi-fag. Immediately the smoke tripled his nausea.

'Just bullshit – not worth reading,' he said and smacked the paper with the back of his hand.

'Gender-led? What does that even mean?' David crossed the room to open the window as she sucked hard on the cigarette. He hoisted the sash and a blast of arctic weather entered. Nausea or hypothermia, he thought, your choice.

'Ruth, this person's written *to these shores*. They've written *a welcome addition*. It's barely literate. It's padding.'

She nodded, and picked at one of her nails. Her cloche hat fell off the sofa to the carpet and she looked at it, making no effort to lift it. She should be over the moon today. A whole new life ahead of her, but she was still a neurotic. Thank God for neurotics. Without them, David thought, there'd be no art at all. He remembered the time he'd reassured her in the echoey hall at Goldsmiths, how tender she'd been, how exposed.

'But to be dismissed in one line by someone you don't know, who doesn't make any attempt to meet your work halfway . . .'

'In fact,' David said, enjoying fording her stream of self-pity, 'let's burn it. Right now.'

'Really?'

'We *have* to,' David said firmly. 'Otherwise it'll just sit here on the table annoying you for the rest of the day.'

Glover entered, carrying a tray with coffee and the Christmas tin of shortbread David's mother had sent back with them.

'We're going to burn that nasty little paragraph . . .'

Glover set the tray down, so precisely that it made no sound. 'We should burn the idiot who wrote it . . .'

David folded the page and tore the paragraph out, leaving a kidney-shaped hole beneath Freud's glare. Ruth murmured, 'I commit thee to the flames. Oh, be careful with it.'

The crumpled bud burned slowly before blooming, suddenly, and then in an instant wilted. David poked at it with his lighter, breaking up the glossy endoskeleton.

Glover dropped another section of the newspaper on the coffee table – loosing a couple of burnt frills of ash into the air – and depressed the plunger of the cafetière with stately deliberation, detonating some historic building. David decided to face the inevitable head-on.

'God, I almost forgot. Congratulations! Have you told everyone? How did Bridget take the news?'

Ruth laughed with a quick defensiveness. 'David! You make it sound like I've some terminal illness!'

'I didn't mean—'

'We just spoke to her, actually. She was delighted—'

'Well, not quite delighted maybe . . .' Glover added.

'She's delighted about coming to London for the wedding, and she's bringing Rolf.'

Rolf was her boyfriend. He was 'inappropriate', being five years older, but was becoming 'a reality with which we'll just have to deal'. David intended to point out the irony soon. Glover switched on the television. Football.

'We've missed ten minutes. You know, you were pretty pissed last night.'

'Yeah, sorry about that.'

Glover told him how he had tried, jokily but persistently, to punch him in the stomach. After that he'd put his head down with an audible bang on the dining-room table. He knew Glover must be exaggerating, but as he kept on talking, David had the faintest sensation of memory surfacing, as if he were hearing the plot of a book he'd loved as a child. Eventually they'd put him in a cab. He didn't remember getting home. He didn't remember getting inside the flat or undressing or making and eating a ham sandwich, the evidence for which, a plate of stiffened crusts, was on the bedside table when he woke.

Ruth had gone to lie down for a while and as David passed Glover's door, carrying the empty plate and cup from his room to the kitchen, she called, 'James.' He pushed gently at the bed-room door.

'Me, actually.'

'Oh hey, you okay? You and Jess really hit it off.'

She lay on her side on the bed, reading. Her baggy brown corduroys and grey wool V-neck made David think of the women, the incidentally liberated, who took the factory jobs after the men went to war. One of her legs was drawn up and the material gathered at the knee in soft corrugations. David set the cup and plate on top of a wine box against the wall, and sat on the director's folding chair, where Glover's clothes were usually draped. He thought suddenly, irrelevantly, that he'd never sat here before.

'She's great. Ruth, maybe it's not my place to ask, but have you told James about her? It's just she mentioned to me that you'd been in a relationship together and maybe James has a right to know ...'

She sighed. 'Oh, it came up last night. I think you might have brought it up, in fact.'

'Really? God, I don't even remember—'

'No, it's fine, honestly. It's just a shame that everyone was drunk. He said I should have told him.'

'About Jess?'

'That I'd been *with women.*' She widened her dark mobile eyes as if this was just hilarious. 'Anyway, it's fine. He likes Jess. So can you believe it? That we're getting married?'

That was evidently the end of the topic. David shifted in his seat. The room looked odd from this new angle, the ceiling seemed lower.

'Not really, to be honest. What happened?'

'We've been getting on so well, and talking about him coming back with me to New York, and it just seemed to make sense. I didn't expect it, but last night we were in the bedroom and he suddenly got down on one knee. I thought he was joking.' She was grinning at the memory; David could tell the story was already crystallizing into myth. No doubt he would hear it again and again. The thought made him very tired. 'He didn't have a ring, so he took this off and put it round my neck.'

She pulled a silver chain from under her white T-shirt, fingered it.

'Huh. It's quite a decision.'

107

Ruth gave a tiny non-committal shrug.

'Oh, let's not be too sensible about it now. I'm at the stage where all I want is somebody who's nice to me, who's kind to me. I've had enough of tortured artists. I want somebody *good*.' She patted something on the bed. 'Have you ever actually *read* this thing?'

It was Glover's Bible, open at some highlighted passage.

'Well, parts of it, of course. At school, and I used to go to church with my parents ...'

She slapped it shut. David said, 'We could burn it next.'

'Don't let James hear you.'

They were being conspiratorial again. She flexed her leg, dissolving the corrugations, and held it a few inches in the air, as if she might start exercising, then let it drop onto the bed.

'I think he might be growing out of it.'

'Really? How come?'

'You'll laugh.'

'I won't.' David raised his right hand, taking an oath.

'Well, he's stopped saying his prayers at night. The first few times we shared a bed, I'd say something and he'd reply, "Can you give me a minute, I'm praying?"'

David pretended to hold a phone to his ear, then turned his head away from it and mimicked Glover's slower, deeper voice: 'Any chance you could give me a minute? God's just on the other line.'

She giggled, rising notes. 'No, we shouldn't make fun. But all that does seem to have gone to the wall. I'm almost sad about it. I find myself admiring those who *can* pray. I go into churches around the Barbican sometimes, in the afternoons, and there's always one or two women on their knees ...'

'Cringing?'

Ruth placed her hand over the Bible, protecting it from David, and said, 'You know I was brought up Lutheran, and I *do* think faith can be a wonderful thing if you can sustain it.' It was typical of Ruth to be so needlessly ambivalent, he thought.

'Oh come on, there's no excuse now for believing in the supernatural.'

'You're making belief sound ridiculous.'

'Because it is.'

She had had enough then, and sat up, swinging her legs down from the bed. She stretched her arms in the air and breathed out loudly, pitching backwards. He could see the shape of her breasts very clearly. He looked away but a little too late: abruptly she dropped her arms, crossing them over her chest. Quickly he said, 'And I'm sorry about last night. When I was a bit drunk. I wasn't trying—'

She held a hand in the air. 'Stop apologizing. Everyone *loves* you.' Then she locked her eyes on David's. 'I know people might blink at it, at first, and they might say the age gap's problematic and, God, how am I going to meet his *parents*? But I really think that James and I ... I *love* this man. I was as surprised as anyone when he asked me yesterday. I hadn't even been thinking ...'

She smoothed a hand over the pillow. David stood up and the movement incited some further disclosure from her. 'I mean, maybe it's premature but why not? I kept thinking to myself, why not?'

David resisted the impulse to itemize reasons. He looked around the room as if it might hold clues to Glover's interior life. It was a small white box, tidy and impersonal. You could tell he rented. It was as if he was camped in it. Nothing nailed to the walls. Everything portable, foldable, packable. The wine crates held his books and a few DVDs. An old leather suitcase in the far corner stored his CDs. He didn't have much. Ruth talked on.

'I just worry that at his age he doesn't know his own mind ... but he seems so *certain* about things, so together. So much more together than I was at twenty-three. God, our generation weren't like that, were they?'

Our generation? Jesus Christ. He was closer to Glover's age than hers. Did she think she was fooling him? She'd *taught* him. David simply nodded and pulled the door a few inches ajar.

'And there's something else James wants to talk to you about today.'

So Glover was moving out, moving to America with Ruth. David would have another month or year or decade of living here alone and then, when he'd grown bored enough to suffer it, he'd organize a round of interviews from *Loot*. The goths, the Aussies, the newly divorced. A knot of toads. A cast of hawks. A bloat of hippopotami.

In the living room, hunched on the edge of the sofa, elbows on his knees, Glover was absorbed in the football. David looked at him expectantly but he ignored him, and lightly drummed the remote control on the tin of shortbread Hilda had sent back with them at Christmas. The crowd's white noise subsided. A whistle blew. When Ruth settled in beside Glover and stroked his neck he dipped his head away, as if even that minute distraction was too much. She drew back her hand, rearranged her black pashmina around herself in two loose loops. David was sifting the newspapers for the property section and noticed.

'Should I turn the thermostat up? Are you a bit cold?'

'*Are* you cold?' Glover repeated, in a tone that suggested she'd refused to answer.

'No, no, I'm fine. This is so soft I was just wrapping myself up in it.' Glover reached out and fingered the material. From where David sat it looked as if the back of his hand must be rubbing against her chest.

'It's really soft. Is it new?' he said, grinning, eyebrows arched.

'It's not mine. Jess left it behind last night.' Glover dropped his hand. 'It's almost unbearably *plush*.' She elongated the sibilant and seemed to gift the word some hidden sexual context. David looked at the toy men chasing each other on-screen.

'You really shouldn't be wearing her shawl. You might get it dirty or something,' Glover said.

'It's a pashmina and it's only Jess's. She won't mind. The *wardrobes* of clothes she's stolen from—'

'You should take it off.' The crowd noise from the TV began building again but Glover didn't even turn to see the screen. There was a little stand-off occurring. David looked down at the newspaper on his lap and pretended to be engrossed by an article on interest rates.

'Oh, don't be silly. If I want to wear—'

'I'm not being silly. It's not yours. Would you like it if you left a coat at someone's house and they wore it round the town?'

'It's not a *coat*, darling. It's a pash—'

'Oh, for *fuck's* sake, whatever it is. Would *you* like it?'

Ruth said nothing. Glover's curse had flavoured the atmosphere, suddenly turning everything a different colour. David read how some experts predicted a rise of another quarter point, while others thought the rates would stay put. The TV commentator spoke into the silence about a superb long ball. The pashmina's inky black made Ruth's body into silhouette. David could see the thinness of her shoulders, the tilt of her breasts, then the angle of the lifted arm that brought a glass of water to her tightened, silent, lovely mouth.

By the time the football match ended, Glover lay like a sick child across the sofa, his head on Ruth's lap. She was playing with his hair, teasing it into separate strands with her fingers. The shawl lay over the back of the armchair. Glover had one hand slid down the front of his jeans, up to the knuckles, and the other was on Ruth's knee.

'He wanted to wait until the soccer finished.'

Glover bumped his head on her thigh in reproof, and sat up.

'The thing is, it's going to be a small wedding, and since we wouldn't even know each other if it wasn't for you, we wondered if you fancied being best man.'

He employed several hand gestures throughout this little declaration and finished, bizarrely, by pointing at David. *If you fancied being* – it sounded as if Glover thought he was the one doing *him* a favour. Still, he supposed he was quite pleased.

'Of course, I'd be delighted. It'd be an absolute honour.'

a red jewel sparkled in her navel

At PMP the A-level students sat their mocks straight after Christmas, at the start of the January term, and it had become traditional that they organize a party to celebrate the exams' conclusion, which – since PMP paid for it – the teachers were meant to attend. The students brought girlfriends or boyfriends, the teachers presented their spouses for inspection and everyone was entreated, like so many Rapunzels, to let their hair down. The fact that a few of the Year Sevens were always technically under the legal drinking age was never discussed. Each year the Mocks Party came and each year David, slightly stoned, with a righteous sense of grievance, went.

The Year Sevens' social committee was headed by Kimberley, an Australian student with a nose ring and a raft of blonde ringlets that provided her with endless satisfaction. If David asked her a question, she'd give them a quick, equine toss before responding. And she talked as she wrote, babbling nervily around a topic. Sometimes her essays actually ended with an exclamation mark – *which all goes to show why Shakespeare is undoubtedly the world's greatest writer!* She had managed to compound the general horror of the evening by staging the party on a boat. They were to be transported, pointlessly, up and down the Thames, which David realized would preclude any early departures.

Kimberley distributed the invites on the first morning of the term, and David spent the entire day worrying. The mad idea of asking Singleton gnawed at him. They were corresponding on a daily basis, and though their talk was still guardedly abstract, though he didn't even know her name or age, they really seemed to *get* each other. There was definitely something there. Even so, a boatload of watching students was not the ideal backdrop for a first date. It would have to be deferred.

That evening Glover, late for work, pulled back the front door to find David tipping forward, key poised, his moon face startled. David tugged out his earphones and asked immediately whether Glover would come with him to the party. He was reluctant, he said he'd heard too many horror stories, but David persisted, persistence being his most significant asset. He promised that it would be interesting for Glover to put faces to the names and he reminded him that he was acting as his best man, and that it was only for one night, and what were they talking about, really? Three hours probably, four maximum. Glover hated to be painted as a man who might let someone down, and finally he agreed, telling David they could always smuggle in a pair of lilos to escape on.

■ ■ ■

On the night itself it took some time to actually locate 'London's premier floating disco', the SS *Carolina*, and they traipsed down several alleyways in Vauxhall before they came across it. Moored close to the riverbank, it was strung with lights and made moist, unnerving slapping sounds as it responded to the river's movements. A slatted wooden bridge took them aboard to Kimberley, the official greeter, who pressed the flesh and flicked her hair and whinnied. David introduced Glover, and then Kimberley presented David with a card from the class, to thank him for his efforts. It featured a quote from James Joyce on the front to the effect that our errors are portals of discovery. David felt that was overly optimistic of them. That class's errors, that class *of* errors, were simply mistakes, fuck-ups due to arrogance and laziness, and misplaced faith in their own capabilities. His students thought self-belief was a good thing. They didn't understand yet that it was the most dangerous delusion of them all. It could ruin your life. Still, it was nice to get a token of their appreciation. He showed it to Glover and watched his gaze skim lightly across it.

David had a fag before going in and the flatmates propped their elbows on the railings out on deck, side by side and mesmerized by the quick, black legion water. Its machinations – turbulent, tubular – left David dizzy. A police launch passed on the far side, lit up and noisy and moving at speed. The boat made a gross sucking noise as the wake of the launch lifted them towards the looming office blocks.

The music had started inside and David was cornered in front of a speaker by Marissa, the teacher who normally ran the debating society. He watched how her mouth, drawn on inexpertly with purple lipstick, made a variety of shapes. The bad nineties pop was much too loud to let him hear whatever she was saying and he simply nodded. She was supposed to be on maternity leave, but had still turned up for the party, proudly swollen in a flowery canopy. Holding her hand was her husband, Benny, a short, bald, bearded Mancunian. He had one of those faces that is also a face if you turn it upside down, and he kept looking hopefully around him as if he might at any moment wake. Faizul pranced towards them and David escaped to Glover and the bar. As he stood against it, awaiting a drink, the underfoot vibrations of the engines began; then the boat peeled away from the bank and London began to scroll past the window.

Glover was looking the girls over with small sly glances, following their progress as they crossed the empty dance floor or stood at the bar. They took their beers and walked down to a booth. For a few seconds David tried to pull the table out so he could squeeze round it, before realizing it was bolted to the floor. Glover smirked and David felt irrationally humiliated, and almost tearful.

Most of the evening David spent talking about American literature with a very serious student called Michael. Michael wanted to 'be a writer', a very different thing, David suggested, from wanting to write. He had white filthy dreads and his paisley-print shirt was too short on the sleeves. Glover was having fun, dancing with Kimberley and a group of her friends. Whatever else Ruth had given him, she had bestowed a new kind of confidence. David had never seen him so happy and fearless. He had two moves – a kind of little shimmy and a clap – but they were good ones. Unlike the other males on the dance floor, he neither overexerted nor embarrassed himself, and he smiled. The faces of the rest were agonies of concentration or frozen in the Caucasian's funky overbite. When Kimberley's group sat down Glover followed. David walked over and hovered until they budged up in their booth. He ensconced himself by Kimberley's sister Rosie, on whose far side Glover sat. She was pretty, David decided, but mostly because she was young, and animated with the same irritatingly jovial manner as Kimberley. David examined Rosie's porcelain blondeness. The skin above her slightly pointy breasts displayed a network of submerged blue veins, a faded river map. A black cropped top showed off a taut, in-curved midriff, where a red jewel sparkled in her navel. David had to make a conscious effort not to stare at it and he fixed his eyes on the rim of his pint. There were six girls around the table, all tipsy and made up and incredibly loud, and he didn't quite know what to say, or where to look, or exactly why he was here. He leant across the table and asked Clare about her English paper; she just smiled and pretended not to have heard.

Shots of tequila appeared, which everyone slammed on the table while David held his beer so it wouldn't get spilt. Later, when Rosie said she was doing international relations at UCL, and David had to stop himself responding *And I'll bet you've done nearly all of them*, he realized he was drunk again. He squeezed out from the table to get a glass of water. At the bar, Alistair, a new history teacher with extraordinary halitosis, wanted to discuss subsidized travelcards; then they were both trapped again by Michael. When David escaped for a smoke, Glover and Rosie were out on the deck, talking intently in a doorway. He was about to join them when he noticed how their heads were inclined towards each other, and how she had laid a hand on Glover's chest.

When they moored again the lights came on, instant and harsh, and all at once everyone was sweaty, bedraggled and grey. Glover reappeared and briskly announced he was heading off to a house party with Rosie and Kim. David said he should get back anyway, that he was knackered, and Glover nodded. David wandered for a while through the night cold, sound-tracked on his iPod by Maria Callas's *Aida*, and finally found a minicab office on Vauxhall Bridge Road. He sat in there waiting, listening to the Caribbean operator swear creatively at his drivers. David was thinking how even by appointing him his best man Glover had just formalized his idea of their relationship: David was his liege, his understudy, his ballboy and his footnote, his Sancho Panza, his Mercutio, there for service, nothing more.

At 4 a.m. he was still awake – on the internet – and Glover hadn't come in. And the next morning his bed was still made. At ten-thirty David heard his key scrape in the door and found him in the kitchen, at the sink, kink-haired and gulping down a pint of water. The radio was on the pirate reggae station and softly played a dub version of Foreigner's 'I Want to Know What Love Is'. He was hurrying, he said; he had to grab a shower and get back into Soho for his shift. David remained in the doorway. Nobody was going anywhere.

'But how was the house party?'

'Oh, fine, fine. Nothing too exciting. I kipped on someone's sofa.'

He was lying. The speech was too rapid, the information given not the information requested. He had prepared, and badly. Now he glanced out of the window, interested suddenly in what the sky was up to, what shapes the clouds were forming.

'And Rosie?'

Glover grinned then, despite himself, and said, 'Nothing. Nothing really.'

David laughed nastily – it was such a childish answer. Glover looked back at him; guilty, a little fearful. The two vertical slits in his forehead appeared and he rubbed at them with his fingers and thumb.

'I didn't sleep with her. Not really. A kiss and a cuddle.'

David said nothing. Glover stepped backwards and leant against the worktop, and the physical movement triggered some internal collapse. His head lolled forward as though a cord had been cut.

'Ruth rang this morning when I was walking to the tube and I couldn't even answer it. I didn't know what to say ...'

'Are you going to tell her?'

He looked up, appalled, rubbed at his forehead again. He was unused to sinning.

'Jesus Christ ...' David said. He leaned in like someone who could help and asked, quietly, 'Were you angry with her? About Jess?'

Glover shook his head, opened his mouth but produced no sound. With his hands clasped together, preacher-like, imploring, he turned back to the sink and looked out on the newly disordered city. David felt an obscene urge to laugh, but instead plunged two slices of white loaf into the toaster; watched the filaments buckle and redden with localized fury.

invisible presences

All Sunday David's mind skittered round in circles. At midnight
he washed two herbal sleeping tablets down with a mug of
Pinot Grigio, and entered violent dreams involving aggressive,
talking eels and keyholes and his Auntie Yvonne's one-eyed cat.
The next morning, after groggily setting his A-level group a
chunk of Chaucer to parse, he locked himself in the disabled
toilet and rang Ruth. She was abstracted, concentrating on
something, and said, 'Sure, of course, come over to the studio
around six.'

By the time he stepped into the cobbled yard the sky was dark,
and although she'd said she never turned the strip lights on, finding such fluorescence too clinical and cold to paint beneath, their
polar glare was visible through the pane of glass above her door.
He knocked diffidently, a suitor.

She was standing in the middle of the studio, at work. Amidst
the mess, the cardboard boxes, the salvaged tea chests and stacks
of canvases, the paints and pots and planks, the easel that she
stood at seemed to David like some long-limbed grazing animal
come on in a clearing, which she was stroking, and which might,
at any second, bolt. She whispered hi and then turned back to
the canvas, so he picked a quiet way through the clutter to the
sink and filled the kettle. Her engrossment gifted him a feeling of
privilege; he was eavesdropping with her on great, invisible pres-
ences. As he scanned for mugs along the cluttered surfaces he

saw the glass heart in its shoebox, crystal and bulky on a bed of scrunched newspaper. It looked finished and was so delicate, David found – as he ran a fingertip along one caulked edge – that he was holding his breath.

The old clock radio on the draining board flashed 00:00. Tuned to a talk radio station, it stayed on all day, but with the volume set too low to pick up the actual conversations. When she was a little girl Ruth would lie in bed in their red-brick walk-up on 67th listening to the muffled sounds of her parents and their friends talking for hours, on the far side of the peach-blossom wallpaper. It still gave her a feeling of safety to know that somewhere people were talking things through, she said, that she wasn't alone in the world. When she told David these things, even after the engagement, he could not quite stop that old stirring of warmth and protection. And he felt it now.

The canvas faced away from him but she stood at an angle to it, and he could watch the whole of her. She looked good in work garb, the hair tangled and held back with a black headband, which on closer inspection became one leg of a pair of tights, tied. On her hands and narrow wrists were smears and spots of paint. The apron, David thought, was strangely flattering, emphasizing the curves of her chest and waist and hips. At the *clink-clink* of him stirring the coffee, she came over and took the mug in both hands, blowing on the top of it and sending the steam to him in a winter breath. He wanted to sit her down and hold her, let her melt into him again; he wanted to tell her everything.

'I'm writing today off. An utter waste of time.'

'I'm sure that's not true.'

'I don't know when to let the thing be finished. I have to always …' She looked up at David suddenly. 'I can't talk about the project now, you know. I have to finalize the exhibition and before that—'

'Oh no, no, that's okay. It was something else, actually ...'

'Hmmmm?' She left her coffee on the table and then lifted up the canvas, turned it round and rested it against the wall, on the far trestle table. For the first time, David saw what she was working on, and set his coffee on the draining board to prevent it spilling. Glover.

The middle band of the painting, from his thighs to his lips, was exact and photographic. Here were his square shoulders and lean chest, the light definitions of his belly. Here were moles on his skin, the raw zip of his appendicitis scar. Faint, whiskery hairs on the pectorals, a thicker line of hair descending to the pubic swarm, and here his narrow hips led in a V to the penis, substantial, whitely luminous, with a fat vein running slant across it. Here were his arms lifted and turned outwards, with brilliantly foreshortened hands beseeching the viewer. But to what end? To seduce or fight? To flee? There was an ambiguity about the pose: the nakedness was sexual, the stance adversarial, the entire thing unsettling. The torso was cropped uncleanly, as if by the two imaginary Tropics. Above the full lips with their cupid's bow, an invisible latitudinal line marked a drifting from focus, and the painting lightened and blurred until a foot or so higher it merged with blank canvas. There was only a mess of a nose, and no eyes to see, no ears. At the thighs the Tropic of Capricorn began, and the same drift and blurring occurred. The legs faded, nebulous. The figure was trapped in the canvas like quicksand.

David felt woozy with embarrassment. He looked away, then back again. The backdrop to the picture was Ruth's living room in the Barbican. She must have been working from a photograph. Ruth had been thinking about those unfinished paintings by Michelangelo that they'd seen in the National. She'd taken the strong lines, the dislocations, the spooky lacunae, and made from Glover this ghoulish, headless, legless, camp-fucked Christ.

122

'Oh, don't look at this. It's not finished,' she said, turning off the main lights.

Gratefully, without comment, David sat down on a tea chest, his back to the canvas, and sipped at his coffee. Ruth stepped out into the courtyard and he heard the soles of her white Converses slap across the cobbles. There was a plate-sized magnifying glass, angled on a bendy stem, and David examined his index finger under it, seeing the whorls magnified to tree rings and oxbows. It was impossible not to find connections when one looked closely at something, he thought. Art itself was a kind of lens, messing with perspective, and it could focus light on a single point, which might catch fire or might not. Art was like prayer; which was like concentration; which was like patience; and patience, David thought, was the most beautiful word in the language. Calm down, he said out loud. Calm down.

He was standing by the door of the studio smoking when Ruth came back from the bathroom and began rinsing brush heads at the sink, refracting the transparent beam of water into its disparate spectral colours.

'What was it you were going to tell me earlier?'

The little nubs of her shoulders in her white cotton T-shirt drew together as she spoke. David looked at Glover's melting face.

'Oh, nothing, really.'

'James said you've been talking to someone online. Have you met yet face to face? We should all go for dinner.'

'No, no, nothing's happened. We're just talking. I mean it's only an internet thing. I don't know that it's even going to get to—'

Ruth turned and put a finger to her lips. Working all day alone had left her childish, solicitous and exhausted.

'Ssshh, don't say that. You never know what's about to happen.'

123

She walked over and held out her hand. On her wedding finger was the smallest diamond David had ever seen. It was a speck of diamond, a grain, a neutrino.

'Isn't it cute? Glover gave it me last night. He'd even wrapped the box.'

exactly what an image does

Ruth was the only person David knew who still brandished a chequebook. She had credit and debit cards but claimed she could never remember her PIN codes. It was the evening of Ruth's opening, and after Jess had got her Campari and soda, Larry his gin and tonic, Walter his whiskey, and the boys their beers, she had pulled the chequebook from her bag and was now waggling it over the bar of the ICA, awaiting her glass of Petit Chablis. When the bargirl noticed the antique method of payment she winced, and said that Ruth would have to wait until Orlando was free. Orlando, the dapper little manager in the ruffled shirt, with slicked-down hair and an apprentice moustache, threw them a glance of practised hauteur, and David was reminded of Proust. He felt, as he supposed he was meant to, daunted and inferior, and he insisted on paying with cash. Ruth, before leaving with her glass of wine, rooted around in her bag and pulled out her fat black purse. She thrust it at David and said, 'No, please, take this. I think there's money in here.'

And there was: three pounds and sixty-three pence, among the business cards and boarding passes.

The evening crawled for David. When Larry pulled Glover forward to introduce him as 'Ruth's partner', David had stepped back and then wandered the rooms, taking notes in case he decided to write something on it. Half an hour later he came upon his flatmate again. Glover was sitting on a plastic chair, by an exit sign, secretly playing Snake on his mobile. He told David he'd overheard a woman ask whether the artist was 'still with us'.

When David stepped out onto the gravel walk to smoke, he found Jess snapping shut her clam phone, having just finished talking to Ginny. The night was chill and dry. Moonlight dusted the paunchy clouds and as the wind changed tack, a faint thudding music from somewhere grew in strength. The Mall lay rigidly in front of them, the park beyond it steeped in darkness.

'Exciting times for Ruth, huh?'

One floor above, someone's arm crooked out through a window, a fat cigar dangling from it, then disappeared again. Jess replied, 'Don't you think the show's a little cluttered? They should have taken fewer pieces and left—'

'I meant the engagement.'

'Oh yes, that.' Jess nudged a cigarette from its packet. He lit it for her, and she took a step back, struck a Katharine Hepburn pose: one foot out and a hand on her hip. 'Tell me: is it for a visa?'

It came as a pleasurable surprise to David, how little she understood.

'No – he's in love. James is very sincere – a God-botherer, in fact. Bible by the bed. Ruth was leafing through it the other day, so who knows ...'

David laughed but Jess just looked up sharply, then she bit her bottom lip.

'Last time I read a Bible ...' She looked at her leather boots and stopped. David did his bit and stayed silent for the dramatic pause. 'Was with Ruth,' she said finally. 'In Sheep Meadow in Central Park. She'd bought it from The Strand to show me something. We'd been staying on Richard's floor in Williamsburg – this was *way* before it was fashionable – almost entirely Polish then – and Ruth had been calling me Naomi for a few days and when I'd ask her why she'd only say, "For where you go, I shall go—"'

126

Larry's laugh interrupted. 'Aha, thought you'd be out here. What are you two plotting? Top-level talks, or can any fool join?'

Jess tucked one end of his grey scarf into the collar of his overcoat and David thought how close they were, how far he was.

'Just a little engagement gossip.'

'Oh, they'll be very happy together ... for a year or two at least.' He gave an outrageous wink.

Jess ignored him and addressed David. 'Doesn't he want to go nightclubbing or skydiving or whatever? Doesn't he want *children*?'

'Ruth's one of the last genuine aesthetes.' Larry jerked his head back towards the door. 'She never got the memo. She's still into *beautiful* things.'

'But why *marry* it?' Jess said.

'Maybe she loves it. Maybe *it* loves her.' Larry offered the sentiment reasonably, cocking his head in a way that even David could tell was designed to irritate his old friend.

'Oh, no doubt,' she sighed, drawing her cigarettes again from some hidden pocket in her drapery. 'He's pretty enough to love.'

What on earth was David doing here among these people, with their casual manners and ironic patter, their insinuation that surface was depth, that appearance was content? And what was Glover? These were not their kind. Walter had no monopoly on being a collector. These people picked other people up and examined them and set them down, and laughed.

He trailed back through the corridors and found the hospitality suite again. The slot on the toilet door read ENGAGED, red letters on white, and his consciousness, associative and drunk, thought of Glover proffering his adolescent silver necklace, on one knee, divinely inspired, then supplementing that with the pinhead diamond ring. David thought of him naked, posed and exposed in the living room for her perusal and her Polaroids. A tableau of supplication, a catalogue of self-abasement ... David had conjured him; Glover's low, urgent voice could be heard from behind the door.

'How could I not? You're amazing. *Amazing.*'

Someone's back bumped on the wood. There was silence. Then the lonely sound of other people kissing. David let his eyeline trace a path from the sink to the ceiling along the vertical and horizontal grouting of the rectangular white tiles. Then he started tracing it back down again. How banal we are, how repetitive, he thought, when we try to speak of love; hate, now that's another matter. Let me count those ways.

Ruth made a puppy's anaclitic whine, then said, 'But aren't you even a little worried?'

'Why would I be worried about leaving?' Glover dropped his tone, asked gravely, 'Or do you mean about our wedding night?'

Ruth shrieked. There was a scuffle on the other side of the door, on the other side of the universe. He was tickling her or had lifted her up, something physical and intimate. David went out to find the toilets for the public, where he belonged.

'I have the whole set now, you know. The last two I bought, with the stars and without the stripes, and with the stripes but without the stars ...' Walter stopped, and turned his flattened nose to Ruth. 'Did you know that? That I had bought the last two flags in Bonhams ten, maybe twelve years ago?'

She didn't respond immediately. First, she lifted a glass of water from Larry's hand and took a sip. Larry acted as if he hadn't noticed; he didn't stop talking or glance down. Then she smiled uncomfortably, keeping her gaze focused somewhere near the mobile phone by Walter's hand. She genuinely seemed to dislike talking about her work. She *genuinely seemed*, David thought. That was it. Two words. Small song of the paradox of Ruth.

'I *knew*, yes. I do follow my pieces out into the world.'

Jess whispered to David, 'Larry sends her updates.'

At his angle, from just behind, a faint line of hair on Jess's cheek was catching the light from the aluminium lampshade that hung low over the bar table. Her cheekbones were high, prominent, and intimated the skull beneath. David felt enormous goodwill for her but wasn't sure why. He thought he might identify with her particular brand of hurt.

She continued, to him alone, 'She says those early pieces are like college friends: she wants to know where they are and how much they're making, but she doesn't want to have to *see* them.'

As she leant closer in towards him, to lift her handbag from the floor, she added, 'We met right *after* college.'

They brought some finger food out to the table and David was educated. He learnt: the ingredients of a mojito; that *The Republic of Women* was based on an understanding that the underlying symbol of nature was the unending, a circle, an egg; that this is opposed to male culture, which is founded on a necessarily linear world view; that this is to do with the arrow, the penis and the pen; that creating a gigantic papier-mâché teapot with a door, and then covering it in silver foil, takes two and a half months and requires three assistants; that this was the spaceship for the Gynaeconaut; that Ruth and Jess had jointly made a bronze cenotaph of names for all the women in Jess's hometown who had reported incidents of domestic violence in 1983; that Ruth had restaged some of the more famous publicity shots from *Star Wars* with female mannequins, replacing the light sabres with neon hula hoops; that Carrie Fisher, according to Jess, has one of the dirtiest laughs in show business; that Ruth had started the *Republic* in an attempt to create an alternative history, and not to present some kind of contemporary Utopia for Andrea Dworkin; that Ruth thought her work had suffered as a result of the media's attention; that Jess disagreed with this; that Walter's mother had been Macedonian; that Susan Sontag had been a fan of Ruth's work, and that if she had been a fan, Jess didn't *exactly* see how Ruth's art could have been robbed of its subtlety.

Ruth insisted the party continue at hers, and since Walter, as usual, had vanished hours before, the five of them fitted in one black cab, although it was still quite a squash. After everyone had settled – with Glover and Jess on the jump seats – David leant across Larry and said to Ruth, 'I didn't know you knew Susan Sontag.'

'Oh, only a little. *Everyone* knew her a little. We ran into each other a couple of times.'

'Where was that?' Larry asked.

'Oh, some bar in New York.'

'Which bar?' Larry pressed. He was heavily resistant to the idea that two people could meet somewhere in the world and he not, in some way, be involved.

'The Henrietta Hudson? I think ... Jess, were *you* there?'

'I was.' Jess was unable to obscure entirely the note of satisfaction.

'Strictly women only,' Larry said, addressing the comment to Glover, who pulled his gaze from the pavements outside and back into the cab.

David could see from his face that Glover didn't like the taste of the words forming in his mouth. He said, a little timidly, a little *childishly*, 'It's a lesbian bar?'

David wanted to laugh. Ruth threw Glover a micro-look but was saying something to Jess about Sontag on photography. Larry continued merrily, 'Oh yes, a whole *shrine* to lesbiana. It's down in the Village. Jess'll know if it's still there.' He glanced at her but she was replying to Ruth.

'... because that's exactly what an image does, or at least the mass replication of an image.'

130

Glover pushed himself back on the jump seat and set his head against the partitioning glass. He knew about Ruth's taste – that tiny, unwilled adjustment – and he knew that Ruth and Jess had once gone out, but still his face had hardened. David could see he hadn't begun to come to terms with the facts, with the anecdotes and dates and debts of her pre-Glover past. He knew they all knew, but he couldn't believe they were supposed to just casually *talk* about it. David wanted to pat the poor bastard's knee and whisper, *Everyone wants something to lie on. It makes no difference what sofa they go for. Taste is not morality.*

The conversation started again. Larry told a story about airport security at JFK and how he'd had to be driven to the gate on 'one of those golf carts for old people' because he was about to miss his flight. David made sounds denoting amusement; Glover made no sounds at all. His withdrawal became total. He turned back to the window and stared outside at the homeward human traffic, the twenty-somethings spilling from the pubs and bars, joking about girls and football and where to go next. At the Barbican he stalked in through the lobby and said nothing as the group ascended in the lift. Jess and Larry kept the conversation going but everyone was aware of the tension. When the doors slid apart at the twenty-third floor, Glover waved all of them out before him, and once in the flat disappeared into Ruth's bedroom. Without meeting anyone's eye, Ruth murmured, 'Give me five minutes,' and followed.

Standing beneath the lit pears, Larry whispered, 'What was *that* about?'

'Actually,' David replied, 'I think it might have been you, mentioning that lesbian bar.'

'Noooo,' Jess said from the sofa, the half-lids of her eyes flipping back like a doll's. 'I thought it was that and then I thought it couldn't be. Why does he care? Ruth says he knows all that stuff and is fine with it … God, he must *loathe* me.' She relished the word, and slid a chunky ring like an abacus bead up and down her index finger.

'No, of course he doesn't.' David moved beside her and patted her shoulder awkwardly. 'I think that maybe he just *thinks* he's fine with it, but when it actually comes up he freaks out. He's very young.'

'Well, look, we're here now,' Larry said. 'There's no point in letting it spoil everyone's evening. Shall we be of good cheer? Anyone fancy a line?' Jess looked up at David, who nodded, making a *Why not?* face, although his stomach stiffened. This was uncharted territory. After retrieving a dinner plate from the kitchen, Larry sat at the dining-room table and magicked a wrap from an inside pocket, which he lovingly opened and set on the china. David watched as it refolded in on itself like some exotic flower at dusk. He had left his wallet on the table and Larry lifted it, extracting his Visa card and expertly chopping out three plaque-coloured, inch-long lines. Then he plucked out the single note, David's last ten, rolled it and offered the plate to David.

It was disgusting: a viscid chemical slick on the back of his throat. But the rush was almost immediate. He felt, yes, joyful, if perhaps a little silly. The other two took their turns. He heard himself talking loudly and very fast. Jess's pupils had dilated so much that they almost eclipsed her irises, which David noticed now were the same tense blue as Microsoft Word. She was biting her lower lip and trying to tell the two men about renting a villa in Tuscany with Ginny but they kept interrupting. All at once David was pleased to be David. It was an unusual sensation. He was pleased that Larry was Larry and Jess was Jess, but mostly he was pleased to be David.

Ruth entered some time later carrying champagne, two fogged-up bottles from the fridge. She had reapplied her citrus perfume and set the drink on the table heavily, with a casual

'There,' as if she'd only been gone a moment and not twenty minutes.

Larry, motivated now to tidy up the tabletop, lifted David's wallet and it flapped open. Something fluttered out. Jess picked it up.

'Ruth, who burst your balloon? You look so *moody*.'

It was the photo from *Time Out* that David had stuck in his wallet, before he'd gone to the Us and the US exhibition at the Hayward. Ruth stood with it under the lights in the living room as David started to explain how he'd had it for ages and had kept meaning to show it to her – but Ruth was much more concerned with the picture itself.

'I look so much *younger*.'

Larry fluently unhooded the seal of a champagne bottle, and rolled the foil into a ball on the tabletop. He said quietly, 'The past tends to do that.'

David too felt low, and realized this was his first comedown: a hypnotic decline, general despair, all sound in a minor key.

Glover appeared, wearing, to David's eye, the sheepish, ruddy grin of the recently orgasmed male.

'Who's this?' he said, joining Ruth under the lights.

'I wanted to make sure I recognized Ruth before that exhibition at the Hayward last year. *Time Out* had printed it.'

Ruth plucked the picture back from Glover.

'The light is *very* harsh. I look like a hooker.'

'A hooker in the morgue,' Jess purred, and stroked the back of David's neck. He hadn't felt someone else's fingers on his body for so long that he groaned involuntarily and his head dropped an inch forward. Ruth retreated into the depths of the sofa and drew her legs up under herself.

'I've left some out for you guys in the bedroom. Larry insisted on gifts.'

'It really should be tax-deductible,' Larry remarked, getting to his feet.

'I'll take you down,' Glover said, which struck David as almost comically proprietorial. The bedroom was about eight metres away. He didn't need a guide. Jess stood up and wrapped her pashmina round herself with two dramatic gestures – a bat arranging its wings to sleep – and settled in by Ruth. Soon they were talking about Jess's sister divorcing, again, and in a manner so familiar David felt at a loss. He went down the hallway to the men and sat a little awkwardly by Larry on the bed, while at the desk Glover chopped out lines. David couldn't quite believe what he was seeing. He'd never even known Glover to roll a joint before, though he'd coughed his way through a couple. But with Ruth as his Eve he was evidently happy to eat whatever windfalls the Tree of Knowledge might provide.

'You've never been?'

'Never. I can't wait.'

'Oh, you're going to have a blast. Her flat's got views across the Hudson and on out to New Jersey. I envy you seeing it all for the first time.'

Larry sped up a fraction when he mentioned the Hudson, afraid, David thought, that he might remind Glover of the conversation in the taxi.

'I mean, I've seen it on telly, of course, and in movies. I have some idea.'

'When do you think you might go?' David asked.

'In the summer, probably, for good. There's not that much to keep us here.'

'There's your friends. There's me.'

'I second that.' Larry waggled a long white finger but Glover didn't smile.

'But you're back and forward anyway, aren't you, Larry? So we'll see you, and David, you'll always have photographs. I'll leave you a couple and you can carry them round in your wallet for the next ten years, maybe knock one out over our wedding picture ...'

Larry quickly snorted his line then left for the bathroom, while David, furious, pretended to read the spines of the books piled by Ruth's bedside. He had already explained the circumstances of the photo. He wasn't going to apologize. Glover looked at himself in the mirror on the door, twisted a couple of the waxed spikes of his hair, seemed to approve, and turned back to David.

'I'm sorry, but it needed to be said.'

After Glover left, David sat down in his seat at the desk and breathed, just breathed. He was very angry. His scalp felt too small for his skull and with both hands he massaged it, trying to ease it. James had done his best to make him feel as small as possible, and in front of Larry. Vacantly, his face burning, he let his gaze trail along the shelves in front of him, willing his attention to fasten on a detail, an object, a fact, a word. Ruth had moved her piles of books and photos from the living room to here. There was a leaning tower of DVDs on the top shelf – Truffaut, Fellini, Hitchcock, some musicals from the forties – and here were the scrapbook picture albums: like a child's, their covers different primary colours, and all with purple, bulging pages. And here were a few loose photos, and on top of them sat the photo of Jess with the pour of dark hair, the columns of Californian redwoods. It was small and hard with laminate.

Larry and Glover were talking in the corridor. David peered around the door jamb; Larry was defensively posed against the wall. He had folded his arms and turned side-on to Glover, who was speaking earnestly to him – though quietly enough so Jess and Ruth wouldn't hear in the living room.

'I don't have a problem at all with her past.'

Larry, plainly agonized, shook his head repeatedly. 'No, of course—'

'Her past is her past. I know it. She's told me. We all have a few skeletons in our closets, right? Right?'

Even you, David thought, especially you.

'Of course,' Larry reassured, reaching out to press Glover's shoulder. 'Well, I'm glad we've squared that.'

Glover wouldn't let it go. The coke had left his mind desperate to gnaw on something. It occurred to David that his flatmate really wasn't very bright.

'I mean, that's exactly what it is. Past.'

'You said it.'

Ruth's bulging leather purse lay on the desk, and beside it her San Francisco Savings Bank credit card. It featured the Golden Gate Bridge strung across the sky, and along its top edge, like accumulating cirrus hanging over the Bay Area, cocaine dreck was smeared. David lifted the photograph of Jess and slipped it into the back of one of the purse's inner pockets, between the stub of a boarding pass and a Starbucks loyalty card.

When David eventually got home that night, alone, he decided to post online an honest appraisal of Ruth's retrospective. Even if Ruth found it by googling herself, which she claimed not to do, there was nothing on the site that could identify The Dampener, and she'd never link it to him. He opened a new section, entitled Art Reviews, and tried to be as candid as possible. Some of the pieces, particularly the early ones, had merit, and a certain contemporaneous interest. However, there was always a great deal of *fetishization*. And the finished picture of Glover exemplified this. It was a child's view, an egoistic, solipsistic vision of the world. I want. I want. I want. Similarly, the treatment of the female body in the artworks seemed to David to posit a very tired view of sexuality. The photographs of vaginas were not far from pornography, though pornography was better lit, and her images had none of the grace of Mapplethorpe. There was also a kind of triumphant lesbiana on show that, at least for this viewer, made one wish for the softer analogies of Oppenheim. He concluded by pointing out that the recent works, making special mention of *The Nearly Transparent Heart*, were sentimental, ugly, and showed a sad reversion to exhausted dialectics. Though he didn't say it, his first response on encountering almost every piece was that he could have made it easily himself. The fact that he hadn't was completely irrelevant.

the republic of no one

Glover was being distant, and his coolness was partly due, David thought, to the fact that David himself must be a reminder of his indiscretion. Ruth seemed very busy and inspired, and was working on into the evenings. In the absence of genuine interaction with her, David had become quite the Ruth Marks scholar. He googled her repeatedly, getting involved in a chat room devoted to international women's art, and updating her Wikipedia page. The internet was useful, too, for learning the fundamental facts, the kind normal people just *tell* you. The online consensus was that Ruth had been born in Syracuse in New York State in 1960, which made her, as he had always thought, forty-five.

In 1979, while at the New York Fine Arts School, she had started the *Republic of Women* project. It was at once proclaimed to be in the vanguard of feminist art, and Ruth was famous. David located JPEGs of some of the artefacts – she alleged she'd found them buried in chests on a farm in Vermont. The lost civilization had comprised only females. Here was the crockery; the diaries; the uniforms and military awards. Here was a news-sheet. Here was some kind of sports racket with two heads. Here was a headdress designed to celebrate menstrual days that coincided with the advent of the full moon. It was barmy and rather wonderful. Ruth had written a rambling essay on the circumstances of the find (gathering mushrooms, stubbing toe) and appended a signed letter from the farmer who owned the land, Hart Skrum, assuring the world of its impeccable provenance.

David found an image online from when she was twenty-one and her hair came past her waist. She looked like a blonde Ali MacGraw, though her eyebrows were thicker and her face a little leaner. *The Republic of Women* avalanched, though not just due to Ruth. The title was borrowed for a play, a TV series, an artists' retreat in Oregon, exhibitions where none of the work was Ruth's but all equal parts rip-off and homage. She had an affair with Bathsheba, a playwright, then moved to Paris, then Barcelona. The common adjective to describe her was 'conscious'.

A few times a week, if the weather accommodated, David began to trek the entire way from Oxford Street back to the flat. It left him sweaty and tired, and took over an hour, but for the first time in years he sensed he wasn't getting larger. He would not be visible from space; his mother would be pleased.

The evening after Valentine's Day, which he spent alone with his computer, he arrived home to a yellow Post-it note in the middle of the kitchen door. It read, in Glover's painstaking handwriting:

Saturday April 22nd, 1 pm?
Islington Registry Office?
DAVID CAN YOU DO?

It reconfirmed something in his mind: what passes for love is imperfect knowledge. Not knowing, initially, allows faithlessness to dress up as its opposite; casts the inarticulate as enigmatic, the selfish as forgetful, the angry as impassioned. Everyone you meet is wearing some disguise, and the lover is the best liar of the lot. Of course, there was the information that they could hardly avoid. Ruth must have noticed that she had no genius in her bed, and as for Ruth, well, no neurotic can hide her neurosis completely. Glover found her insecurities disarming; they made him feel necessary, but that would soon become exhausting. Already David could see the thing weakening. Ruth's interaction was so exclusive and entire that when she turned her attention elsewhere, as she had to, Glover grew cold and irritated in the sudden shade. Ruth had told David once that no feeling was for ever, and Glover had nothing of the quality of patience he possessed.

David pulled the Post-it off the door and stared at it, a gambler studying form. There was hope yet in those question marks that grappled up the side of the thing, that hung on. The air of haste about the enterprise suggested bluffing on both sides, as if each expected the other to buckle and backtrack. Glover had a peculiar, faraway smile that appeared every time Ruth was mentioned, and when David had called her the previous Friday to fix a time to talk about their project, she'd barely listened, and then responded by telling him how James had forgotten his scarf that morning, the brick-red one.

That night David decided to go to work on the project by himself. To raise her interest again in their collaborative enterprise, he knew she would have to be pushed a little, and a week later he arrived, unannounced, at the studio. He'd put together a folder with printouts of digital photos he'd taken over that weekend (graffiti, road signs, billboards), some poems and lines and notes of his own, and a worksheet listing in bullet points some ideas on how they could match words to the imagery, on the style of the thing, on what tone it might have. Her interest could not fail to be snagged.

The door was ajar and Ruth was standing in the middle of the floor, staring fixedly at a canvas – at one of the canvases – of Glover's torso. The room smelt as if methylated spirits had recently been spilt. As he knocked, she twisted her body round, startled, then smiled and raised a coffee mug a few inches in greeting. Her apron was rigid with paint. It must once have been as white and pristine as any worn by his father, and it struck him as strange, and then as not strange, that the vestments of destruction should require spotlessness.

'That thing could do with a wash.' He pointed at the strange impasto down her front.

'I couldn't do that.' She lifted the apron's bottom corners as if carrying apples in it. 'It's battle-scarred. I couldn't wash it any more than I could throw it in the dumpster.'

'So you've set a date.'

Ruth beamed, dropped the corners and gave a little twirl. Stiffly the apron swung outwards. 'James was going to check it was all right with you.'

'Oh no, he did. It's fine. It's great.'

David placed his satchel on one of the tables and drew out the project folders. He silently handed over her copy, then sat on the edge of a crate. Ruth gave a baffled smile and opened hers, then took her seat by the trestle table, adjusting the Anglepoise so the light fell away from her. He started explaining and when he'd run through all his suggestions, said, 'And for a name I'd thought: *The Republic of No one*, or *Scenes from the Republic of No one*. Like an update.'

Ruth gave a single lengthy nod. 'Yeah, I'm kind of keen not to go backwards.' She stood, leaving the open folder on the table, and hugged herself. Under the apron she wore only a white T-shirt, and a reflex muscle in her forearm fluttered as she talked. Her skin was stippled with goosebumps. 'A lot of artists do one thing, and it's successful, and they end up doing that for the whole of their lives, you know.' She was talking slowly, David felt, explaining to the unsophisticated, to a commonplace intelligence. 'And I'm just not interested in that.' She looked down – David was staring at his folder – and her tone softened. 'Though I...you know, I do *love* some of these ideas and your photographs are terrific. There's a real awareness of framing.'

He nodded, tucking some of the flesh of his cheek between his teeth and biting down on it. She picked up some pieces of glass lying on discs of emery paper by the polishing machine and, as if about to shoot craps, jiggled them in her palm. 'I get a kick from *new* stuff.'

David felt desperation rise; it felt like being left by someone and knowing everything you say from here on in will only make them want to leave you more. It was like Sarah going to India. Like Natalie leaving college.

'We don't have to stick to what's written down here. And we could *easily* change the title. I just thought it could reference your most successful work ...'

It was out of his mouth before he could stop it; and he compounded the mistake by falling silent. He looked up from the folder, but Ruth had her back to him now. She dropped the rounded shards with a clatter on the table and said, 'I know you might find this difficult, David, but I think it's a misjudgement to confuse fame with success.' She turned around. Her face had hardened; the curves of her generous mouth had straightened. 'And it's certainly a mistake to judge success *by* fame.'

Another pseudo-profound chiasmus. David wasn't at all sure there was a difference in the two things she'd said, but he nodded thoughtfully, his face veneered with empathy. She started filling the kettle and, to be heard above the running tap, raised her voice a pitch. 'And for the record, my *success* was also pretty weird and mostly unpleasant and brought me a lot of grief, jealousy, all the wrong kinds of attention. It almost *killed* me. That's when I ended up in Europe the first time.'

She docked the kettle in its plastic base and switched it on. He closed the folder and clutched it across his chest, bringing his chin to rest on its sharp top.

'It must have been difficult.' What *was* difficult was for David to say the sentence without sarcasm. 'I just thought that *The Republic of Women* was so impressive, you know, so richly imagined …'

Ruth wrinkled her nose with distaste. He changed tack.

'And with everything that's happening in America, you know, it could be *The Republic of No one* because so many of the American people simply *aren't* being represented. And this could be … If you look in the folder you'll see I made certain political signs. I found one at a bus stop.' He opened his file again but Ruth, resting against the sink, made no motion to pick hers up. 'You can see it there, on page … twelve. Where someone had added an H to the sign so it said "BusH Stop". It would have been better as an imperative, I thought, you know, "Stop Bush" rather than a plea, but—' Ruth held up a paint-speckled hand and David stopped talking. He was out of breath. She had closed her eyes at some point during his speech and now opened them, slowly, as if the effort it took was immense and unknown and could never, ever be explained.

'I appreciate the trouble you've gone to with this, David, but it's not something … This isn't how my art works. It's not that baldly political, and even talking this way makes me feel slightly nauseated.'

He closed the folder again, and stared at the PMP crest on the cover. It was yellow and outdated and ridiculous. The motto in its gothic script: *Stet Fortuna Domus.*

'Ruth, there's no need to insult me.'

'Oh, David, I don't mean to.' She came across the studio, untying her apron and flipping the string of it neatly over her head. She was about to touch his shoulder and then seemed to decide not to, veering away to the sink.

'It's just our ideas are so different. Of course, we can work on it. We can do something. Just not that. I just don't want to spend any more time making artefacts or images for some non-existent republic. You've got such a neat view of things. You can't …

Everything's really messy, David, where art's concerned. Stuff just comes out.'

David watched a volley of steam rise from the kettle's underbite, and then it clicked decisively off.

■ ■ ■

At 2.17 a.m. that night he came to a decision. What was best for Ruth and Glover amounted to one thing. Glover had said he wasn't Catholic, that confession wasn't the deal here. He'd erased Rosie's phone number from his mobile the day after, and along with it the event itself. And Ruth was obsessed, fearless, painting him, praising him. In eight weeks' time, a wedding.

Stet fortuna domus. The situation needed Michelangelo's *disegno*, the most sublime problem-solving, and the solution would be a work of art reflecting the continuing conflicting calls of function, site, material and subject, verisimilitude, expressivity and formal beauty. Not to mention freedom and restraint.

Thus he spent two hours on Wednesday evening, in the empty flat, opening an account in the name of Kimber1986@ hotmail.com and drafting an email from Kimberley to Ruth. Larry's email was on the Barbican website as her representative, and David decided to send it to him. Why not? People are odd. They do odd things.

To: larryfrobisher@thefrobishergallery.com
From: Kimber1986@hotmail.com

ONLY FOR THE EYES OF Ms RUTH MARKS
Please forgive me writing you. This is a very difficult
thing to write. I found your contact email on the Barbican
website where I understand you are in a residency.
I wanted to warn you about what you are getting into with a
certain man. In January we had our Mocks Party on a boat

on the Tames, and our English teacher Mr Pinner, brought
a friend of his called James. My sister Rosie, whose an
undergrad, had a situation with James and she ended up
really liking him. She asked me to get his number and I've
since found out from Mr Pinner that he's engaged, and to
you, Mr Pinner's friend the artist. James came on very
heavy with my sister. He told her he was single and said
he'd ring her but that was all just to get her into bed. I had
a boyfriend Simon Moffet for two years who was cheating
on me and I would have wanted to know. And afterwards it
turned out everyone knew what was going on and had said
nothing to me. Mr Pinner told us all about your exhibition
and some of us from class have been to the ICA to see it
and I know that you are a good person, as well as being a
good artist. I knew that the right thing to do was to tell you
what happened that night on the boat.

Yours in sisterhood and friendship
Kimberley

He sent it at 8.27 p.m. on Friday night. He knew Larry probably didn't work weekends, but he still felt disappointed when
he woke the next morning and nothing had changed. There were
no texts, missed calls or emails; no consequences. After skim-
ming the newspaper websites, he ate a few rounds of toast
sodden with butter, and a bowl of porridge and honey. Then he
climbed back into bed in his dressing gown. Too anxious to do
much, he smoked and listened to a Sibelius symphony rise and
fall on his iPod, then picked up the anthology that lived by his
pillow. He wanted a poem to fit the blankness of his mood. He
started in on Coleridge's 'Frost at Midnight' and dozed off almost
instantly.

In his dream he was lying on the herringbone parquet at the
back of his classroom in PMP, paralysed like Gulliver, when

Sarah appeared at his feet. She looked the same as fourteen years ago, mad-eyed with those dangly fish earrings, except she wore a white butcher's trilby and a tie-dyed apron. She walked around him without saying a word, then dropped suddenly to her knees and started pressing piano wire down onto his neck, cutting through the flesh. She was screaming. He woke with a jolt as if dropped from a height onto the bed; Sibelius's Fourth crashed in one ear. He reached up to his neck and rubbed at his Adam's apple. One of the iPod's earphones had come out and the cord had wrapped round his throat.

It had already begun to get dark, which meant he'd successfully squandered the entire day. His mouth was parched, all the liquid in his body having sweated out of his back. He peeled off his T-shirt. He didn't smell so good. He needed a glass of water.

Glover's jeans were lying on the hallway floor, pointing to his bedroom. He must have dropped them when he was doing his washing. As David bent to pick them up, some movement in his peripheral vision made him glance through Glover's doorway. They were here, in the flat. Between the door and jamb there was a gap of a few inches and, his back to David, Glover stood naked at the foot of his bed. Ruth was on all fours in front of him, wearing only a silver ankle bracelet. He watched as Glover's fat little ass grew and then wrinkled and shrunk with each thrust. The skin was paper white and his hips seemed very narrow. The parts of Ruth that he could make out were browner, softer. One hand held her by the indent of her waist and the other was curved under her, holding a breast. David could hardly see it. It could have been anyone. Her blonde hair shifted in and out of shot, as did her ass, which rode in the air, receiving, pushing upwards against Glover – it was a standard pornographic image; it lacked imagination. It almost came as a relief. David stood there, naked himself apart from his black silk boxer shorts. He could hear himself breathing.

The time of the voyeur – like the time of the victim – is slow. Each movement extended before him, *for* him. There was something automatic in the action, the hydraulic effort of those nodding donkeys that drill for oil in Texas. He crept backwards into his room and lay on the bed. He thought of women on the internet, of their expressions as they got fucked like dogs: how they'd close their eyes and pout and pant and moan and beg and sigh. Sometimes they might scream and yell and bite the pillow, taking it. He listened to the propulsive sounds from the next room, and masturbated rapidly, coming into the sweaty T-shirt that he'd left lying on his pillow. Afterwards he put on his dressing gown and softly opened then loudly shut the door of his bedroom. He heard Ruth make a whimper of surprise, not joy, not joy. Glover's bedroom door was slammed. David walked around the flat, banging cupboards and turning up the kitchen radio; then ran himself a bath that came, when he sat in it, right up to the brim.

around about one

i carried you

When David awoke on Sunday, Ruth and Glover had already left. He walked listlessly through Borough market, stopping at stalls to try the morsels on cocktail sticks, and bought nothing. The place was filled with couples holding hands and wearing scarves and paying twenty quid for geometric hunks of cheese. He wandered home and blogged about how shit the market had become. He was involved in four arguments – on a film blog, a poetry forum, the International Women Arts website and a newspaper comment section – and he posted new replies. He chatted to Singleton online but then she had to go to see friends. She'd suggested, very casually, that they could meet for a drink but he hadn't really taken her up on it. Nor had they swapped photographs yet. He felt uneasy about setting himself before her, for judgement, for review, and he was sure she felt the same. He lay on the sofa for an hour, imagining lines he might use when Ruth or Glover eventually called, when the email from Kimberley eventually surfaced. It had been released into the system; it was waiting, primed, in Larry's inbox. David couldn't believe there were people who went a whole weekend without checking their email, but it wasn't until the Monday morning, as he stood in the staff room at 11 a.m., waiting for the coffee to percolate, that his mobile rang. 'James-Mob' flashed on the screen.

'Ruth knows.' He sounded piteous. 'Kimberley sent her an email. Can you believe she sent her an email?'

David stepped out into the corridor. 'Oh *shit*. I didn't mention it, but she's been asking about you. Last week she stopped me after class and said Rosie wanted your number. I told her you were engaged to a friend.'

Glover's breathing was hoarse. He cursed, gave a short moan, sniffed several times.

'It's going to be all right,' David said soothingly. Whether, in fact, this was true now lay within his power. Glover had called the right man.

'I think I've still got Rosie's number somewhere,' Glover said. 'When I get back I'm going to ring her and find out why the fuck she's doing this.'

'You have her number? I thought you erased it.'

'She wrote it on the invite.'

David slid this info to the back of his mind before moving on to the little speech he'd prepared. 'I almost feel responsible. I've talked about Ruth's work in class, she had the name and I suppose—'

'And that's the other thing.' There was a pause. 'She sent it to Larry. Ruth thinks the whole gallery's read it. I've humiliated her.'

Silence again. So much depends on what people believe about the texture of a silence. Then Glover began to cry; softly, tenderly, a mourner who knows the dead are dead and can't be helped by tears. Finally he stopped and sighed, and murmured, 'I sabotaged myself.'

It hurt David to hear him like that; he assured him again that it would all be fine. Friendship is full of these economies with the truth. A little theory: just as artists would rather have imperfect knowledge of their art (that is, they'd rather think their art is perfect), so we would all rather be loved for what we *seem* to be. For Glover, it was the end of 'seeming', and David felt strongly that his tears had the flavour of a liberation, though he knew he would not thank him for it.

Ringing Rosie, obviously, could not be allowed to happen. It would transpire that she hadn't known her sister was going to write to Ruth, and then it would transpire that her sister had done nothing of the sort. David had a free period before lunch and he hurried to Oxford Circus and caught the tube home.

First he tried the pockets of Glover's jackets that were hanging in the hallway, but turned up only loose coins and receipts. Glover always closed his bedroom door when he was leaving the flat. David didn't think it was, particularly, to keep him out: he was just that kind of person, a drawer-shutter, a turner-off of lights. He knocked lightly, even though he knew that Glover was in the Bell. His room was much tidier than David's: the inch-too-short blue curtains were drawn back and the white duvet had been smoothed out, creaseless as icing. He tugged the wardrobe open and went through the jeans folded on the shelf. Two almost-empty packets of gum. What had he been wearing? His brown leather blazer, battered and scuffed like some seventies pimp's, was hanging on the back of his door. In the inside pocket David's fingers met stiff card and he pulled out the invite – **The End of Mocks! All Aboard the SS _Carolina_!** On the back, neat in red ink, a phone number and _Rosie_.

David smiled at himself in the wardrobe mirror, then sat down on the edge of the bed. A spring in the mattress emitted a short resonant belch, and for a minute he stayed very still, listening to the nearest thing to silence London had to offer. The fridge hummed in the kitchen. Traffic sounds rose and fell. Someone was shouting very loudly and very far away. Carefully, he lowered himself down onto his back.

So this was the view from here, from his bed, from his pillow. This is what it was like to be Glover.

Here was his Artex ceiling, the cream paper globe of his lamp-shade. David turned his head to the right and here was his wall: magnolia, matt, bumpily plastered. To the left, here were his photographs, his books, his clothes; and here was something else, his smell. In the mornings, after one of his lengthy baths or showers, he'd slope into the kitchen redolent of milk-and-honey shower gel. By the evening, though, or after he'd come back from the pub, under the smell of stale beer and ash there was a hint off him of forest, timber, sap. And now it came from his pillow. David inhaled again. Was Ruth's perfume in there? Some part per million of the atmosphere suggested her, a citrus sweetness somewhere. Maybe he imagined it. He heard a noise and sat up quickly. A pigeon, plump and sleek, had landed on the windowsill. It swivelled an unblinking eye towards him, jerked its plush head twice and dropped from sight. Where was its collective noun, David thought, its group, its flock, its kind?

On top of the three wine boxes Glover had stacked by the bed sat a framed picture of Glover and Ruth on a deserted, freezing beach. Already there were photographs; already there was hard evidence. The camera must have been on self-timer and placed on a *soft sand* sign or a life-ring box. Glover's hair was plastered to his forehead and Ruth's cheekbones were pinkish, scrubbed-looking. He stood squarely, facing the camera in his black anorak, while she wore his blood-red cagoule, and was pretending to climb him, her leg raised to his thigh and her arms around his chest, like one of those vines that grows up its host tree, eventually strangling it. The sky behind them was pale as paper, the sea a band of wet cement beneath it, and a haze of light rain scumbled the scene. In one corner the picture was flecked where the lens had been hit by a raindrop. Despite the weather, they wore huge foolish grins. David knew it was Norfolk, though it looked like the edge of the world.

A few weeks before, they'd come in from the cinema to find David slumped in an armchair, browsing through an old

National Trust handbook, cracking pistachios and trying very hard to be nice. When he reached for the remote control on the coffee table, to turn down the volume, he upset the bowl of empty shells he'd balanced on his stomach. As he trawled the depths of the armchair for the last remaining bits, Ruth had leafed through the handbook and lightly mooted the idea that *we* should take a weekend away somewhere. A few days later David heard Glover on the phone telling Tom he needed the weekend off. When Glover came into the kitchen afterwards David was making an omelette. He asked if they could borrow the Polo, and David realized that his fears had come true: the *we* did not include him. They spent three days rattling down the hedge-walled C-roads of East Anglia, treading across the drawing rooms of dying mansions, and taking photographs on wet deserted beaches. Although they filled the petrol tank, there was sand in the creases of the car seats and all over the foot mats. Glover had returned on the Monday night when David was watching *EastEnders*, having dropped Ruth at the Barbican. He asked him whether they'd called in on his parents and Glover grinned.

'I don't think Ruth would have been up for that, and they'd probably have been out anyway ...'

David set the photo back on the wine boxes and spotted that the drawer of the wooden bedside table was open a little. He pulled it out a few inches further. Towards the back was an *Auto Trader* and on top of it sat Glover's Bible. When he touched a Bible, David liked to say, he wanted to go and wash his hands. Bound in black leather, it had several ribbons marking places in its gilt-edged pages. It was tagged and highlighted and as dog-eared as an exam text, which of course it was. Paperclips like knots upset the straight grain of the pages, bookmarks peeped from the ends and sides. David pulled out a bookmark that featured the story of the man who is looking back over the journey of his life. He sees two sets of footprints and notices that, during the most testing periods, one of the sets disappeared. He asks God, who as it happens is standing beside him, what it means, why He abandoned him when things were at their worst. God replies *Those were the times that I carried you.*

David flicked through the Good Book and the tiny breeze from the turning pages made him blink. A starchy smell came off it. There was something desperate and saddening about Glover sitting in here among his cricket almanacs and *National Geographics*, underlining mad and ancient rules to live by. Glover was so *young*. David thought of Shylock: *I hate him for he is a Christian.* He turned to the glued-in frontispiece and read:

To James, Happy 16th Birthday Darling, Love Mummy and Dad xxx

As he laid the Bible back in the drawer he noticed a loose sheet poking out from under the *Auto Trader*. It was a quick pencil sketch of a face – the heavy brow, the almost feminine jawline – and yet it couldn't be anyone but Glover. David was amazed at how few lines it took to replicate someone. It needed just the barest adumbration. Evolution takes the shortest route and our most remarkable ability is *picking out.* We learnt to piece together moving specks of colour in the canopy and resolve them into creature, into enemy or prey. We see faces in the clouds, make gods in our own image. Ruth had signed the sketch with a swollen R. David set it back, under the motoring bible and the real one, pushed the drawer shut and thought how he should really leave for school.

On entering the living room though, he let himself collapse on his back on the lumpy sofa beneath the window. It was a bright cold afternoon and the curtains were half-drawn. The room was sliced with shadow and light. He patted the folded invite in the pocket of his shirt and felt content, swollen and sated by the two packets of prawn sandwiches he'd wolfed down on the tube. Let's see what happens now, he thought. There was no way Ruth would be able to bear the shame, at least not alone, and he would be there for her. He lay completely motionless and watched the dust ride in and out of the pilastered sunlight. It was like the smoke that wreathed his father in the glass box of his porch. It flittered, hovered, hung like plankton; and when he pursed his lips and blew, it scattered. He thought how every time he spoke these particles and fibres were being driven and dispersed before him, and he was entirely unconscious of it. Perhaps these tiny specks could be resolved as well, could be pieced together into … For the split of a second he found himself thinking, *Is it really so improbable that God exists?* The sunlight was warm on his hands and his face, and he remembered how faith felt, how cosy it could be, how collective and safe; then the moment passed.

He locked up and walked to the station quickly, stopping outside the entrance. He slipped the ticket for the boat party out of his pocket and tore it in half, then in half again, and tossed the pieces into the mouth of the litter bin. If there is a God, David thought, why the fuck should it not be me?

That afternoon, between lessons, he tried to ring Ruth, but her phone was turned off. He heard nothing from either of them until the following morning. When he logged on and signed in at 8.07 a.m., there was an email from Ruth, eleven minutes old, tersely stating that she knew now and wasn't angry with him for not telling her. They were 'going to try to work through it'. After checking the Kimber1986 account – she hadn't replied to it – he decided to phone her.

'Oh, hey David.'

Her voice was blowsy with reverb: she was already in her studio.

'I'm so sorry, I didn't know what to do. I was caught in the middle. Do you want me to come over?'

'Of course not, no one died. I'm fine, really.'

'Oh, come on, it's me. You can't just be *fine*.'

She sighed, releasing some of her real self. 'Oh, I don't know … In a way I'm relieved. I'd been thinking that it wasn't realistic—'

'Realistic?' David couldn't help it. She was refusing to take this *personally*. He held his dressing gown closed and put his head out into the hallway. Glover's door was open, the room empty. He must be at Ruth's, still asleep in that king-sized bed in the sky.

'Look, obviously I'm embarrassed about it. Larry had to forward the damn thing to me and I know the girls at the gallery have read it. And I'm annoyed that this girl – that these sisters – have come into my life in some way, and I guess I'm upset, but, you know, I'm almost *pleased*. It's sick, I know. I want us to stand a chance of being happy and you *have* to be realistic … I know it sounds crazy but I want James to be *with* me, not *resent* me, not find marriage some constricting obligation. He's only twenty-three …'

David thought of Kafka, finding new sources of pleasure in his own abasement. Another sigh and she said nothing for a moment. He responded in kind, and she spoke first, as he'd known she would.

'People *want*, David. It's what they do. They're machines that run on desire. We just have to deal with that as best we can. And James needs to have experiences. I never thought of monogamy as a condition of marriage. Really, it's just what happens …'

So it went. She kept talking and David went about his morning routine – the things he had to do before he went out to the world of work she could never imagine, a world she was privileged not to have known. Ruth was free of that, of the stain of utility. But that makes it sound as if her privileges were only of the kind defined by class, and as he put the phone on the sink and splashed water on his face, listening to her self-justifications on the loudspeaker, David saw that this was much too limited a vision.

There is no privilege as great as that enjoyed by those 'To Whom Things Come Easily'. Class *is* a part of it; talent is a part also; sometimes, as it was with Glover, dumb pretty looks will do the job. They are anointed with luck. They don't make it. There is no effort. There is little danger of fragmentation, of personal destruction. Since they are accustomed to getting, to having, the risk of loss is small. Their run of fortune will continue and they know it. When they mourn, when they are betrayed or lost or alone, their responses will be effortlessly elegant. Even their feelings, David realized, were better than his.

natural disaster

The following Sunday, when they exited Borough station hand in hand, David realized the revelation had not worked, or at least not in the way that he'd hoped. He'd expected to spend the week comforting her, or him, or both, but in fact had heard very little from Glover, and from Ruth nothing at all. And then late on Saturday night he'd received a perfunctory, mysterious text from her asking him to meet them both at twelve the next day by the station, if he was free, as they needed to canvass his opinion. The neutral venue. The monumental time of high noon. He imagined the three of them would sit in the snug of some pub, and Ruth and Glover would outline all their feelings for each other, and he'd preside over a difficult session of accusation and counter-accusation, and then, at the end, he'd lean forward, his eyes glossy with tears, and advise them that only a total separation would work.

Instead Glover's arm was lolling across Ruth's shoulders, her fingers appeared from around his waist. They were presenting a united front. Blinking enthusiastically in a way that made David clench his fist in his duffel coat pocket, Glover said they'd decided to have a pre-wedding get-together on the eve of the service and they were heading to the South London Tavern to check out the private room upstairs. The news perforated David, and all his excited, nervous energy leaked from him. They stopped at a newsagent's so he could buy a can of Coke, and he watched through the window as outside Glover pulled Ruth to him as if they were jiving.

As they walked Ruth described how the reception would be in Larry's house in Regent's Park, a huge terrace in a row designed by John Nash. It was six floors tall, with an iron spiral staircase from the kitchen to the landscaped garden, where they planned to erect a small marquee. Larry had a superb collection of contemporary art – and David pretended to be excited about seeing his Hodgkinson, his Kiefer, his Twombly and Riley.

To have the pre-wedding drinks on Borough High Street was to add contrast, David assumed. According to Glover, Ruth had liked the idea of the Tavern at once. Tom had offered to have something in the Bell, but that was in Soho and had no private room. Glover's keenness to have the party locally suggested he was trying to hang on to something, some part of himself. Aware, David thought, that some of Ruth's interest in him stemmed from his authenticity, he was not above playing up to it.

They often drank in the Tavern. About four years ago the whole place had been gentrified and gourmandized, but it hadn't really taken. The paint had begun to peel again and the locals had started to return. A handsome Rasta called Kevin led them into the back and up the stairs. The room was large and perfect for a party. After the busy lunchtime pub, it appeared very still and calming. Nowhere seemed more tranquil to David than an empty barroom with lots of seating: the silence was charged with absence, the same absence of noise you find in a shop selling musical instruments, where the guitars and violins and flutes hang, unplayed, on the walls. In fact here, too, a piano stood, unopened, in the opposite corner from the little bar, and a few tables were grouped around it. The two external walls each had three sash windows, and two leather chesterfield sofas sat beneath them, green, battered, basking in the afternoon sun. David perched on the arm of one and set his satchel on the table; the surface was heavily franked with the postage of past drinks.

'You can bring your own music, CDs or an iPod,' Kevin said. 'We've got an adaptor in here *somewhere*.' He reached down below the bar and bobbed up offering a black lead as thick as one of his dreads. 'And we can do food if you like. Have you spoken to Phil downstairs?' Glover shook his head. 'Well, he's got menus for you to choose from, hors d'oeuvres and whatnot.' He sniffed hard, once, punctuating his little speech.

Glover, leaning on one elbow against the mantelpiece, nodded his head a few times to some inaudible beat and said, 'Well, I think it's pretty good and it's free on April 21st, is it? On the Friday?'

Kevin flipped loudly through a large black book by the cash register.

'Uh-huh. Yep, it's free.'

'And what's the capacity?' Glover asked. He pushed himself off the fireplace and looked around again. He was wearing one of his new outfits – a pinstriped blazer over a red T-shirt – and he buttoned the middle button of the blazer now while adopting a serious, officious expression, the look of a house-buyer who's about to start knocking on walls and turning on taps.

'Around sixty. There's no minimum bar charge. It's one hundred and fifty all in, and you can book it by leaving a deposit of half. You'll have a bartender for the evening – if you're *very* lucky you might even have me.' He flashed a set of gappy teeth and bobbed his head again, as if his neck was sprung.

'So what do you two think?' Glover called across to Ruth and David, who were by the sash windows.

Before either could answer, Kevin chipped in, grinning over the bar, 'Mum and dad paying for it, are they?'

Glover reacted ludicrously, laughing very loudly and then staring at Kevin with ill-disguised anger. Ruth simply smiled through it all, embarrassment and distress apparent in her eyes. David was surprised to pass for Glover's father, even if the insult was offset by the suggestion that he and Ruth looked like the natural couple. For a few seconds he had to face the window to hide his expression. Poor Kevin. But it could only do them good to realize how the entire world saw them. When they got downstairs David suggested that they have Sunday lunch in the pub, but Glover said he wasn't really hungry, and wanted to go home.

■ ■ ■

If a wedding can be likened to a natural disaster, it's the avalanche it has the most in common with. The answer to a question echoes, setting off a trickle that builds until a body struggles and flounders through billowing white. Ruth and David were in a wedding-dress shop, which is to say they had entered the heart of the avalanche. The walls were white, the curtains were white and all the gowns were part of that family: ivory, cream, parchment and ecru and pearl. They were not entirely serious about their presence here, and the sales assistant, Tonya, who in a show of recalcitrance wore a plain black cardigan, appeared to be aware of it.

They'd passed the wedding-dress shop on the way back from the Tavern. David had never noticed it before and that was surprising, since the window display compelled attention: two mannequins stood in wedding outfits, each wearing Disney masks (Mickey Mouse groom, Goofy bride) and cutting what looked like a real cake. To David, the masks emphasized the prescriptive and oppressive elements of such a ceremony. They suggested the absurdity of funnelling the entire population into the same rigid sliver of tradition, of expecting everyone to wear for ever either one mask or the other. *Bride or groom?* But not everyone, David thought, is a spouse in waiting, as he perhaps was here to prove. Romantic love was over. It had lost its sweep and power, even as a symbol. *We will have no more marriages.* Still, the shop was open.

David insisted that he and Ruth should just pop in, just to see the kind of thing they had, and Glover said he'd see them at the flat. The presence of Tonya, who'd stomped through from the back, embarrassed them, and they were suddenly polite and serious. She explained that they were lucky, as she was only in for two final fittings later on, sisters, marrying on Wednesday in a double ceremony. It was apparent that Tonya deeply disapproved of double ceremonies, though David and Ruth, she insisted, should feel free to look round.

Ruth hovered near a rack of hanging dresses, too fazed or repelled to actually touch them, and David fingered a card from the stack on the table. *Tonya Kazmierska, Wedding Dress Design and Hire.* Tonya, back on her white sofa in the corner, was hemming down a cloud with pins.

'I mean, I can't wear white, obviously. That'd be farcical. But maybe a dress … You know, I've been married three times and I've *never* worn a dress of any kind. Isn't that strange? But maybe I'm too old for it now. I'd just look … ridiculous.' Something in her voice made David turn towards her and he saw that her eyes were wet.

She pushed past him out of the shop and David followed. She was walking stiffly ahead and David said, 'Hold on.' She stopped but didn't turn round. She was crying, and looked so raw and misused, so thin-boned and tender and broken. When she tried to speak, a sob cluttered her throat. David put a hand on her shoulder. It was his dramatic moment, and he filed frantically through his mind for the right thing to say.

'Oh God, you shouldn't be ... You shouldn't even be thinking about the wedding after everything that's happened. It's a charade. I can't believe James is forcing you to go and look at places for a reception—'

He tried to embrace her then but she gave herself a brisk wet-dog shake, casting off sadness, then looked up at him.

'James isn't *forcing* me into anything. Grow *up*, David. Can't you grow up?'

'Me grow up? I'm just trying to—'

Ruth clasped both his hands suddenly. 'I know you mean to help,' she said, slowly, 'but I'm just trying to explain to you: I'm a little upset – but it's not apocalypse. It's just been a tough week.'

'That's all I meant. I *know* it's been tough.'

'Okay. And I'm fine, really. It's been good in a way. We discussed a lot of things we hadn't, and which we needed to.'

The tears were wiped away quickly and she was back; the quality of play-acting returned to her voice.

'I guess it's good to be humiliated once in a while, though I wish it would stop now.'

But as they walked slowly to the flat, with David making Ruth laugh by doing impressions of Tonya's accent, she asked suddenly, 'You met her, didn't you? The girl.'

'The girl? Rosie?'

'Yes. Are you going to make me ask what she was like or could you just tell me?'

'Pretty, you know. Dull. I mean, she was young and blonde. Your typical whatever. Not my thing, but I can see how ... I think she studied international relations. She had her belly button pierced. Am I describing her? Does it matter? To grown-ups like you?'

The details he'd given would echo inside her when she stood at the mirror, when she'd lean in and examine her complexion, the creases at the corners of her mouth, at her eyes, when she'd stand back and appraise herself, naked, and turn to the side and hold and inhale, and think of the girl with the jewel in her navel. It would not be easy to deal with. David knew enough of jealousy; after its introduction, like some rapacious non-native species, it spreads out and destroys, transforming the landscape for ever.

menus

Jess arrived with the spring. She was in London for the first truly warm week at the start of March, styling a shoot for *Vanity Fair* with a skeletal starlet Jess had heard was 'a gold-plated five-alarm bitch'. David had emailed her some of his reviews, to see if it was the sort of thing that Ginny's journal might be interested in, and he knew from her replies that she'd been having a hard time.

She had got married in one of the first same-sex civil partnerships in America. Ruth had shown David a picture of Jess and Ginny in one of her scrapbook photo albums. Ginny was dressed in a bespoke tweed suit, trim and sensible, and a black cane buttressed her left leg. She peered out benignly from behind enormous dark-rimmed glasses, more like flying goggles than glasses, and she was smiling, though not looking anywhere near the camera. This would not have been particularly remarkable except that the twelve people flanking her were, and this image constituted the wedding photograph. One of the twelve, small and perfected in a black trouser suit with a French blue scarf knotted at her neck, was Ruth.

At the end of January Ginny, taking the few steps from her cab to her doorway, had slipped on ice on the sidewalk and broken some 'tiny but, you know, vital' bone in her foot. After contracting pneumonia, she'd been kept unwillingly in hospital for ten days.

Ruth's assistant Karen arranged a dinner for Jess in a Japanese restaurant in Fitzrovia for the night she got into town. Browsing menus had become so familiar an activity to David that it had lost its thrill, and been replaced by despair that everything was so expensive. It didn't matter if he chose the cheapest dish: some unwritten constitution decreed that all bills were borne equally.

David had the feeling Ruth had invited them – Larry, Glover and him – because she feared that Jess was going to try to talk her out of the wedding. As it happened, Jess was too tired and glad to be out of New York to do much but smile bravely and drink sake. She'd taken the whole of February off to look after Ginny, and upon seeing her enter the restaurant, it was apparent she was unsuited to the role of nurse. Her hair pulled back tightly in a ponytail, she had applied dramatic eye make-up but left her face pale and drawn, to suggest perhaps the depths of her privation.

When Ruth stood up to greet her and said something David couldn't catch, Jess, after making a wet click in her throat, replied, 'It's been hellish.'

Then they hugged for an age, with Jess's houndstooth coat bunched up awkwardly round one shoulder.

During the meal Ruth did her trick of singular focus, cooing and fussing over Jess as if the rest of the table had disappeared. Larry was his jovial self, managing to flirt with the waitress merely by lovingly stroking his left eyebrow when he was ordering. He had a gift for being amused and bored and politely lascivious all at the same time. Out of the blue he asked David whether he'd proofread some catalogue copy for him – his usual reader was having a baby – and David accepted immediately, then spent the rest of the meal wondering if he'd be paid anything more than Larry's huge smile. David realized the way to be liked by Larry was not to be funny or clever or kind; it was to make yourself useful to Larry. Across the table Glover was trying very hard to stay in good form, but the only time his eyes relaxed was when he began explaining to David how the Son of Star Wars weapons system worked, utilizing the chopstick rests, the sake cups, the soy sauce and the pot of wasabi to represent targets, lasers and missiles.

Afterwards, as they walked down to Larry's club, Jess and David fell into step at the back of the group, and when the traffic lights changed on Charing Cross Road, they found themselves left behind.

As they waited to cross, a group of elderly Japanese sightseers joined them; and under the baseball caps their faces were tense and dismayed at the sights they were seeing. David had read once that tourists from Japan sometimes experienced such enormous disappointment when they visited London that they actually collapsed in the street. It was a story to fill the gap and he told it, quietly, to Jess.

'Their expectations are so wildly different – Dickens, the Queen, Sherlock Holmes – to what they actually encounter – overcrowding, rudeness, squalor – they can't cope. Last year in the capital there were fifteen cases of hospitalization from it. Hospitalized with disappointment. I'm surprised it hasn't happened to me.'

Jess smiled emptily but David pressed on; he was going to write to the Mayor, proposing a new slogan to counteract the unrealistic hopes of visitors: *London – Really Not That Great.* Everyone was being forced to live their lives dissatisfied, in that fracture and rift between the advert and the reality, between the hard sell and the actual purchase, between the . . . Jess reached into her bag for a cigarette and he stopped talking. She murmured, 'London's got its problems.'

It was obvious she wasn't referring to the city, so David asked her, in a low-pitched tone, as if he'd patiently been waiting for this very opportunity, 'But how are *you* doing? You've been through such a lot recently.'

This did the trick. Jess slipped her gloved hand into his and squeezed it. The leather felt odd holding tight to his fingers, official, fascistic, *thrilling*.

'Frazzled. It was tough enough when Ginny was actually in St Katherine's, she looked so small and helpless, but afterwards was worse ... When they let her home I'd wake and creep into the bedroom to check she was still breathing. It really got into her lungs and listening to her struggle for breath was just so awful ...'

'I can imagine,' David said, which wasn't true. The lights changed and the urban herds began to cross. They walked for a few metres without speaking, then David asked, 'Did you ever get a chance to look at those articles I sent you? I mean, I suppose Ginny's been too ill ...'

'I read a few of them, but to be honest I haven't passed them on to her ... Don't you find it *exhausting*?'

'Find what exhausting?'

'Writing all those bad reviews. Detesting everything.'

'I don't detest *everything*. There's lot of things I value—'

'I guess ... I found the tone a little wearing. A little depressing.'

David managed to laugh, and said the truth took no prisoners and was a stranger to pity. He gave her his line about artists and imperfect knowledge. She said nothing and looked straight ahead, and he had an urge to punish her, to disgust her. They could have been Virgil and Dante, descending through landscapes of excess and pain. He pointed out fresh horrors: a pool of vomit by a lamppost; head sunk in his arms, a homeless man crouching on a doorstep; a middle-aged woman in a pink miniskirt waggling a broken stiletto, her leg bent up behind her like some farm-fed flamingo.

To pass on his sense of injustice and anger, to direct it somewhere, he brought up the 'whole incident with the girl' as their new topic. Jess exhaled sharply. 'He's a child. Children shouldn't marry.'

'Well, *exactly*.'

'He accuses her of going through his pockets and stealing this girl's number? Is this the playground?'

'Really? Did she steal the girl's number?'

Abruptly Jess turned to him. 'She's forty-five years old, David. Of course she didn't.' Jess frowned at her cigarette and threw it aside. 'She was upset enough to have Karen book her flight back.'

'No!'

How close he'd come. A hair's breadth. And no one had told him.

'It was difficult. James was crying, she was crying. He begged and begged. He loves her – that's the pathetic part.'

She sighed. There were moments when David wondered about the damage done to Jess. What was it? How early had it begun? She fixed her mustard scarf and then hugged herself as she walked.

'I can't pretend to understand ...' She spoke more slowly now, trying to follow her thoughts as best she could. 'But I guess waiting for the perfect thing will leave you ninety or stone-dead by the time it comes, if it ever does. If you can't love another person you've got no right to be here.'

Another set of lights delayed them. Trafalgar Square lay off to their right, floodlit in its depression, busy as a skating rink. David could smell a hotdog stand somewhere, close by, and wanted one immediately. The thought left him almost giddy. With ketchup. A white bun. He tried to ignore it and breathed through his mouth. On the pavement beside them, an Indonesian in an orange tea-cosy hat was selling roast chestnuts, waving his hand over them to waft away the smoke and reveal the little flashes of yellow pith where the papery charred skin had split. The others – Ruth and Glover and Larry – had long since vanished from sight.

When she stopped and stepped into a doorway, drawing her cigarettes from her shoulder bag, David said, 'And I suppose you and Ginny had a similar age gap to overcome.'

She lit one, blew out smoke and then gave a little purr of demurral. 'Twenty years. It's different for women ...'

He lit his and although he couldn't fit in the doorway with her, leant against the stone jamb. They were standing in St Martin's Lane. A few doors up a play had finished and the theatre disgorged spectators onto the street. They stopped in groups of two or three, like them, and were lighting up, were talking earnestly and quickly. David had a sudden sense of a community responding, of group debate, and felt oddly resistant to following Jess as she started down the street. Then here was the alley, and here was the door in the wall where no door should be.

When he got in that night a cheerful, flirty email from Singleton was waiting for him, along with an email at his Damp Review account from Tickertape Films. As part of their publicity drive for Kent Gray's new movie they were sending out tickets to respected film bloggers, of which he, apparently, was one. They were invited to a press viewing in a multiplex in Leicester Square, and could bring a guest. He tried to make himself ponder whether his going would be immoral, and then told himself not to be ridiculous. He emailed Singleton to ask her whether she fancied seeing the movie, then lay on the duvet, his fingers intertwined over his stomach, and imagined what she might look like. She had revealed, in an email headed *Full Disclosure*, which sounded somehow Hollywood and sexy, that she was thirty-four and from Stockport, which didn't. He kept thinking of Ruth at twenty-one, the blonde hair down past her waist, the cheekbones, the hips, the waist and breasts ... He thought about Jess and what she'd said about falling stone-dead.

■ ■ ■

The week Jess was in London Glover spent all the time he wasn't working in the flat in Borough. David thought he'd be spending his off-hours at the Barbican, metaphorically pissing in the corners to mark out his territory, but no. He said Ruth's place would feel too crowded with three of them in it, and what did he want to hang around with two women for a week for? There was a touch of falsity in his tone and David decided that he was repeating Ruth.

In the last few months Glover had begun to show a certain reluctance to demonstrate enthusiasm about anything David said or did. Particularly in front of Ruth. He felt that Glover's comments were usually aimed at chipping a little bit off him, at reducing him. But that week they had fun. They consumed indiscriminately: sitcoms, video games, takeaways. David thought Glover seemed relieved to be hanging out and talking shit like in the pre-Ruth days. During *Top Gear* he made David laugh for ages when he said it was like Christmas not to have to listen to Radio Fucking Four.

stalwart

The press screening was at four in the afternoon and David managed to leave school in time to arrive at the Leicester Square multiplex ten minutes early. Singleton arrived five minutes late, pushing a boneshaker and wearing a leopardskin coat, both of which she had warned him about. He watched her from the lobby as she chained the bike to a lamppost using a large padlock and a thick chain that she pulled from her rucksack. She had abundant pre-Raphaelite hair, and as she entered the lobby and looked around, he saw she had large brown timid eyes set deep in an apple face; and she was a little apple-red and flustered. She was so sorry she was late, she'd forgotten her glasses and then had to go back. Sorry, sorry, she was Gayle, with a Y. No problem, they had plenty of time. Don't worry. Breathe. He was David, with an I. She laughed politely and, after they'd shaken hands, disappeared into the lobby toilets. Another five minutes passed, and when she still hadn't come back, he found himself seriously considering the possibility that she might have done a runner, that she might have taken just one look and scarpered, but then she came out, banging the toilet door on the wall and pulling an endearingly silly face at the noise. She had re-made up and, in gratitude for her reappearance, David decided that she was cute. Particularly if he focused on her big brown eyes and tried to ignore the babyish rotundity of her face, and her depleted mouth.

174

In the screening room they sat in the row behind two newspaper critics that David recognized from their byline photos. They, the critics, were going to Cannes and seemed to want everyone else to know it. David raised his eyebrows at Gayle and she rolled her eyes back at him; it was a bit of British bonding. He took his notebook out and wrote down the gist of what the loudest critic said, to post online and satirize.

Seeing what he was doing, Gayle whispered, excitedly, 'Oh, you're terrible.'

He decided she definitely *was* cute, and pretty even, though a little plump. Botticelli would have loved her. David Pinner, so far, liked. The conversation didn't flow quite as it did on IM, though they both smiled a lot, and agreed how weird it felt to meet face to face, to hear the other's voice. When she pulled a freezer bag from her rucksack and offered David a peeled carrot he took one – more from solidarity than desire. She hadn't seen much of the director Kent Gray's previous work and had come straight from her office in Stockwell, where she worked part-time on a medical journal, a job which she wanted to quit in order to travel in India, or maybe China, though she'd been to Hong Kong once before, when she was very young, with her whole family, to see an uncle who worked in the army and was stationed out there. She chattered on nervously, nibbling at her carrot, and watching her made David feel very stalwart and substantial and rational.

Even so, the darkness came as a relief; any silence now could no longer be described as awkward, only anticipative. In their baggy jeans, her knees were much further away from the seat in front than David's, and he found that this too pleased him. Contentedly he sat and listened to the tiny bumps and ticks of ice cubes blunting in his carbonated drink. Then the movie started.

Afterwards they stood and talked for a while when she unlocked her bike. She had quite enjoyed the film, found the cinematography innovative. David thought it total rubbish, with a ludicrous plot, an unconvincing denouement and two-dimensional characters. She had to get home now. She blogged mostly on books but was, she said, going to start doing movies. The evening was pleasant, David thought, not world-shaking, perhaps, but certainly pleasant. He rode all the way home on the tube standing up, strap-hanging, hurtling through the earth, watching the blasted rock speed past, since that was without doubt what a man would do.

flicking between channels

'You wouldn't believe the number of forms they make you fill out.'

London was petty, repetitive, tiring. The tube had gorged itself on commuters and when it seemed to David that his carriage could not possibly take another soul, some chancer had flung himself against the bodies and forced another shuffle and commingling. He'd been squashed against the connecting door, where a pallid, abruptly nosed woman in a business suit, forehead dappled evenly with sweat as though she'd used a pastry brush, had spent ten minutes coughing her illness into his face. The city felt expended. Nothing was clean. David had a hankering for something mint and shiny. He ignored Glover and went into the bathroom, where he washed his face viciously to separate the evening from his shitty day.

A thick folder of official-looking documents lay on a cushion on Glover's stomach as he lounged on the sofa and leafed through them.

'I said you wouldn't believe the amount of forms they make you complete.'

He was pretending to be exasperated, but his tone was excited, proud even: he saw himself responding supremely well to a devilish challenge.

'Who does?' David slumped in the chair. No *hello*. No *how-was-your-day*.

'The Americans. At the embassy. They make you fill out a ton of forms when you're applying for a visa.'

'Since when have you said *fill out*? The English fill *in* forms. We've already lost you to the Yanks.'

Glover wiggled a little on the sofa, adjusting the cushion under the forms, and said, 'Well, whatever, there's a billion of them.'

David fired the TV on with the remote and immediately turned it off again. He was not in the mood to be distracted, patronized, misinformed or sold something.

'Now, do you mean an American billion or a British billion? Do you even know the difference between them? Shouldn't you check that out before you move there?'

Quickly, Glover shifted the cushion and got up. He didn't look at David as he stepped lightly over his extended legs.

'*Okay*. You win. Your crap mood trumps my good one. I give in.'

'Don't you mean you give *out*?' David shouted after him. He heard Glover's door pull closed. After a few minutes he got up and drank a glass of London's worn-out water, then rolled a three-skin spliff while sitting on the toilet. The rest of the evening he kept his door closed and worked on his best man's speech. He'd been writing it for days but that night it really came together. He tweaked and fine-tuned it, rehearsed it softly, then out loud, varying the emphases. No reply to his thank-you-for-a-nice-afternoon email to Gayle. She was obviously uninterested, or busy, or both.

Glover claimed that he didn't want a stag night, and David didn't try to persuade him otherwise. The idea of organizing a weekend's, or even an evening's, activities for a drunken all-male troop of baboons didn't appeal. But on the Friday evening two weeks before the wedding, Glover texted to say he was 'involved in a session'. He'd stayed on in the Bell after the day shift, and by the time David arrived he was already flushed and far gone. The current pressing concern seemed to be not the rise of fundamentalism or global warming or the decline of the NHS, but how many beer mats you could balance in a stack on your elbow and then catch when you jerked your arm down.

Glover was chewing a matchstick, and the way it pinned his mouth up made it look as though he had a cleft lip. He plucked it out, then pointed it at David and said, 'Compadre, welcome. Tom you've met. Eugene, another member of the Bell and Crown family. We're having a drink. Tom in fact might be a bit drunk.'

He winked and nodded towards his cousin, whose response was to give him a zingy punch, hard, on the shoulder. The manager of the Bell was as bullying and charmless as a barrow boy shouting in a market. He was muscular but small-framed and had given himself a curved back from working out so much. His mousey hair hung to his shoulders, parted in the middle, and though around David's age, he dressed more like a Brooklyn teenager: a loop of chain hanging down from oversized jeans, an enormous New York Knicks T-shirt. His face was permanently changing, grinning, frowning, smirking, as if someone sat inside him flicking between channels.

It is quite something to be sober when everyone is drunk. You're a genius crash-landed in the valley of the imbeciles. Eugene, a kind of ghost-man, pale as flour, was probably the drunkest. His freckles made his face harmless and as endearing as a child actor's, though when he opened his mouth each sentence was garnished with a swear word. David unfastened the toggles of his duffel coat and draped it over the back of the chair, which promptly tipped to the ground with a muffled bump. When he retrieved it and straightened up Tom was smirking conspiratorially at Glover. David knew they didn't really want him here – he was outside the circle, a bore, a drogue – but he tried hard to win them round. He jollied along, laughed tremendously, and kept a firm grip on his dislike of Tom.

They wandered then, the four of them, through guilty neon Soho, sticking to the patch bordered by Shaftesbury Avenue in the south, Charing Cross Road in the east and Oxford Street to the north. They must have been to six or seven pubs – the Rising Sun, the Three Brigadiers, the Coach and Horses, Fluid, the Moon and Sixpence – standing shoulder to shoulder in a ring, necking pints and shorts and reminding Glover that he was soon to be at the altar, haltered, retrained, restrained, worried, harried, sorry, married. They returned triumphant to the Bell and Crown for last orders.

Della, Tom's new girlfriend and – not coincidentally – the Bell's new barmaid, triple-bolted the doors as soon as the last customers were cajoled outside. Tom directed her to some lights behind the bar and the atmosphere dimmed.

Pints tended to make David inward and morose, and when a Smiths track he liked came on – 'Death of a Disco Dancer' – he found that he had been unconsciously ripping apart an empty box of Camel Lights. Like an undone jigsaw of the sky, the pieces lay scattered before him. Tom was talking.

'*That* I understand, but I only met her once and she was wearing some yellow coat that covered everything up, and so the question is, is she stacked?'

Glover's only response was to laugh. Normally his features looked closed and forbidding, like a soldier on parade, but when he laughed something winning and vulnerable entered the equation. His mouth was slightly overpopulated with teeth and his eyes narrowed. There was nothing intimidating about him when he laughed. It made David want to dive in and join him. And now he did.

Glover lowered his pint and said, still smiling, 'She's curvy, and she's *extremely* sexy, Tom. She should carry a health warning.'

He was amusing himself. What David envied most was Glover's valency, that talent he possessed for combining with whatever element he moved in.

'David knows her. Ask him.'

As to Ruth, one of the foremost feminist artists of our time, Tom still required a certain specific confirmation.

'So has she got a rack?'

David grinned at Tom and then turned to Eugene's farm-boy face, the porous freckles.

'Ruth beggars all description. She has an exquisitely straight nose. And her eyes are a deep intelligent brown.'

'An exquisitely straight nose?' Glover laughed.

'Like Cleopatra's,' David said. Glover grinned at him with bemused approval; he couldn't quite gauge his seriousness.

With deliberate crudity and iambic stress, Tom said, 'But whát abóut the títs?'

'Yes, she has those,' David replied, nodding wisely to the general laughter.

Glover stood up slowly and unsteadily, as if being inflated, then plucked the unlit cigarette from between his lips. He announced, 'My friends, the tits are magnificent.'

'Well, there you go,' David added, but Glover wasn't finished.

'*And* she gives great head.'

A cheer went up from Tom; Eugene nervously raised his glass in a toast; David looked at the table.

■ ■ ■

They went home some hours later in a taxi. As David tried to get the key into the door, Glover took his arm and told him that he was a great guy, and that he'd helped him out, and that he really loved him. David wasn't particularly touched. He manoeuvred him into his room and helped him climb onto the bed, setting a glass of water on his bedside table and leaving his plastic bin and a towel beside him. Glover lay there fully clothed, groaning every so often, but as David was leaving he spoke, in a soft anxious voice.

181

'I have to say my prayers.'

David remained standing at the door but didn't respond. He thought Glover was about to pray aloud, but a few seconds later he turned over onto his side, to face the wall, and murmured, 'Sleep well, Swell.'

He wondered if Ruth said that to him when they lay in bed together. Maybe that was all his prayers comprised now. He stood and watched the tiny rhythmic crumpling movement of the duvet and listened to the waveform of Glover's breathing, then left to write a long post for The Damp Review about the death of love. He wrapped himself in his brown fleece blanket, propped himself up on his pillows and booted up the laptop.

Gayle had finally emailed. She said she had been in Swindon on a course for work and was now in Bristol with her sister. She'd be in touch when she got back. David didn't buy it for a second. He was a little drunk himself and anonymously left some comments on her blog poking gentle fun at a couple of her entries. To be honest, he wasn't interested in seeing someone who found Kent Gray's heavy-handed style of direction acceptable.

He started on his post. Glover had transferred his faith in God to faith in Love. People used to believe in nature too, as a way to teach them how to live, at least until evolution came along, and people looked at gardens and saw not the symbols of grace and harmony that Marvell did, but fresh patterns of competition, auctions of light, acres and acres of selfishness. Where do we find ourselves? Where is the analogy for good? Glover believed he could become himself through love, that love would move him to the centre of his life, to his true place in the sun. It was the first time he had fallen for such a lie, and only a first-timer, an amateur, could fail to notice that love had died in the culture. It wasn't serious. Only a child credited love now. Only a virgin. A millionth visitor. A religious nut. It all required the same kind of faith, the same vanity and weakness. But, David thought, God is dead – as is Nature, as is the Author – and Love has followed them into the grave.

Information killed it. People know all about infidelity and opportunity and pheromones, about natural spans of lust, about the genetic imperative. We know that the man who leaves his wife for his secretary will be the same man in three years, and will feel the same way that he feels now. A new partner is at best a temporary salve; believe it, they will not save you. But poor Glover never had a chance. First love is sentimental. It is *romantic* and we've moved beyond that. The meaning of love, in fact, follows the meaning of that word. Romantic used to refer to an expression of deep feeling (see Wordsworth) and now it's become nothing less than an insult, meaning one is unrealistic and possesses an idealized notion of the way things should be. David typed quickly, checked it, then headed the post *Wanking Ourselves Senseless: The Death of Love in Modern Culture.* That should bring in a few hits.

He turned off the computer and the bedside lamp. The curtains were still open and out to the south, over zone three and zone four and zone five and onwards, a silver bank of cumuli had aggregated. It was shining eerily, lanterned from within by an invisible moon.

a series of short rises and swinging stops

Even though Glover and Ruth had eschewed the usual trappings (no photographer, no morning suits, no limousine or string quartet), David didn't think Ruth had done any of her real work – any art – for days. When he managed to get hold of her, she was trying on shoes in South Molton Street or having a facial in a spa in a basement in Chelsea. Bridget and Rolf arrived on the Thursday night, a week before the wedding. On the Friday she was taking them shopping, then to the Tate Modern, and then – at Glover's suggestion – up on the London Eye.

They were to meet Ruth and co at six o'clock on the Friday night outside County Hall. It was bright and clear but a chill wind loitered on the river walk, rising and fading and rising again. David was sensible in his black woollen gloves and duffel, but in the walk from Waterloo had broken out in a sweat. If the Thames is London's artery, the South Bank is its cholesterol: book stalls, tourists, street theatre (meaning buskers and painted immigrants standing still on upturned buckets). David had the impression there were a lot of first dates occurring. Optimistic couples walked past, glowing with mendacity, and far enough apart not to bump hands. A businessman loosened his tie as he strode towards them and then violently yanked it out from his collar, as though it had turned into a cobra. This was the end of work and the end of the week. Night was arriving and the darkness was welcome. It licensed an adjustment of mood.

As Glover and David approached the Eye, its lights came on suddenly, transforming it from the capital's mill wheel to a fairground ride, a mega-Ferris. David looked up when they reached its base and swayed for a second under the vast rotation. The prospect of sailing above the city left him tiny and dizzy. Glover tugged at his sleeve: he'd spotted Ruth. She was standing with Bridget and Rolf by the entrance to the aquarium, and they made an uneasy group. Rolf had dirty blond hair, combed aggressively to the side, and a high forehead that he began to nod vigorously. Leaning his elongated frame against the Portland stone, he appeared to be agreeing with his girlfriend, who David could see from even twenty feet away – now fifteen, now ten – was exasperating her mother. Ruth's head was inclined forward and she seemed to be staring at the shopping bags that petticoated Bridget's legs. The daughter was a dark rejected second of the mother, hands dug into a maroon denim jacket she had customized with silver sequins.

When the two men arrived beside them Bridget kept on talking. David imagined she might hold a palm up to them as Ruth had done to the Chinese waitress, but not even that acknowledgement was made. Obediently, Glover and David stood delayed at the edge of convention. David felt he couldn't just stare at Bridget without an introduction, so he turned away. Beside them a miniskirted gum-chewing teenager was holding a plush toy, a white baby seal. The father, talking softly on his mobile, his tweedy back to her, had bought it as some kind of compensation. She held it as if she was weighing it, and it was found wanting, and when two boys her own age walked past, David watched her slip it under her arm.

He turned back to Bridget, who welcomed him now with the tiniest widening of her eyes. They were the same sad-brown as her mother's, but disdainful where Ruth's were pleading. Her whole manner was tense, and David recognized such demeanour for the thing he witnessed every day: self-conscious

185

youth in its ugly full bloom. Their presence jogged her to a finale:

'...which is why Rolf and I know what our shit's about. We're not children.'

At this namecheck Rolf stopped leaning against the limestone and straightened up. His movements were distracting, gawky, goose-like. Ruth didn't reply to her daughter but kissed Glover, then David, hello. David felt the brush of her emerald scarf as incredibly soft and her cheek as porcelain-cold. Continuing to grip his woollen fingers, forcing a brightness into her voice, she said, 'Well, you two made it just in time. Any later and you might have missed Bridget scolding me. James, my darling daughter ... Rolf ... my friend David.'

Bridget shook her head dismissively. 'Not scolding. Pointing out inconsistencies in your position. You want to get married. *I* want to get married. It's called hypocrisy.'

The hair was dyed jet black and held in a ponytail by an ordinary rubber band: some strands weren't long enough to make it and these were guided back behind her ears, repeatedly. As James bent to kiss her on the cheek, she ducked her head and held out a limp hand, quick enough that it might have been a genuine mistake.

They queued, shuffling along the narrow path trammelled by metal barriers. In his boredom, Glover would grip them like parallel bars and suspend himself half a foot from the pavement. Rolf watched him with an unblinking avian interest. After David's first look at Bridget, he had precisely zero interest in chatting to her about teaching and was hoping the idea, like so many Ruth came up with, had been forgotten or shelved. He was pretty sure her daughter knew what a school was like, having attended one for fifteen years. However, rounding one of the barriers, when the conversation had fizzled out, he found himself standing between them.

Ruth smiled at him and said, 'Oh Bridget, David's agreed to have a talk with you.'

To be fair, Ruth had made it sound as though he'd offered to donate his one good kidney to her. Bridget stared coldly past him at her mother. 'Why would we do that?'

Ruth didn't react. There was no embarrassment, David sensed, to which her daughter had not already conditioned her. He found he was trying to absent himself physically from their conversation, pressing the small of his back hard against the metal bar.

'I thought it'd be great for you to go into school with him. We thought maybe you'd like to sit in on one of his classes.'

Bridget turned to swap a glance with the human goose, but he was loading a film into his camera. A strand got tucked behind her ear.

'I think I'm okay, thanks.'

'Bridge' – Ruth's tone was a mother's again, too tired to go softly – 'if you're going to drop drama after two and a half years to go and teach in inner-city Detroit or LA or wherever, after all your hopes of acting, then I think you should do *some* research into—'

'*My* hopes of acting ...' Bridget whispered. Ruth decided not to hear.

'I just want you to go into this with your eyes *open*. There'll still be teaching jobs when you've finished your degree. Maybe you could even major in education.'

David looked up and down the queue, which was beginning to tune in to their broadcast of radio drama.

'Well,' he said to cut through the thing, 'why don't we just meet for a sandwich Monday lunchtime? We don't have to talk about teaching. I know I won't want to. We could talk about anything. The Norwegian suicide rate. Cow-tipping.'

Bridget looked squarely at him, trying to work him out; then she smiled, a little abashed, David thought, and looked much younger than her twenty years.

'Okay,' she said.

Ruth flashed a smile at David. He had the impression she was assuming that if anyone could put Bridget off teaching for life, then he was that man. She seemed scared of her daughter, at pains not to upset her, but unable to abase herself to quite the extent Bridget required; in turn Bridget was illuminated by a thousand-watt resentment. They queued for less than fifteen minutes and David noted that her anecdotes were twice introduced with *Ruth won't remember this, but...*

It was dark by the time they entered the glass pod and the door was lowered, sealed and bolted. There was a series of short rises and swinging stops as more pods were filled, and then they started ascending properly. David pressed his forehead against the glass. Rolf was explaining to Glover why 35 mil is still way better than digital. His voice was somehow wrong, a spy trying to pass for American. The luminous landscape unrolled in every direction, and the wheel kept rising until London was laid out around them, a litter of constituent parts and components nobody knew how to put back together. David's forehead had left a smudge of grease against the glass and he wiped at it with his sleeve. Glover pointed out Cromwell Tower, where Ruth's flat was, to Rolf, and he obediently took photographs in its general direction.

A seagull, angelically lit from below by the wheel, hovered in an updraught not far from the pod. David looked down with it along the flat river, at the scatter of buildings and chaos of lights. There was so much *place* – and all of it sparking and spilling and flickering into the mischief night. Modern life is the city: modernity has atomized society. The human now must move in Brownian motion, not in a shoal, not in a pack or a team or a herd, not in a chain. We don't lie in family plots. We don't work our father's father's land. Randomly, repeatedly, we knock against people, and spin off like particles elsewhere. How hard it was to form a bond, to stick. We have slipped our own collective nouns. He scribbled his thoughts into his Moleskine to post online later.

The wheel moved very slowly. Nothing was swung heaven-wards, nothing cast to the abyss. After the first circuit David's contemplation returned to the surface of things. He'd seen the city; he'd examined the other passengers; and by the second descent he was ready to exit. The others seemed to feel it too. David began talking to Rolf, who still toted his camera but with none of his earlier pep. He was nice and presented a happy, vaguely confused expression, as if he'd learnt that the only safe thing to do was smile. He'd grown up with German-speaking parents on a small farm in Missoula, in Western Montana – hence the accent – and David wanted to tell him to run for those hills. It was apparent that the driving force behind his engage-ment to Bridget was Bridget, and that their imminent wedding (though no date had been set) was a way of antagonizing her parents.

By the third revolution of the Eye, they had regrouped. Bridget was preparing herself for something: she resettled her shopping bags against Rolf's forest-green corduroys. Her eyes shone.

'So James, do you know what you're going to *do* in New York?'

Glover tried to smile warmly; it came off as tepid, possibly hostile. 'I thought I might do some voluntary work initially. And then your mum and I've talked about me working with her on large installations. I studied mechanical engineering, so I know a bit about—'

'Volunteer work? Really? So what will you live off? Or, sorry – who?'

Ruth, conversant with Bridget's strategies, wore a glazed calm-ness. But David could see her prospective father-in-law having difficulty not getting snagged on that little hook of Bridget's half-smile. Glover turned, addressed his non-answer to Rolf.

'Yeah, I looked some stuff up online. A lot of churches in Manhattan run outreach centres and mentoring programmes—'

'Oh, don't go through the Church. You'll end up giving flyers out for Jesus,' Bridget said, and then a short unhappy laugh escaped sideways from her mouth. The pod rocked faintly as it started a descent. Ruth laid a hand on Glover's shoulder, and not for balance. Bridget said, 'I've got some friends who run a drop-in centre in Harlem. I'll get their details for you.'

David watched expectantly but Glover only nodded tersely. Sensing the opening, Rolf spoke very quickly: 'Actually, Bridget and I were thinking of the Peace Corps for after we're married.'

'*If* I don't start teaching right away,' Bridget added.

The wheel was slowing down: a gigantic brake had been engaged somewhere. Ruth brightened. 'I think that's a very good idea. You'll get to travel and—'

'God, Ruth, it's not about *travel*. It's not about personal fucking development. It's about helping people without inflicting our own religious and colonial impulses—'

The discussion continued as they were lowered, in uniform arcs, to the ground. Glover grew increasingly irate, his brow declining by millimetres, his voice more intense. The level of discourse, David felt, was fairly low – his debating team would have wiped the floor with either of them – but Bridget he was beginning to like. She was sequinned and fearless, a little bristler. As they tramped down the gangway to the pavement, she swung her shopping bags as though she might clobber someone with them if they came too close.

Goodbyes were said, and David saw her give Glover a peck on the cheek, which was progress of sorts. She seemed the type to be cheered by any interaction, even if it happened to be corrosive. They were off to see Stravinsky's *Pulcinella*. David hadn't been asked. He would get on with his marking and, as Glover was due in the Bell and Crown, they wandered back along the river eastwards. Before he clanged energetically up the metal stairway to the Embankment footbridge, Glover's summation of Bridget was 'some piece of work'. Watching him take the steps three at a time made David resolve to walk home, and he'd just reached the Blackfriars Road when he felt a drop of wet on his scalp. He stood under a bus shelter and watched. Localized to each lamppost's pool of light, the rain fell in angled stacks. He waited but it kept on falling, and then a bus came and he got on.

landfill

Gayle-with-a-Y hadn't replied to the email he'd sent her that morning. He'd read her blog about the findings of the latest government inquiry and thought, just like the inquiry, that she'd utterly and deliberately missed the point. He left a comment as The Dampener, explaining how it was irrelevant if the idiot actually believed his own lies. If he did, then he was alone, and his sin lay in failing to listen. Culpability resides also in neglect. He can't just decide he's right. There are good books apart from the Bible. And, Mr Pride, here is your fall: his whole crooked pack should be brought before a war tribunal. Betray the mandate at your peril. Who does he think elected him? Twelfth-century crusaders? Esso? No, not even that. He thinks us insignificant.

Then David spent some time researching Gayle the Singleton properly. He found her address in Stockwell by searching the electoral roll online, then found her home phone number on 192.com. On the land registry site he found out how much she'd paid for her flat when she bought it two years ago. A trawl of a few medical journals turned up where she worked. Some photos of a work party on her colleague's Flickr account showed her looking larger and a great deal drunker. He printed one off to remind himself of what she'd actually looked like, and then set another picture of her as his desktop, photoshopping the buffoons on either side of her out.

The next morning Glover arrived back at ten carrying several flattened cardboard boxes that he'd picked up in the Sainsbury's off the High Street. He was going to start packing up his stuff, and seemed very matter-of-fact about the whole operation. The unmade boxes leant against the hallway wall all morning and every time David passed them he felt himself tense. He drove to his parents' for lunch and when he returned three of the boxes were in a row in the hallway, filled and Scotch-taped. Glover's books were gone from the living room, as were his DVDs. His huge QPR mug – for his morning pint of tea – had disappeared from the kitchen cupboard, his digital radio from the windowsill. Entering each room with trepidation, listing the small depletions of the flat, David knew what it was to be burgled. He lay beached on the sofa, taking it in.

Later, when he wandered down the High Street to buy something for dinner, a short, bespectacled, nondescript man passed him outside Specsavers, trailing an adult fox on a lead. A fox. On a lead. Red-furred, bushy-tailed, white-chinned, with the intelligent eyes and the haughty snout. David had seen weird things in Southwark before: an Indian man, thin as a rope, naked save for a tiny pink towel that didn't quite meet at his hip; a greyhound strapped into a pushchair; an old woman who wore on one hand a glove puppet, a dirty grey monkey with two matted arms joined round her neck with Velcro paws. She had cornered him outside Tesco's last summer and repeated into his face, her breath startlingly sweet with cider, 'I know who you are. You're one of them.' David had responded – like Simon Peter – by denying it, and pushed past her with his shopping bags. And as he'd walked away he'd heard her shouting after him, 'I've seen you. I know who you are. You're one of them.' Once he had crossed the car park, and got beyond range of that witchy, crumbling voice, it occurred to him to feel relieved that she hadn't said what might have been more awful and more true: *I know who you are. You're one of us.*

As for the fox on the lead, David gawked, recovered, and then tried hard not to read it as a symbol. One could believe in nothing, no guff about magpies or ladders or mirrors or gods, but still have a hankering. Allegories multiplied in his mind. The world seemed like a sequence of patterns that he was endlessly spotting, though the patterns themselves were unreadable. In another time he might have made a living as an interpreter of dreams, but now he caught himself, and looked away, and watched the exhaust fumes of an empty flatbed lorry at the traffic lights clamber upwards and dissolve. Glover was not a fox; Ruth was not a little man in horn-rimmed glasses and an anorak; marriage was not a choke collar.

On the Monday at lunchtime he met Bridget on the steps outside the school, where she was sitting smoking, a little ostentatiously, and listening to her iPod. She was reserved but polite, and David led her into the noisy canteen in the basement. It was very busy, and he became conscious of his students watching him with this unidentified young woman, so he suggested they nip around the corner to a sandwich shop that wasn't colossally expensive. Bridget seemed less brittle when she was away from her mother. She didn't have to play her role. London was kind of grey but their hotel in Covent Garden peachy. They had stayed up half the night watching movies and eating ice cream from the minibar. Rolf had loped off now to Tottenham Court Road to find some Xbox game where you could be an elf and defeat some defined and final evil. Bridget thought that kind of stuff was *so* pointless, but then smiled to suggest it was just another sacrifice that lovers had to make. She was going to look for a summer dress after this. The way she said 'after *this*' made David remember their purpose. He'd been dumbly watching her, marvelling at how her eyes were just the same as Ruth's, how her cheeks were convex where Ruth's were scooped. Did she really want to teach? She nodded.

'I really do. You know, Ruth doesn't have the vaguest idea of what's happening in our cities. I've seen some of those places. I've driven through them. You know what we spend on education? And what we spend on defence?'

Rather sweetly, David thought, she was conflating social justice with standing in a room full of ten or twenty or thirty young people whose sole job was to hate you. Had he been like that once? Shaking his head sorrowfully, David wiped some mayonnaise from the side of his mouth with an abrasive serviette and said, 'But shouldn't you finish at NYU first?'

She sniffed and her nose crinkled. That short nose, with a tiny fleshy bulb on the end, must have been a paternal gift. He watched the hollow at the base of her throat deepen as she spoke.

'Actually, if I were to leave right now, I mean like tomorrow, I'd already have enough semester hours to make my teacher training just a year long, and if I stay for another year and a half it's going to be the same.'

'Aren't you enjoying it?'

'It's … fine, you know. New York's really pricey and living there can be pretty intense, and drama is very … competitive. I think Ruth expected me to be acting on Broadway by now.'

She gave her hurt little laugh: it bounced along – *ha ha ha* – like something hard had dropped and skittered on the tiled floor. The thick-waisted redhead behind the sandwich counter stared at them, even though she'd managed not to make eye contact once when they'd ordered. He stared back and she looked away eventually, wiping two stubby hands on her apron.

Bridget squashed her empty water bottle into a third of its size, and screwed the lid back on. It held its form. Seeing him watching, she added, 'For the landfill sites.'

He tapped it gently on the lid and it spun round to point at her. 'You could probably get that shown in one of your mother's exhibitions.'

195

Bridget gave a reluctant half-smile. 'Don't tell her I said that ... As far as I can see, you know, your mum's proud of you whatever you choose to do.'

Even as he was saying it David knew it was a lie. His own parents were not so much proud of him as sporadically tolerant, and he guessed that Bridget felt something similar from Ruth. He lifted his empty Coke can and buckled it in his two hands. Liquid dribbled out of the split, and Bridget looked pityingly at his sticky fingers.

'Listen, David, you seem like a nice man and you're, you know, clearly a fully paid-up member of her court, but what's between Ruth and me is not really up for discussion.'

The small speech had left her tremulous. For an awful second he thought she might cry. He hunched forward and bandaged serviettes around his fingers.

'No, of course not. I didn't mean to intrude into ...'

'It's guilt with Ruth. It works in mysterious ways, and just because she pays for stuff does not mean she has the right to have a say in my life.'

'What does she have to feel guilty about? As far as I can see—'

Somewhat dramatically, Bridget interrupted him by slapping both of her small hands face down on the table. Her nails were bitten raw.

'When I was eight, she walked out. She's "Ruth" to me, you know? "Mom" is kind of overstating the case.'

A strand of hair was swept behind her ear and immediately fell back again.

'Well, that's a terrible thing to have happened.'

'Things like that don't just *happen*.'

They sat in silence, David rubbing at his fingers. He'd stepped in a puddle to find it was three feet deep. He felt ashamed of himself. The only thing to do was unpeel the lid of his yoghurt and begin eating it.

'It wasn't that I didn't like Gloria. But you know Ruth brought her into my life and now I still have to see her. She's living in Chicago and we keep in contact but she and Ruth don't even speak. When she was in the clinic I was the one who visited her ...'

The anti-laugh again.

They wandered in the cold sunshine around the block, passing students of David's who assumed, he assumed, that Bridget was a prospective attendee at PMP. The girls looked at her closely, which confirmed to David that she was pretty. At a travel agent's window, bricked up with white cards showing last-minute flights, she stopped.

'God, eighty-nine pounds to Prague. It's so cheap for you guys to get to Europe.'

'Yeah, though I don't really take advantage of it.'

'I love Europe. My dad met Dylan in Prague. They jammed for like two hours or something,' Bridget said, in a low, serious tone. He could tell Dylan was the godhead for her, though she had not yet perfected Ruth's ability to drop a name into the conversation and then wait for the ripples to settle round it. She couldn't help continuing, 'Dylan. Can you imagine?'

Parting on the PMP steps, they agreed that as far as Ruth was concerned they'd fully discussed Bridget's teaching career, and that David had been very helpful. After David had kissed her goodbye, Bridget asked him as an afterthought whether he knew where she could buy James and Ruth a wedding present, something antiquey maybe. David had no classes tomorrow afternoon and said he was intending to go to Alfie's market on the Edgware Road. They'd be welcome to join him.

■ ■ ■

When he got home David saw that he'd had a visit from Singleton's IP address. But there was still no email. He responded to some of the arguments he was involved in, and then updated his blog. Glover got in from a run when David was going through his best man's speech. He still had his iPod in, and was half-singing along, making tentative little demi-notes and yelps and murmurs. The speech, David thought, wasn't bad at all. It had a few witty one-liners, but was, primarily, a masterwork in evasion.

Over a Chinese takeaway, eaten on their laps, Glover mentioned that Jess and Ginny were arriving that evening. Ginny was being collected at Heathrow by her niece and going down to West Sussex to stay with family. On the pretence that she had business in London, and with Ginny's blessing, Jess was avoiding her in-laws.

She was staying at Ruth's for the week, Glover said, and changed the subject then, telling David how Eugene had had his bicycle stolen from the lamppost outside the Bell and Crown. Glover had a nebulous fear of Jess. He had no handle on her. Later, as he washed the dishes and David dried them, David asked him outright if he minded that Jess was staying in the Barbican. He batted the question away with 'Why should I mind? They're old friends. She's got a right to see her old friends.'

A few seconds later he added, 'It throws me – I don't know. Her own daughter can't stay there but her ex-girlfriend can?'

'It was a strong thing between them. She's a loyal person, Ruth – that's what's great about her.'

'A strong thing? Spoken about it with you, has she?'

It was a question pushed towards him scornfully, like a counterfeit coin, and David saw the fear on its flip side.

'Yeah, sometimes she says stuff.' David moved beside him, pleased with his use of the present tense, and fished the dishcloth from the murky water.

'Like?'

'Oh, you know, this and that. You should really be having this conversation with Ruth, James, not me.'

'You think I'm stupid. It's stupid, I know.'

'I don't think it's stupid. Maybe it's not sophisticated ...' David trailed off.

'I don't know, man. How d'you get sophisticated feelings? I can't manage it. You feel what you feel ... There's always going to be *aspects* of the relationships she's had with women that I just can't replicate.'

'Yeah, I can see what you mean.'

Glover looked tragically thankful for this. Rice and sweet-and-sour sauce had been spilt in transferring their takeaways onto the plates, and David wiped the kitchen table in broad sweeps, leaving shiny channels on the dark wood. 'But, you know, you're only twenty-three. You should maybe also think about whether or not you want to be getting so serious.'

Glover turned around to face the room, wiping his hands on a checked tea towel.

'David, understand. I'm *absolutely* serious about this. I can't imagine being anywhere she isn't.'

a toast to Mrs Glover

'I think that maybe this is too large?'

Rolf was addressing them both, gesturing towards a wrought-iron birdcage that came up to his chest and looked as though it belonged in a fetish club. David laughed but Bridget just nodded and continued flipping through the rack of prints. They'd been here for almost two hours and had not found anything suitable, although David had purchased, rather recklessly, a first-edition Graham Greene and Bridget had tried on several vintage dresses, buying a pretty gingham pinafore that was very, as she said, *Little House on the Prairie*. It had been a pleasant afternoon. Rolf was always checking to make sure they didn't lose each other and he carried Bridget's shopping for her. David intended to report such attentiveness back to Ruth.

As some of the dealers were starting to shut up shop, fetching in furniture from the passageways and using long poles to take down hanging bags and clothes, they had to find something quickly. David was beginning to panic. Glover and Ruth had insisted they didn't want presents (actually, specifically, Glover had said, 'We don't *need* anything,' which David felt was off-message), but as best man he couldn't turn up empty-handed. Bridget had just decided that she wanted to get them two prints of street scenes from sepia London – ideally one of the Barbican area and one of where David and Glover lived, but even this was proving tricky.

On the wall behind the rack of prints that Bridget was perusing was a framed picture of an English country cottage. Pink briar roses twisted round the door and a stream ran through the foreground. Off to the side was a proper forest, dark and deep, the kind that represents the subconscious in fairy tales. The thing was stiff and twee and awkwardly done. David glanced at it quickly and away, and then spotted a little brass plate on the bottom of the frame. It read *Puzzle Picture* in a gothic font and he looked again at the image, then realized the stallholder, a stooped, diminished man in an overwashed white shirt and a navy tank top, had appeared at his shoulder. He was smoothing his spivvy pencil moustache and smiling with nervous field-mouse eyes. Around his neck his glasses hung on ordinary white string. As they came in David had noticed on his desk, beside the *Daily Mail*'s half-completed puzzle page, a pack of Benson & Hedges, and as he stood beside him now the proprietor's breath was stale and laboured.

'Lovely, isn't it? An original Currier and Ives.'

From the back of his throat, David surprised himself by producing a mooing sound of interest.

'American printmakers. Nineteenth century. The puzzle pictures being particularly sought after. I was *very* lucky to find this one.' He unfolded his spectacles and slid them on. Little nodules of Sellotape bulked the arms where the string was attached.

'Have you spotted all the animals? I think there's five of them. Or six maybe.'

As the dealer spoke, the English country scene seemed to refocus itself. David suddenly discerned a leopard crouched in some branches; a crocodile half-submerged in the foam of the river; the face of a horse in the cottage thatch. He saw that the fissure in the path was not a fissure but a snake, or no, not a snake but the tail of a rat, its body formed from a rock and a tussock of grass. A wolf, his jaw ajar, looked down from the clouds.

'I picked it up in Devon. Or was it Somerset? They're really highly collectible,' the dealer said, a little faintly. An aura of despair had settled on him like a pungent eau de cologne. David was finding it difficult to breathe. He took a step forward, away from the man, and examined the picture again. The odd thing was that once he had spotted the hidden creatures everything became different; he saw a face in the line of a branch, a wispy figure in the twisting roses, a dagger hidden in the ferns. This was paranoia. The dealer wanted one hundred and thirty, though he took, unhappily, a hundred in cash.

Under David's direction Bridget purchased a 1927 print of the dome of St Paul's, with a few black boxy cars on the untarred road, and one for Glover of The Cut in Waterloo. It was from 1910 and featured a shopkeeper standing in front of a grocery store, arms folded, ready to sell. A striped awning extended behind him and in its shade two long tables of fruit and vegetables stood piled as high as any harvest festival.

■ ■ ■

Wednesday brought the kind of wet that only these little islands can manage. It started in the small hours of Tuesday night and stirred David awake. As he lay curled beneath his 20 tog duvet and listened to its hiss and thrum, then to the gathered contrapuntal drips landing on his windowsill, he felt a deep primeval gladness to be dry and warm and horizontal.

By the morning the rain was fanaticized. The roads and pavements had turned to waterways, and black cabs swished past like hovercraft. At lunchtime David braved Oxford Street to buy a new ensemble for the wedding, settling, finally, on a fawn-coloured double-breasted suit with two splits at the back of the jacket, which, as the Italian shop assistant slickly suggested, 'the bigger man normally prefers'. David realized, again, that he was in danger of joining the fat men's club. The next step would be a suggestion that he might want to try these, which have an elastic waistband. Or maybe this muumuu. He bought an umbrella and walked back to school slowly, not really caring, and had to spend the afternoon sitting at his desk in bare feet, with his desert boots and socks drying on the radiator behind the bookcase.

By the time he walked from Borough station home, it had eased to a light simmer. As he closed the door of the flat, Glover's voice greeted him from the living room.

'David, know where Ruth is? I've been trying to catch her all day.'

David watched the new brolly he'd just propped in the corner fall slowly over, drawing a wet arc on the wall. His flatmate appeared in the hallway then, in a thick grey polo neck David didn't recognize.

'Nope, neither seen nor spoken.'

He had to step round him to hang up his duffel. Glover's voice dropped a register. 'Every time I ring they're at lunch, or in a bar, or drinking wine on the sofa – I don't know what kind of organizing they're doing.'

He was smiling and pushing absently against the door frame with one hand, wanting reassurance. David wasn't in the mood.

'Unbelievable outside. You'd think the Thames had burst its banks.'

In the bedroom he tried his new suit on again and thought, this time, that he looked like a free-range egg. When he turned in front of the mirror he saw how his posterior caused the jacket flap to stick out slightly, like tail feathers. Chicken or egg. Front or side. How do you want me? He should have gone for black. Just then an email from Gayle arrived, a copy of her post about seeing some pop singer in a Brixton pub. Apparently he'd been rude to a barmaid and had then been chucked out for smoking weed in the toilets. David began to reply that listening to puerile descriptions of the detritus of society was like being back at school – but then he looked at the picture of her he'd printed out and Blu-tacked to the monitor. She appeared to have a dimple, though it may have been a fleck of something on the camera lens. In the picture she was laughing, rubbing a balloon on her jumper – on her not-insubstantial chest, in fact – and holding a bottle of Becks. He deleted his unsent message and drafted another, beginning *It's always struck me how our culture, such as it is, gets the celebrities it deserves.* Then he elaborated on how 'slebs' had taken on the roles previously occupied by the pantheon of gods. Then he discussed the tendency of even the global village to need its stereotypes and scapegoats, and a pretty girl to sacrifice. Marilyn Monroe. Princess Diana. Heather Mills McCartney. The last was a joke and he showed this by writing (*Joke!*) after it. Then, at the end, casually, he invited her to Glover and Ruth's party. She was online and messaged back, immediately, that she wasn't sure but she thought she'd be able to come, and that she'd definitely try, and that she was glad that he'd asked her, and that she agreed about celebrities – though she couldn't pass up the chance to skim through *Heat* when she was in the hairdressers. Despite the wayward punctuation, David found he was smiling.

■ ■ ■

On the Friday – their last Friday as flatmates – David came home from school and tidied up in case anyone came back that night after the Tavern. He hoovered the living-room rug, emptied the fridge of some rancid yoghurt and a block of colonized parmesan, and pushed the kitchen table against the wall to make a decent space for socializing.

Glover was in his bedroom, finishing his packing, and he said Jess and Ruth were having cocktails in the Savoy. The Tavern was booked from eight but he doubted if anyone would be arriving before nine. His black holdall was open on his bed, clothes folded inside it. The boxes were going to be collected next Saturday: David would have to wait in for the removals company, as if he'd nothing better to do. He'd get used to the empty flat, he told himself. That was the lesson of the last six months. One could get used to anything.

There had been no word from Gayle. David had sent her a reminder email with the details, and his mobile number, and checked MSN to see if she was online, but her account had been set to private for some reason. He searched for her on Skype, just in case, but she wasn't listed. He had her home number now but didn't like to just ring it, at least not yet. There was a chance she might turn up at the pub, no doubt late and flustered, the Rossetti hair everywhere, the flapping leopardskin coat.

'Do you think you could listen to me run through my speech tonight? Just to check I've covered all the bases?'

David was about to tuck in to his pasta, but he nodded, and Glover rested against the kitchen counter, holding a sheet of A4, flexed, psalter-like, in front of him. Awkwardly, he clutched his left elbow with his right hand. David twirled spaghetti carbonara on his fork as quietly as possible.

'"On behalf of my wife and I..."' he nodded to an imaginary Ruth beside the toaster, '"I'd like to thank everyone for coming, particularly those who've travelled far and wide to be here ... from Felixstowe and even the USA, and particularly Bridget and Rolf, who should right now be studying—"'

'Too many *particularly*s. And I don't think people *travel* far and wide.'

Glover let the sheet drop and gave a wolfish smile. He had a little sliver of theatricality in him.

'Can we keep the comments to the end, please? I just need to practise running through it first. So…"the first meeting between my wife and myself was very strange indeed. She thought that I was following her from the tube station, and it's fair to say that our first conversation was less than friendly. In fact she screamed at me in the street."'

Glover paused for audience reaction. David smiled as he might at a small child who was blocking a doorway he needed to get through. His flatmate was sufficiently encouraged.

'"Immediately, I knew that Ruth was going to play a big part in my life. She swept into it like a hurricane."'

Another look towards the toaster.

'"I've never met anyone like her. And she's introduced me to a new world of ideas and experiences. Some good, some bad and some downright ugly."'

Another pause. David stared at his spaghetti, trying to divine things from it.

'"Everything about Ruth is unexpected. She can recite, in alphabetical order, the names of all fifty states. On her right foot her second toe is slightly longer than the first, the big toe, or the King of the Toes, as she calls it. She has eleven freckles on her back and doesn't like beer or frozen yoghurt or the Beatles."'

David didn't know about the frozen yoghurt. Or the freckles.

'"She can't drive, though she *does* make the most wonderful passenger. But even more exciting than the things I know about her are the things I don't. I love the fact that we're only beginning a journey towards getting to know each other, and I'm sure it's going to be interesting … Working at her art is, as you all know, what Ruth has dedicated her life to. And I wake in the mornings delighted to have found *her*, a work of art to which I can dedicate mine."'

The sentiment caught David off guard with its neat reversal, and he felt it for a second. The range and draw and compulsion of it; the unlikelihood made it more remarkable not less. He loved her indeed; that was not in doubt – though neither was it the point. There were no impediments left to love, no restrictions or barriers or secrets, and thus love had lost its power. It did not make the world go round: that was, at least according to Glover, the conservation of initial momentum and the gravitational field of the sun. David tuned back in.

'"... pursuing artistic perfection, she recently had the good taste to ask me to sit for her, or stand, actually, in the nude, which has obviously brought us even closer together ... Ruth is beautiful, as you can see, maybe the most beautiful woman I've met"' – David very much liked that *maybe* – '"and not just on the outside. I don't think she could make such beautiful things unless they reflected the beauty inside her."'

David imagined Larry's face, not knowing what to do with itself, pulled between sincere irony and insincere politeness. And Jess! He began willing Glover to make more declarations, to go higher and faster and deeper; but he had come down to brass tacks.

'"Of course, I'm aware there's an age gap between us, and some of you might even say she's old enough to be my mother, but well, my mum's here today, and you can see the difference. No offence, Dad!"'

He grinned at David and scratched at the acne scars on his jaw, confirming that this was indeed a gag, and David's cue to laugh. He did so, and genuinely. Something seemed to free itself. He laughed and laughed.

'"And Ruth may be older but that doesn't make her wiser. Our relationship is not simply one-way. I've taught her several important things about English culture, which means the pub, a topic I'm something of an expert on. I've also taught her how to use the iPod she'd had for a year and which was still in its box. In turn she persuaded me to finally try sushi, which I now *know* isn't for me ... So I'd like to thank Ruth for a terrific six months, and for having another go at marriage. I assure you all that this time it's for good."'

David pouted and sucked in some air. 'Do you really think you should say that this time it's for good?'

'Why not?'

'Well, is it not a bit like saying the other times it wasn't right, or even the other times it was for bad or something?'

'She didn't stay with those people.'

'I'm not sure that's quite how it works. Is it not better to think that relationships are right for the moment? That they're all provisional?'

'They don't have to be.'

'But something can be provisional for your entire life. Your entire life's provisional anyway.'

He shrugged his boxy shoulders, then snapped his ardent gaze across to the toaster again as if Ruth really *was* there in the corner, and he expected her to support him.

'Look, let me finish it ...' He gripped the worktop's edge and propelled himself up and sat on the counter. '"We're delighted that you could all make it today and support Ruth and me. And we'd like to invite any of you, all of you, to come visit us in the Big Apple."'

The Big Apple! David saw Bridget crushing ice in her vodka with a straw, Jess raising her eyebrows at Larry.

'"And so I'd like to invite you all to join me in toasting my wonderful wife Ruth."' He raised his tumbler of Diet Coke. '"A toast to Mrs Glover."'

Glover told David once that he couldn't trust people, but in fact the opposite was true. He had too much trust. It would be tough on him. He regarded everything as fixable, thought relationships were just machines that ran either well or badly, that they had cogs and springs and circuits. He believed that all the operations of the earth accorded to the laws of Newton, that cause and effect were linked by the simplest equations. But these are complicated times, and the mechanics of the adult life are quantum. Such principle that can exist is of uncertainty.

David told him that his speech was perfect.

where one might pin a medal

'Can I use your printer? I want to change those *particularly*s and mine's out of ink.'

David had just lowered himself, gasping, into a too-hot bath when Glover knocked on the door.

'Sure, you'll have to email the speech to yourself and open it up on my laptop. It's all plugged in.'

'Cheers, matey.'

Ten minutes later David's temperature had adjusted, though perspiration had broken out on his forehead. He was soaping his crevices with pomegranate body gel when Glover shouted something through from David's bedroom.

'You what?'

'I said, I didn't know you had a blog, Mr Dampener!'

David sat up straight, sending a backwash up over the bath rim and onto the lino. He dropped the plastic bottle against his thigh, where it bobbed merrily.

'Don't read it! Please don't read it!'

'Why not?'

'It's private!'

'Don't be daft. It's online.'

Both were shouting but only David had panic in his voice. He struggled to get up out of the bath, a pink soft thing, water cascading from him like Botticelli's Venus. He felt faint from the heat of the water and had just tucked a towel round his waist when Glover banged very hard on the door.

David slid the lock across and Glover gave it a sudden shove. The base of the door stubbed David's toe and then Glover was in the bathroom with him, very close and very angry. Ineffectually, David tried to push him away as he jabbed a finger in his chest.

'What is *wrong* with you?'

A pearly fleck of spittle flew from Glover's lip and landed on David's collarbone. He grabbed David by the arm to pull him out of the bathroom. Strong as Glover might be, David had weight on his side, and he stood inert and doughy, gripping the sink with one hand.

'Get into the fucking living room.'

'James, *fuck off.*'

When Glover stalked from the bathroom David slid the bolt across, but he hadn't finished pulling on his dressing gown before Glover banged again.

'What?'

'*What?* Well, let's see fucking what.' He heard plastic bump against the wood and realized Glover was holding his laptop. The mirror had steamed up. Suddenly he couldn't bear to see himself erased, and wiped it with his hand, which gave his face the aqueous distortions of a funfair mirror. Glover started reading.

'"This tired view of sexuality ... this triumphant lesbiana ..."' What the fuck is *triumphant lesbiana*? '"Fetishistic ... the new painting, *James the First*, features a young emasculated neutered male, his torso a site for the conflicting demands of hatred and sexual tension ... the banality of resorting to tired dialectics ..."'

'They're just opinions,' David offered in a dwindled, childish voice.

'"Ruth Marks has embarked on a series of romantic adventures, all of which have ended badly ... She left her first husband for a woman …"' Glover fell silent, then asked in a clipped, lowered voice, 'Is that true?'

David wiped at the mirror again and looked at himself, then widened his eyes in greeting. *Hello, David, how do you do? I'm fine, David, thanks for asking. How are you? No, how are you really?*

'I think so. Bridget told me.'

'When did she tell you that? When you had lunch?' The panic was in his voice now, but the anger came back, and the disgust. 'What's *wrong* with you?'

David loosely knotted the cord of his dressing gown and sat on the edge of the bath. He should have been more careful. He mopped at his forehead with his towelling sleeve.

'I suppose I felt a bit let down …'

There was silence and David pulled the lock across. He swung the door open and Glover was still standing there, still staring at the screen of the laptop.

'Please. Don't read any more.'

'"Wanking ourselves senseless"? "The Death of Love"? You bitter little fuck. Is this you? Is this who you are? Is this who I'm living with?'

'I don't know. I don't think so. Please. Give it to me.'

David tried to grab the laptop and Glover held on to it; then it fell to the laminate floor of the hallway, and bounced open, almost flat. David screamed as a viridescent liquid spread across the screen and red vertical lines appeared.

'Oh fuck – sorry,' Glover said, polite till the end.

David dropped to his knees and ran his fingers over the screen, then tried pressing some buttons.

'No, no, no, no.'

Why should a dog, a horse, a rat have life, and thou no breath at all? The laptop was fucked. He shut it, clicking the screen softly in place as one might close the lid of a coffin. When he looked up, Glover was gone.

David was at a loss. He set the laptop on the lid of the toilet and locked the door again. Unsure what to do next, he climbed back into the bath and lay there, corpse-like. A spreading pink welt had appeared on his chest where Glover had jabbed him with his finger, above the left nipple. When the bruise came it would be where one might pin a medal. He turned the hot tap on again and watched the rising water threaten the desert island of his stomach. It lacked only a palm tree. No man is an island, thought David, apart from me. Then he dried and dressed himself slowly, and slunk into the living room. There was nowhere else to go.

'James, I'm … sorry. I think I'm depressed maybe. I don't know why – I don't really think that stuff about Ruth, or her work, or any of it.'

Glover didn't look up from the property show on TV. 'Will your insurance cover the laptop?'

'I don't have insurance.'

'Well, maybe I can give you something towards replacing the screen. It's probably just the screen.'

'I'll take that stuff down from the website as soon as I sort out my computer.'

'Yeah, I don't want to think about that.'

'But I feel—'

'I don't give a fuck about what you *feel*, David. Let's just forget it. I'm sorry your laptop got broke but I don't want to talk about this any more. I don't think Ruth needs to hear about this. It would upset her too much. She thinks you adore her, if you can believe that.'

'I do adore her. I do.'

'You seem to hate her.'

'Of course not.'

'You know, I'm out of here tomorrow, and I cannot fucking wait.'

How might David explain it to Glover? Real emotions were not distinct. They were like colours, they ran into each other. When does the day become the night? The neck the shoulder? Everything laps and overlaps. But for Glover to every thing there was a season, right was right and man was man and wrong was wrong and woman woman, and every single object his righteous eyes could see appeared to have been edged with a thick, black line, like the scenes from a colouring book.

■ ■ ■

Though they left the house to go to the party together, they were not speaking, and when David stopped off to buy cigarettes, Glover didn't wait. By the time he came out of the shop, his flatmate was stalking off in the distance. Feeling ridiculous, David followed.

He had a sense it would end up being a very long evening. Not to mention a very long weekend, a very long life. Tomorrow he had to dress like an egg and give his ludicrous celebratory speech. His phone vibrated and he clawed it from his jeans. Ruth.

'David, hi. I'm trying to get hold of James.'

'Oh, I think he's turned his phone off. His mum and dad kept ringing him.'

'Listen, we were at the Tavern but Jess has just gotten a call from – oh no, hang on, I see you ...'

The phone cut off and a black cab pulled up abruptly beside him. The window slid down and Ruth appeared, mouthing something.

'You're going the wrong way,' David laughed before he realized there was a problem. He could make Jess out on the far side of her, crouched on the edge of the seat, talking forcefully into a mobile phone. And behind the cab, past the traffic lights, unnoticed by Jess and Ruth, he could see Glover's broad receding back.

'Jess just got a call from Ginny's niece. She's sick. She woke up from a nap with pains in her arms, and you know what that can mean. We're heading straight down to Chichester now.'

'Well, you'll have to get a train. Or maybe I could drive you there. You can't take a cab the whole way—'

Ruth waved the notion impatiently away.

'It's fine. But listen, can you tell James, and tell him I'm sorry not to be there to see his parents.'

A bus had pulled up behind the cab and the driver gave a long blast on his horn. The taxi was blocking the bus stop. David looked angrily at the driver, a Sikh with a very narrow face, who wagged a many-jointed finger towards the bus stop sign.

'Tell him I love him and can't wait for tomorrow.'

David nodded stupidly. 'I hope everything's all right. Ring me on my mobile. I'll tell James to turn his on.'

David ducked a little to try to smile in at Jess but she was busy, somewhere between angry and scared, saying sharply, 'Oh, Miriam, just tell me what he said. I'm not a child.'

The horn of the bus blasted again; Jess twisted her willowy body around to wave her phone through the back window at the bus driver. She wanted to tell her news to the world; then it would part for her like the Red Sea. The taxi began to pull off and Ruth shouted, 'Give our love to everyone.'

In the Tavern David saw Glover sitting with Eugene and Tom at the table in the hidden snug downstairs, obviously having a quick shot or two before heading up to face the party. David pretended not to have seen them and no one called him over. Though he normally found entering parties uniquely stressful, that evening he just straightened his back and walked fearlessly in. He had a secret and it lent him purpose. He checked the room for Gayle, but couldn't see her. Larry was slouched in a corner with a pretty girl and David headed towards him. He thought he might know, that Ruth might have called him, but he seemed oblivious, and

215

David felt curiously reluctant to pass the news on. Larry would take charge and tell everyone. He would organize flowers, an airlift, a satellite link-up to Chichester hospital.

David let the conversation drift through the week's weather, the forecast for tomorrow, and then, unexpectedly, the girl's admiration for Ruth's art, particularly her paintings. David informed her that Ruth wouldn't be attending tonight. She'd been here for a second but had been called away. Larry wanted details, predictably. David could tell he was itching to stand on a chair, let his beautiful assistant tap her wine glass for silence and then announce that he had an announcement.

David grew vague, said that Jess and Ruth had had to hurry off and that he must have just missed them. He said he wanted to speak to Glover before he said anything more. Larry was nodding; he couldn't push too hard because it was becoming obvious that he was not, as David was certain he'd represented, Ruth's closest confidant.

David recognized Glover's parents, Robin and Jane, from the photograph in his flatmate's room. They were sitting on one of the green leather chesterfields, in a manner that a body-language expert would describe as closed. The sofas had been moved close to face each other, and opposite them sat David's parents. His mother, dressed entirely in citrus yellow, had spotted him and was waving as if he were partially sighted. Obediently he trotted over.

'James not arrived?'

The volley of love that was his mother's first question.

'No, I haven't seen him yet.'

'I'm James's father, Robin. You must be David.'

The fingers were overlong and travelled too far round David's hand. They *applied* themselves to the skin. That must be a requirement, David found himself thinking, for playing the accordion; he glanced around, just in case Robin had brought it.

'And David, I understand you're the best man for this what-ever-it-is tomorrow.'

Jane threw a horrified, nervous glance at her husband. Whatever agreement they'd made, he was breaking.

'Apparently Ruth's here. Have you seen her? Can you point her out? Let's hear what *she's* got to say.'

Robin's nose was a shark's fin, and there was something similarly predatory about his thin-lipped mouth. The eyes were wide and blue and similar to Glover's but lacked his son's good nature. For a religious man, he was a little too fastidious, the cuffs just so, the hair swept neatly apart with the comb tracks still showing. David would bet any money that something unruly raged in the heart that thudded under his checked sports jacket. David wouldn't, for example, want to be a young woman trapped in a lift with him. Anyone who used his name so much was trying either to con or convert him – which was, of course, much the same thing.

And David could tell that Jane had been conned. She smiled and smiled and smiled, but you knew that in an ideal world she'd have cut her husband's throat many years ago. She had made bad decisions, including the one to disguise the hair on each side of her upper lip by dying it. Now white whiskers curved around the corners of her mouth. Coupled with the twitchy nervousness, the impression left was of a kitten caught lapping at another kitten's milk.

'Robin, *please*,' she said.

Alcohol was the way and the light here, and David began with Jane: 'Can I get you something to drink?'

She started. 'Oh no, no thanks. Not for me. Maybe a Shloer. Would they have Shloer in here?'

Robin asked for a fizzy water – a *fizzy* water, Hilda repeated to her son, as if such an adjective-and-noun combination was extremely unlikely. Then she shifted her buttocks to pat the leather under her thigh and check it for stickiness, adding that

217

she'd like another orange juice. David could tell by the coral tint to her cheeks that the depleted one in her hand had been diluted by a shot or two of vodka, and realized she was fitting herself to the Glovers, from shame or neediness or a desire to be liked. It was a family trait! He saw himself in her suddenly, looking out, and looked away to his father, who tipped his Guinness at him, nodded.

disegno

Kevin bobbed in, smiled at each disparate group as he looked for Glover or Ruth, and David realized that in their absence he was in charge of the party. He went over and agreed with Kevin that, yes, some music would be a good idea. He had his iPod in his duffel, and he settled on a playlist of some 1930s big band jazz.

At the bar a female administrator from the Barbican patted David's sleeve and asked whether this was the leaving party for Ruth Marks. She didn't even *know* Ruth was getting married.

There was movement at the door. Bridget and Rolf had arrived with several friends, part of the mass of American youth that haunts the globe, and in one stroke they doubled the party's loudness and halved its average age. For a second David thought Gayle was among them, but it was another girl with long dark curls. Already Larry was heading towards Bridget, steering his pretty companion by a hand in the dip of her back.

Bridget offered David a desultory kiss on the cheek, and Rolf, to atone for her coolness perhaps, stepped lankily round her and enclosed him in a massive hug. It was like being restrained by rubber straps. David asked Bridget whether she'd spoken to Ruth and she sidestepped the question, introducing him collectively to the nearest circle of her group: Daisy, Zoe, Sarah, Maud, and a large-eared boy called Rooster. Then she sighed dismissively and said Ruth had texted. Raking her gaze around the circle to check for its full attention, she shrugged, saying, 'But that's Ruth.'

Rolf tried to second her – 'How about the time she missed her flight at JFK because she'd taken a cab to Newark? Bridget?' – but his girlfriend had moved on, and was whispering something into the ear of Daisy or Zoe or Sarah.

On the parents' sofas Robin was demonstrating something to Ken by smacking his palms against each other, playing invisible cymbals. The far side of the room appeared to be lit solely by David's mother's outfit. Jane was nodding her practical bob and squinting at Hilda with a faint, dazzled smile. It was already nine o'clock. Gayle wasn't going to turn up. And she hadn't even had the manners to leave a message. If she wasn't interested, why didn't she just say, instead of doing this? Instead of playing him along? And Glover should really come up from below, face the big band music. He must have spoken to Ruth by now and realized he'd have to go it alone.

'Will you partake in a pep-up?'

The voice was very close to David's ear and he jerked round, bumping his nose into Larry's head. He smelt wonderful, expensive, and David noticed he'd disturbed the silver plumage by his temple. Larry quickly smoothed it into place and David followed him and his companion into the L-shaped toilet. As the girl fiddled with the drugs on the edge of the sink, he and Larry stood behind her, against the radiator. This was Larry's version of sneaking a fag behind the bike sheds. He bent his knee in its marl-grey worsted, sliding his leather sole up the metal with a scrape.

'We can't stay long, really. Pity Ruth and Jess had to go.'

'I heard there was some story about Ginny. I hope she's all right.'

'Oh really? Well, she's *always* all right. I'm just going to wait to wish James luck and then we're going to disappear as well, grab some dinner.'

The comments were addressed to David but designed to reassure the girl. She was magazine-lovely, with TV hair, and her slinky black dress was accessorized in such a way that her extremities – her fingers, toes, clutch bag and hair – all glimmered with crystal and silver. She had her back to the men and was swaying her hips very gently in time to the music. David realized Larry and he were both watching her and turned away. He had assumed until recently that Larry was gay – until Ruth had mentioned how his divorce had halved his art collection. And it was a small shock to see him with anyone, or looking at anyone with intent or desire. David had thought him too refined to actually *want*.

Now he decided that with Larry his women must always be girls, and they would always be pretty; and no doubt they were filed indistinguishably in his mind under the heading Pretty Girls. There wasn't room in there for anyone else, for anyone serious. In some ways David considered Larry and himself to be similar creatures: their energies were directed to their friends.

Glover had arrived in their absence and was standing at the bar in the middle of Bridget's squad, with his head tipped back and a bottle of Heineken pressed to his lips, sounding Reveille to his father's cymbals. Beside him Eugene raised his own bottle, answering the call. Then Tom wrapped his bulging arm round Eugene's neck, in either friendship or threat – with Tom, it seemed impractical to differentiate. Bridget was playing up to her friends again, describing how her mother hadn't made her graduation ceremony.

'. . . and she was all wham-bam I'm here, I'm here, and I just shouted down from the window, "It was this *morning*, Ruth, and you missed it."'

Confirming that he was by now a little drunk, Glover gave David a hug and said, 'And how's my best man? Have *you* heard from Ruth?'

'I assumed you'd spoken to her.'

'Battery's dead. Kevin's trying to find me a charger but none of them fit. Tom was insisting on drinking games.'

David explained. Then he expanded: 'They said that something had come up with Ginny.' He placed a drifting emphasis on *said*, to leave it open to interpretation. The coke had made him edgy and he shredded a tissue in his pocket as he talked. Then he added that Ruth had mentioned she was nervous about meeting his parents. Glover frowned – the two lines, the umlaut, appeared above his nose – and he shook his head, trying to dislodge the thoughts that were crowding in on it. He put his mouth close to David's ear and whispered that Bridget thought Jess and Ruth were probably too wasted to stay.

'Well, that's not true. I mean they'd had cocktails at the Savoy but they weren't wildly drunk. They'd caught a black cab on the High Street and they stopped when they saw me. You'd gone on.'

'I can't believe she's left. My mum said she heard someone say she rushed out hand in hand with some tall woman. She didn't even come across to say hello to them.'

'I'm sure she didn't want to go.'

His eyes were slightly bloodshot, uncertain. 'What did she say? Can I ring her on your phone?'

'Sure. I think Ginny had a turn or something, and she and Jess had no choice.' David handed over his mobile.

'You think she had a turn?'

'I mean Ruth told me she'd had a turn.'

Glover dipped his head slightly so their eyes were level. David touched his arm to reassure him and Glover shook his head, so he placed his two hands on his shoulders and looked directly into his face.

'She just didn't want Jess to have to travel down alone—'

'Who *knows* what she and Jess wanted? It's not like she'd nothing else on tonight.'

His phrasing struck David as a fine example of litotes, though he didn't say so.

Larry was listening to Bridget, and the Pretty Girl had been cornered by Tom between the bar and a leggy stool. When David joined the group she spotted her chance and slipped off to the bathroom.

'Is that your daughter, then?' Tom said to Larry, semi-pleasantly, semi-aggressively. Larry grinned, unembarrassed. The chances of Tom discomposing him came in at precisely zero. Larry had the endless good grace of a career politician.

'God no, she's doing an internship at the gallery.'

'Not bad,' Tom said and nodded, considering her figure as she crossed the floor. Bridget shot them a disdainful glance. Tom had already been blacklisted by her group: her girlfriends' backs were ranged in unison like shields against him.

'No, my *own* daughter's built like a tank,' Larry mused, plainly buzzing. He pointed at David. 'She looks like him in a wig.'

Tom laughed, and David walked off, not smiling. He was still pretending to study the playlists on his iPod when Glover came back. It had been a short conversation. He handed the phone over and as a return gesture David passed him the player.

'Everything I pick seems more suitable to a funeral. Is everything cool? Did you speak to Ruth?'

'I told her to get here now and she hung up on me. "Ginny's ill. Jess needs me." Incredible!'

Glover swallowed hard and blinked. David saw that Robin was staring blankly at his son from the other side of the room, and Glover saw it too. He set his jaw to the side in an unconvincing expression of endurance. His forehead was perspiring and he looked to David as if he were melting, and wilting, and failing.

At 10 p.m. David decided to ring Gayle at home. He went outside to the dry chilly evening and sat at one of the pub's chained-up picnic tables. Apart from a bloated pigeon that plodded along the edge of the kerb, too fat or sick to fly, he was alone on the pavement. He shooed the bird away so he wouldn't have to identify with it, and it waddled off contentedly. Then he scrolled down to find her number – saved under Singleton – and called it. A man's voice, shrill and Northern, answered immediately. David asked for Gayle and the voice chirped, 'Who's that then?'

'David, David Pinner,' he replied, already embarrassed. He slipped his thumb onto the hang-up button but didn't press it.

'Okay, give me one sec.'

. . .

'Hello?'

'Gayle, hi, it's David. I'm just at the pub and I was wondering—'

'How'd you get this number?' She sounded perplexed, and strangely antagonistic.

'Oh, I just did a search on 192.com. With your name and London. I wanted to check whether—'

'No, I can't make it tonight.'

'Really?'

'I have people here.' David heard her take a few steps on a hard surface and then close a door. She hissed, 'David, if I'd wanted you to have my number I'd have given it to you. I don't think you should just ring me in my own house.'

'But you're listed. I was only trying to see … Who was that who answered the phone?'

'It's none of your business.'

He heard a door open and the man with the high voice ask, 'Who *is* that?'

'I have to go now. Goodbye.'

It might have been the television or her visitors, but David thought then he heard a child crying in the background.

One of Bridget's friends liked Glover. She was Midwestern, dark-haired and wide-hipped, with a pretty corn-fed face and long, prominent teeth. She twirled her hair for a while when they talked and then sucked on her straw, head down, big puppy-eyes looking up. She was making, David thought, the blowjob expression.

Ken and Robin came to the bar to speak to Glover, Robin's hand arriving first, tentacle fingers enclosing his son's shoulder.

'I think you've probably had enough now, James. Still no sign? What do we reckon? Cold feet?'

He barked a lifeless laugh and then his fingers began to contract on Glover's shoulder, digging into the collarbone. Glover had told David once that he and his father communicated physically, and now David witnessed what that actually entailed. Robin extended his other hand towards his son and grabbed at his left wrist, twisting it. James set his pint on the bar and what ensued was what the broadsheets would call a brief scuffle. David stepped back beside Ken and they watched. It was not entirely good-humoured, ending when Robin said, 'Ah now, not my bad finger, that's my arthritic finger.'

David felt his phone vibrate in his pocket but waited until he was in the toilet to check it. Perhaps it was an apology from Gayle but no, it was Ruth.

James, don't be so absurd. Jess is my friend. I love you.
I need you to be mature about this. Ginny is very ill. Have
a great evening.

He deleted it.

Eugene and Rolf had discovered a joint love of online multi-player gaming. Both had spent several weeks completing a certain quest in World of Warcraft and were now describing it to David at length. Nearby Tom was talking very seriously to Glover who rested, loose-limbed but attentive, against a table. Tom was itemizing his arguments by counting on his fingers. Everyone in the room seemed to be shouting.

The parents exited together. Hilda's goodbye to her son had an edge of resentment: she thought David had not spent enough time with her and proffered her cheek without attempting to kiss him. Sealing their handshake with his other hand, Ken said to Glover, 'And we look forward to meeting the lucky lady tomorrow' – which caused Robin to raise his eyebrows at Jane. When Robin shook David's hand he said, 'David, God bless,' and David again got the sense that here was a very bad man. Jane closed her eyes and held on to her son tightly, as if a tornado howled at her back. Then Robin said, 'Right-o, come on,' and they left.

On Glover's insistence, Eugene and Tom came back with them. David told him he was crazy, that they had a huge day tomorrow, but he wouldn't listen. David didn't want them in the flat and when they sat down in the kitchen, he moved to the living room and turned on the telly. After a few minutes Eugene came in and offered him a spliff. There was some pity in the gesture but he seized upon it anyway, engaging him in a conversation about the debt-consolidation advert playing. Eugene's eyes had a pleasing way of growing larger when he listened, and he was so ginger that his skin appeared to be transparent, like rolled wax. All the pigment from his body's hinterlands had moved to the freckling conurbations that spread across his face and arms. He might have been splattered with orange paint and, perched on the arm of the easy chair, he wiped his fingertips over his forehead as if trying to rub some off.

Glover entered, balancing a tray of mugs and bottles of beer. Tom followed, saying, 'Yeah, though not as fit as Larry's intern. She was something else.'

Apparently contemplating a woman's beauty caused Tom physical pain, and he winced. David lifted his tea from the tray, sipped it and watched. No one picked up Tom's remarks, so he soldiered on alone, saying to Glover, 'I suppose you'll have to put all that behind you now.'

'I can still *look*.'

David could see Tom wanted to say something cruel here, but in the event it was innocent Eugene who delivered the perfect knockout. A music video of a black girl holding a baby had come on and Eugene asked, 'When do you think you'll have kids?'

Sitting on the sofa beside David, Glover answered tentatively, 'Yeah, I'm not sure I want kids.'

'Ruth's quite a bit *old*er,' David added, informing Eugene of some fearful affliction. 'I don't think children'll be an issue.'

'What do you mean older?' Tom demanded with his usual charm.

David wondered for a second if he might be on steroids. Plus he had after all met Ruth, albeit briefly. Glover frowned but his eyes didn't leave the TV. He might have been discussing the weather forecast when he said, 'She's in her forties.'

Tom gave a low whistle and Eugene said, 'Huh,' as if he'd learnt of an interesting minor coincidence. Tom raised his beer bottle to his mouth – the stripes of his shirt arched round his bicep – and then decided not to take a sip.

'When you say she's in her forties – is she like forty-one or forty-nine?'

'Neither,' Glover said, and David chipped in.

'She's forty-five – though you thought she was forty, didn't you?'

Glover turned to his flatmate and his eyes were visor slits. 'Why don't you shut up?'

'It's true.'

'I didn't know you'd got a thing for the blue-rinse brigade, Jimmy. Gran's still single, you know.'

Tom laughed, by himself. Glover was staring at David, and David realized that whatever anger and frustration and embarrassment Glover felt about the conversation – about the evening, about the entire ridiculous relationship – he was going to take it out on him.

'David, I know you're upset about me getting married but you don't have to act like *such* a cunt. I've let you hang around Ruth and—'

'You've *let* me?'

'Yes, I fucking let you. Even after we found that you were carrying photos of her around in your wallet. And then tonight I find out—'

'I explained that.'

'He's writing crap about Ruth all over the net – he's taken it upon himself to review my wife.'

Like a toddler, Tom clapped once with glee. Eugene, startled, retracted a digestive biscuit from his open mouth, unbitten. Somehow, simply by saying that Ruth was too old to have children, simply by telling the truth, he'd provoked him. And now Glover'd done his best to humiliate him in front of his moronic friends.

'The photo was there for reference,' David said, not much louder than a whisper.

'Whatever you say, champ, whatever you say.'

A few minutes later Tom held one bottle of Budweiser between his feet and angled another upside down against it, leveraging the caps. The Bud came unsealed with a hiss and Tom handed it to Glover; but when he lifted a second unopened bottle and tried to repeat the trick, there was a gritty crunch, an Anglo-Saxon oath, exuberant foam through his fingers, and brown shards in the tatty grey rug. Tom humped off to the kitchen and they heard the tap running. He'd cut his thumb. David was happy to accept any amount of Tom's blood as a distraction.

'You might still tap-dance but your piano-playing days are over,' Glover said when Tom came back, kitchen roll wrapping his hand. He was trying to lighten the mood, but Tom was not cheered. A bully, he was incapable of being the target for wit. He aimed for David.

228

'Don't know what you're so fucking excited about.' Heartened, Tom turned back to Glover. 'Here, if I'd known you were going to ask this prick to be best man, I'd have said yes after all.'

David turned to James. 'What?'

'Don't like speaking in public, mate.'

Glover looked at David and gave a shrug of relaxed defiance. 'He is my cousin.'

'I reckon even with the dyslexia, though, I'd have done a better job than you.'

'Shut up, Tom,' Glover said equably.

After they'd gone, David followed Glover into the kitchen, where Glover started rinsing glasses at the sink, keen, it seemed, to erase any last remaining traces of his presence in the flat. David felt strangely calm; he was actually glad that Glover was leaving, and removing the splinter of resentment he'd been feeling these several months. By going, Glover was writing him the blank cheque of a new life, and he could decide how it was filled in – or filled out. They were almost at the end. Tomorrow it would be over and Glover and Ruth would be gone.

And he wouldn't miss having mouth-breathers like Tom hanging around, though it was intensely annoying that he'd been second choice for best man. It turned out he was not even Glover's understudy; he was Tom's. Heavily, he sat down at the table, scraping it close to rest his elbows on.

'Nice evening,' Glover said. Was he being sarcastic? David didn't know. He watched his shoulder blades trowelling under his shirt. David's Sunday-school teacher, in a bare dusty hall in Kennington, had once told his class that their shoulder blades were the stubs left over from angel wings, which they'd lost when they fell from grace. The very memory angered him. All that venality and self-importance and superstition. God has chosen to make … you. You are the millionth visitor, the goal of evolution and the absolute reason for the existence of the cosmos, and the BIG CASH PRIZE of heaven awaits. Just click here.

'I'm sorry. Again. But you didn't have to mention the photograph – make me look like a freak.'

James set an upended mug on the draining board, then stopped the tap with three sharp twists and turned round.

'You *are* a freak. And Ruth was freaked about you carrying a photo of her around. Pretend all you want, but it can't mean nothing. It means *something.*'

David felt quite tranquil. *Disegno.* He had material and subject. He had freedom and restraint. He had invention and respect for the tradition. It was possible to solve the problem properly. *Stet Fortuna Domus.* Let luck attend his house. Say it.

'You should look in her fucking wallet, then.'

'What?'

'You're not in there. Jess is, though. What d'you think *that* means?'

'Bullshit.'

'I've fucking seen it. At her exhibition. She gave me her wallet to pay for drinks and there was a photo of Jess in it. For all I know, she might have one of each of her husbands too. Everyone she's fucked.'

David watched with interest as Glover tried to re-enter the current of his emotions at another, safer spot. He blinked.

'You lie, David. We know that now. You lie and lie.'

David held an artful silence for a few seconds. In it, he hoped that Glover found his answer. David once thought he was a painter; then a novelist; then a poet. Right man, wrong mediums. His gift was for silences.

'Look, I don't know anything. I don't even know if it was Jess that Ruth left Bridget's father for. And you don't know either, clearly.'

David did know, of course. What was she called? Gloria. Something gothic happened to her. Bridget had mentioned an asylum.

'Why are you trying to fuck things up, David? Why are you trying so hard?'

Glover slammed the kitchen door behind him. David sat and listened to the stoic refrigerator humming, then heard Glover, speaking softly in the hallway. *Ruth, it's me. Can you ring me, please? I know it's late but I need to talk ... I just really need to talk to you. Where are you? Are you with Jess? Call me.*

A minute or two passed and David continued to sit, very still, in the kitchen. It was late. The dark glass of the window reflected the bulb hanging over the table and it seemed as if one could cross over and enter that reflected world of liquid shadows and black depths, of antimatter and all its possibilities. He heard Glover scrabbling around for taxi cards in the drawer by the phone, then listened to him talking again, asking for a cab. *You've got nothing, nothing at all?*

David stood up and lowered the blind in the kitchen, banishing his murky twin. Glover was sitting on the floor of the hallway, the Yellow Pages open on his crossed legs.

'It's three in the morning. Do you not think—'

'I'm going to Ruth's. I'll get a cab from somewhere.'

'Look, I can drive you if you really want, but will this stuff not wait until tomorrow—'

'Let's go, then. Or just give me the keys. I can drive there myself.'

'You're drunk. I'm not giving you the car.'

'I'm no drunker than you are.'

'That's as may be, but you're not insured.'

David lifted a half-bottle of whiskey from the booze cupboard above the kettle.

'We'll need this.'

The street was desolate and freezing, and all the houses appeared to be in darkness, though a hip-hop beat was just

231

audible from somewhere. The Polo wouldn't start but Glover, even in his present state, insisted that if David kept gunning the ignition he'd flood the engine.

As they waited between failing, scraping attempts, Glover asked, 'Are you trying to protect me? Do you know something?'

It was so touching. He sounded so small and forlorn. It was such a generous interpretation of his actions that David was genuinely moved.

'I know they loved each other once. I saw that photo. I know what you know. I want you to be happy, mate.' He tried the key and the engine kicked in. 'Here, take a swig. I really shouldn't drink any more.'

variegated bruise

As they drove across Blackfriars Bridge the night was about to break. A grey sky was dully emerging. With difficulty a young woman walked in high heels beside the bridge railing, a man's suit jacket unevenly draped round her shoulders, though there was no man to be seen. Glover was silent, staring out of the window, travelling through his psychic geography. What was it they'd said? Despair 8 miles, Contentment 26? David had left Despair far behind and was heading for Contentment; Glover was making the opposite journey. David judged the next words carefully.

'Look, what does it matter if Ruth carries a photo of Jess? Ex is ex.'

Glover tipped the Jameson back and took a nip, then gasped. 'It doesn't. I just – I don't want to lose her.'

'You know what it is? It's this thing when it's the first person you've really loved. It can all seem enormously important.'

'I've had other girlfriends.'

'Sure, sure, but Ruth told me you were a virgin.'

'Did she?'

'She was surprised I think but ... anyway.'

Glover sat in silence as the Polo came off the bridge and coasted into a roundabout, as smooth as if it ran on tracks.

David stopped on Whitecross Street, by the metal shutters of the Peking Express where Ruth and he had eaten all those months before, the night she told David about her feelings for Glover. David started to say that he'd wait and Glover cut him off, telling him to go on home, then abruptly he jumped out. David watched him jog down the white broken line in the middle of the road.

Then he got out of the car and followed, hiding behind a van in the courtyard of the block when Glover waited in the lit lobby for the lift to come. After the steel doors had closed their maw, David buzzed the porter, and then waved his wallet at the pensionable, shaved head squinting at him from above the counter.

'My friend, who's just come in, left this in the car.' He walked past without waiting for an answer. He would say that he was worried, he would say he was just making sure that everything turned out okay.

He heard Glover as soon as the lift slid open on Ruth's floor. The front door of the flat was ajar, and he was shouting. Ruth's boxes were stacked in the hallway and David crept round them and down to the kitchen. The voices came from round the corner, from the living room. Glover was demanding to know where her handbag was. Ruth didn't understand.

'James, *please* keep your voice down ... I think it's hanging on the hooks by the door. What the hell is wrong with you? You're drunk. You stink of drink.'

'You have a good evening?'

Ruth replied, 'No, as it hap—' but Glover had already stamped down the corridor and grabbed the bag. David heard him drop it on the carpet, and he edged his head round the dividing wall.

Glover was on his knees, shaking out the contents of her bag. Ruth, in a copper-coloured hooded sweat-top and black silk pyjamas, sat in the armchair with her head in her hands, blonde tufts poking out through her fingers. She was appearing in a different play. David thought she was expecting Glover to notice her pose and join her onstage. She didn't realize what was happening, what

234

mood Glover was in; then she glanced up. She fired herself out of her seat, shouting, 'What are you *doing*? Those are *my things*.'

'Have you got a photo of Jess in your purse?'

'What? No. Why?'

They both made a snatch at her wallet and then James grabbed the hood of her top, and yanked her away. The zip caught at her neck and she banged her hip off the arm of the sofa. She screamed briefly, a shocking animal sound. He was emptying the wallet out onto the carpet and then he lifted something and straightened up. Ruth had collapsed to a sitting position, Buddha-like, with her back to the side of the sofa, and was clutching her throat. She was silent, terrified, and looked up with incomprehension as Glover waved the photo of Jess in her face.

'What are you doing? What is that?'

'It's fucking Jess. Everywhere, always. Why are you lying to me?'

He tossed it at her and it bounced off her shoulder, spinning under the sofa.

'I had no idea that was in there. But what does it matter anyway? Why does it matter in the least—'

'Ruth, why are you here?'

'What do you mean? James, you're drunk and—'

'Why fuck me? Why not fuck Jess? Or anyone else?'

She opened her mouth, closed it again, then said, 'Oh my God. Not this. *Again.* Not now.' She pitched her head back, displaying the dark bags under her eyes, then she let out a sigh and slid her jaw to one side with contempt. 'I've probably fucked her enough already.'

Glover stooped slightly, as if he might help her get up, but instead David saw his arm lash out, saw him hit her with the back of his hand in her face. He heard the sound, fleshy and dull and definite.

He was there. He was watching. He pulled Glover off her, though by then he was trying to hug her, and pushed him against the wall. Glover's shoulder hit a picture, a Miró print, one of Walter's, and it fell to the carpet without breaking. They were in shock. Glover stood there dumbly and Ruth just stared at the carpet and held the lower half of her face. David was between them, saying, 'It's all right, it's all right,' knowing it wasn't even close to the truth. Glover started sobbing, great gusty, whooping sobs, and his face was all twisted. David knelt and took Ruth in his arms.

Jess appeared then in the living-room doorway, an apparition in a white sweatshirt with San Diego written on it, and grey jogging pants. She dangled a box of tissues, a finger hooked into the hole on the top.

When he saw her, Glover stopped crying and said, with a half-hearted flare of defiance, 'What the fuck? What the fuck is she—'

Jess's face was swollen and blank. 'My Ginny almost died.'

She glided across the room, not seeing the contents of the bag or the fact Ruth was holding her jaw with two hands or that David was even here. Then Ruth repeated it suddenly, screaming at Glover, 'Ginny almost died! You stupid boy! You child!'

There it was: 'child'. It hung in the room like a beautiful paint-ing, so undeniable and true that no one could look away, that everything near it lost lustre and interest. The apartment had started to grow light. Outside London was coming to, waking up. The long night was over. David told Glover to get out and he edged towards the door, but didn't go through it. He was still wearing his black anorak and held both elbows to stop himself shaking. Then he began rubbing a palm vacantly up and down the door frame.

Ruth, sitting at the foot of the armchair, pulled a tissue from Jess's box and held it to her mouth, where it bloomed with an acid red. Jess had sat back on the sofa, waiting for something, and now stared impassively at Glover. Ruth said, 'Please *go*. David, thank God you're here. Get him to leave.'

Her voice was hoarse, digitized by the tissue pressed against her lip.

'Thank God *he's* here? What the fuck is he here *for*? Why don't you look at his blog? Check out The Damp Review if you want to see what he thinks—'

He was stopped by David pushing him through the doorway. For a second he tried to resist but then the anguish went out of his face and he turned, walked meekly out. They heard the door of the flat close. David's breath came quick and shallow. At the sink he unreeled some kitchen roll and wet it under the tap, then sat beside Ruth on the carpet. Gently, he inclined her compliant head towards the pear lights and dabbed at the cut on her lip. She started to cry again. He helped her up onto the sofa and he and Jess sat on either side of her and hugged her. Then he made tea.

■ ■ ■

They had been in the taxi when the news came that Ginny had suffered a series of small strokes, but Jess had begged Ruth not to tell anyone at the party, not to spoil their evening too. When they arrived at the hospital Ginny's niece Miriam had hugged Jess for fifteen minutes straight. Miriam said she'd stopped talking, mid-sentence, and was then put on a respirator. They'd stayed at the hospital for three hours, by which time Ginny was well enough to insist that they leave. She said Ruth needed Jess at her wedding, and besides, she'd still be here tomorrow evening. 'You will be,' Jess said, as she finally agreed to go.

They'd arrived back in London around 2 a.m. and the shock of it had started to hit Jess. She never handled things like this well and Ruth had given her two Temazepam, and heaped blankets on her. She was still a drug-zombie and now Ruth and David walked her down the corridor and watched her climb awkwardly into the mound of bedclothes.

Ruth perched on the edge of the sofa; knees pressed tightly together, elbows propped on them, head shored up by her fists. She was withdrawing herself from the world and spoke softly, her gaze stalled in mid-air. She'd never seen a man behave in such a way, had never in her life been shouted at like that. And never, never, never had someone actually hit her.

David, lying back in an armchair, sat up and unbuttoned his shirt, and displayed to Ruth the variegated bruise on his chest – his medal – that Glover had given him. He told her how Glover had punched him there only last night when he was trying to have a bath. He was out of control. He'd been angry about some tiny thing that David had said, and he'd then grabbed his computer and thrown it against the wall. The screen had been smashed. David didn't know what was wrong with him. Ruth shook her head repeatedly, clearing the scales from her eyes. It was the depth of her error that astonished her.

She needed some air. He helped her climb into her yellow coat, then followed her out onto the balcony. There was a cold wind this high above London. Out east, over the finance district's glass and steel, the curry houses of Brick Lane and Aldgate, Hackney's estates and undredged canals, the sun released an anaemic downy light. No heat, not yet.

Ruth shivered and David placed an arm around her. Twisting away from him suddenly, she snapped her hand into the air and lobbed her mobile phone over the hammered concrete wall. They listened for a couple of seconds, expecting somehow to hear it land, but they were too far up, and there was only silence. David laughed a little nervously and Ruth said, without emotion, 'I'm too old to take that kind of shit.'

Our culture is too old for love, David thought. You must rescue yourself and you know it. The impulse inwards has overcome the impulse out. Who wants to relinquish autonomy, be whisked up by someone else, be enthralled and helpless? We are busy. We are surfing for porn. We are watching TV. We are waiting at the counter for our turn to describe the size of the slice of Brie we want, or Gorgonzola. Glover and Ruth would thank him, if they knew enough to know how he had saved them. He had given them back reality. He had demythologized them.

How foolish they were to think they could become purposeful and whole through another human being. The process of existing, of growing a soul, is allegorical to making art, not love. The answer might not be One, true, but we know it's not Two.

Expectations are different. Our plays do not end with a marriage now, or if they do, we expect that that marriage too, one day, will end. We have absorbed various crystalline truths, and one of them is this: people love each other all the time, and leave.

David assured her he'd take care of everything, that she should spend her time with Jess and Ginny, and Ruth turned on her computer to print out the guest list with phone numbers. She was almost too tired to be emotional now, and did everything woodenly. David was watching as she called up the files. She exhaled with a slight hum.

'I didn't know you were one of these bloggers everyone talks about.'

'Oh, it's nothing. It's not working anyway at the minute.'

'What's it called?'

'I'll send you the link.'

Ruth went to check on Jess while the printed pages swooned onto the carpet. David lifted and ordered them, and called softly down the corridor that he'd be back in half an hour or so. He descended into the morning and started walking in the pale daylight towards his car. The sky was a weak medieval blue. Glover was nowhere to be seen.

Upstairs Ruth walked barefoot back into the kitchen. She filled her kettle and turned it on. A cup of Indian chai would settle her.

Jess was out cold and she noticed the computer still open on the dining table. She plugged in the internet cord and then called up the *New York Times* website to see what other momentous things had happened on this, the day her life, again, had come apart. Her lip hurt and her tongue pushed out over it, feeling the foreign swelling. How strange it was, that impulse to push against something and feel a new sensation, even if it was only pain. She had made so many mistakes, and he would not be the last. She thought of James standing there in her living room and turned now to see where the Miró print had fallen. David had leant it against the wall. What was the name of his blog?

James Glover sloped from the lobby, moving his body as if it wasn't a part of him, as if he were wearing it. Still crying, he sat on the pavement outside a locked pub and saw how the sleeve of his anorak was shiny with snot and tears. The back of his hand smarted where he had ... where it had ... She had looked at him as if she didn't know him. He should cut it off, it had so offended. He was a stranger to himself. Two nights ago they'd lain on the bed, face to face, their foreheads almost touching, and she'd played with the soft skin of his ear lobe and stroked his hair, and said he shouldn't be fearful, that maybe it would last ten years, or five, or two, and he'd frowned and made her promise it would last for ever. He kicked off from the pavement and started to walk south, into the abandoned square mile of the City.

A street away, long-shadowed in low sun, David turned and decided to go back to the lobby. The porter had put on a black tie over his white shirt and eyed him with unqualified hatred.

'Do you think I could borrow your computer? Just for a minute?'

'Are you a resident here?'

'Well, no, but I'm a close friend of Ruth Marks. She's in 23A.'

'Can't you use hers?'

'It's not working, unfortunately. Her laptop was dropped and smashed.'

The porter sighed. 'It's not up to me. There are rules.'

'It's extremely important. Here, I can pay you.'

David pulled out a crumpled twenty from his jeans and straightened it on the counter.

'No, don't bother about that. Put that away.' The porter gave a cursory glance round the lobby. 'But be quick. It's just in through there.'

Ruth typed into the search box. The Drab Review. The white line turned blue as the search came back with nothing that looked likely. The Damn Review? She tried again. No. This wasn't it. She got up to make her tea.

Glover was running. He'd walked down Finsbury Circus, and the gentle slope had started to speed him up and then, without deciding to, he'd started running. He had trainers on and baggy combat trousers – though his anorak was really too bulky – but he kept his arms loose, and his back straight, and began to enter the pattern of movement. The banks and law firms were closed up and the pavements were empty. He would ring her when he got to the flat. He would ring her and explain how he'd misunderstood everything – he realized now – and his behaviour had been completely unacceptable. A bus passed him and he upped his pace. He just couldn't bear the thought of someone else touching her. She must understand that. David would speak up for him, would explain how much he loved her.

In the back room of the lobby, David called up his blog and turned on the Under Construction page. Then he highlighted the three-page demolition of Ruth's exhibition and the artist's biographical note, and deleted them. He quickly typed in a bland, rapturous one-paragraph panegyric. *At the forefront of artistic endeavour. A world artist in the full sense. We live in the time of Ruth Marks.*

Upstairs Ruth took her tea to the dining table and sat at the keyboard again. David had told her once that he'd been named after his uncles, all of whom were named after the apostles. No, disciples. David and what? Matthew. No, Andrew. Mark. Was Mark a disciple or an apostle? Or was he the evangelist? She'd thought the name had fitted David somehow. His defeatism and his airlessness. Of course, his hands, they were always slightly damp and clammy. The Damp Review – and, oh, here was the page. She clicked on the art section, and smiled sadly. This was really too much.

He might have been barefoot on the sand at Cromer. It might have been the summer after his first year at uni, when each morning he'd gone whipping along the beach, new and lean and fast. He'd been running now for fifteen, twenty minutes. Had come to Blackfriars Bridge and crossed it, then dropped down to the river and kept going – figuring he'd stop at some point, that he'd have to stop at some point. He carried his anorak bunched in one hand and his white T-shirt was drenched with sweat. An African woman clutched her handbag as he slipped past, scared he was about to grab it. Glover didn't notice. Now he wasn't even trying. Endorphins surged through him and gorgeous momentum carried him on. He couldn't have stopped if he'd wanted to. He was being propelled along the curve of the earth, frictionless, oiled and perfectly made to maintain this motion. The skip of his feet on the paving slabs was something mesmeric and primal. Each morning he woke, together, apart, and he thought of her. He was not always thinking about her, but he was never not thinking about her. On the third night they'd made love and then they'd had sex on the dining-room table, in the shower, on the sofa. He'd made her come that last time, on the sofa, and she'd moaned and he'd never heard a sound before that had given him more pleasure. They'd built a nest of pillows on the carpet and wrapped themselves in her massive duck-down duvet and watched *Strangers on a Train*, drinking champagne and eating toast with French jam and a bag of sweet mandarins. It was the most amazing thing that had ever happened to him. Broken nights when they'd slept in her enormous bed and woken late, at noon, and once she'd kissed his nose and said he had the nose of a very pretty girl, and then said that she loved waking to the sound of someone breathing. And he would wonder afterwards how it had come about. How he had found himself replying to her, half-asleep, a bad taste in his mouth and semen caked and flaky on his stomach, 'Maybe you should get married.' Now he swerved around a bench and resolved to jump the next one. It had never occurred to him how it might be taken, how in any case he hadn't meant that she should marry someone in partic- ular, really, until one of her thin, skilful hands had crawled down to his balls and cupped them, and she'd said, 'Well, maybe *you* should.' And softly, semi-conscious, hypnotized, he'd replied, 'Maybe we should.' And she'd known, she'd known. And then he'd done it properly the next night, on New Year's Eve, and got down all serious on one knee, and they'd both cried and laughed and cried ... He vaulted the next bench and scattered the pigeons pecking round a litter bin. He was reaching the plateau, the moment when he left the realm of gravity and entered outer space, when his limbs forgot that stasis ever existed. He held his head straight and tensed the muscles in his stomach, extending his stride and his speed. He would ring her when he got back. He could save this. Love did not appear so often that one stupid incident could end it. People made mistakes. Without sin in the world there would be no place for forgiveness. He was almost sprinting but the pitch was weirdly easy to maintain. He felt as though he could run for ever, as though he could run so fast he could evade everything – his childhood, his parents, David, his job in the Bell, the events of the evening, even his own swinging arms and shunted breath, his legs and his head and his heart, as if he could leave himself behind completely and funnel forward to purest movement, a particle that travels on a beam of light, then quicker than the speed of light.

daggers, crosses, hearts and bells

David sat outside in the Polo for half an hour, cancelling arrangements. He phoned the registry office first. The woman didn't seem surprised at all, and then he rang his mother and gave her the details of the guests. It wasn't his place to explain to them and it was the kind of task that she would relish; she could be officious and mysterious; she could make out a list and cross things off it. She was delighted. He promised to give her more details later.

In the Somerfield on Whitecross Street he bought Jess and Ruth three newspapers, hot croissants, juice and Danish pastries, anything to take their minds off what had happened to them both. Then he had another thought and collected the wedding present, wrapped in glossy silver paper embossed with wedding bells, from the boot of the car where he'd stored it on Tuesday, safe from Glover's eyes.

Ruth's lip was swollen now, like a botched collagen injection, which is what he imagined most people would think it was. She said if she opened her mouth too far the cut opened again and bled. She was touched by his compassion. He insisted that he wanted her to have the present anyway. She started to cry again, and hugged him. He made her unwrap it and she said the puzzle picture was wonderful, that she'd always loved kitsch, and this was the definition of that: so bad it was good. It reminded her of Dalí's elephants and swans, and David said he remembered that picture and then, for a few moments, they were student and teacher again. The swans and trees are reflected in the lake as elephants, and she said Dalí called the technique paranoiac-critical, where hallucination and reality seem to merge, where one thing is always becoming another.

'I think Dalí is an artist for people who don't like art. All those details and pellucid glazes. It's so *cold*-looking.'

He was nodding along. David thought it was helping her to be able to tell him these things, to be restored to a position of authority. He noticed that there was a box on her dining-room table wrapped in pink newspaper, and that Ruth had painted little black symbols on it: daggers, crosses, hearts and bells. He asked her about it and she murmured it was a present she'd been going to give to James, after the ceremony; then she said, decidedly, '*You* have it.' He tried to stop her but she insisted, and David wanted to make things as easy for her as he could. That's how *The Nearly Transparent Heart*, an original Ruth Marks, came to be sitting on his passenger seat. It was beautiful, he thought, and, left on his bedroom sill, would throw lovely patterns of light on the wall. Maybe he should get the project folders back out again, and change things round a bit. Ruth would have more time now. Or maybe he should just have a go at doing it himself. He'd seen how easy it was.

As he drove home London was warming up. The day was promising. He'd take Glover to a beer garden, maybe even to the George on the High Street, to sit outside in the very courtyard where Shakespeare staged his plays, and then he'd tell him that he'd have to move out. He'd made arrangements. He could have a day or two but that was it. No doubt Glover would be fine, would right himself and tilt back towards the light. He should pray for God's forgiveness, in the absence of Ruth's. And David wasn't always going to be there for him. He couldn't stay with him now, not since he'd seen what he was capable of doing. For this next passage of his life there would only be a single set of footprints in the sand, awaiting the sea's deletion, and no one was being carried.

ACKNOWLEDGEMENTS

Many thanks to Natasha Fairweather, Clare Reihill, and Zadie Smith. For reading an early draft, thanks to Richard Young, Ben Turrell, Alan Turkington, and Sam Wallace. Lastly, special thanks to Lorcan O'Neill, Tom Bissell, Angela Rohan, Ruth Scurr, and Nik Bower.